THE ITALIAN SISTER

The Wine Lover's Daughter, Book One

THE ITALIAN SISTER

The Wine Lover's Daughter, Book One

Christa Polkinhorn

Bookworm Press

Bookworm Press
1223 Wilshire Blvd., #1054
Santa Monica, CA 90403

Cover design and author photo: Diane Busch
Cover images: www.bigstockphoto.com

ISBN: 978-0-9600135-2-4

Printed in the United States of America

In memory of my father Heinrich Umiker who inspired in me an appreciation of good wine.

PART ONE: A SECRET

Chapter 1

Tears rose to Sofia's eyes and her heart clenched as she looked down at the urn next to the small mound of dirt that would soon cover it. She was still unable to comprehend her father's sudden death. He was so vivid in her mind. She saw his tall, somewhat square figure lumbering across the yard of their home in Santa Monica, his longish light-brown hair, streaked with gray, fluttering in the breeze. She still felt his arm around her and smelled his aftershave, a light citrus fragrance.

Another image that lingered in her mind was the way he held a wineglass toward the light, checking out the color of the wine, then slowly turning the glass and letting the red liquid swirl around. Because wine had been Henry Laverne's passion; the growing and making of wine, its history, and everything connected to it. He'd written about wine in several trade magazines and had published books about the history of wine and winemaking. In spite of his passion, Henry had been a very moderate drinker, but he savored each drop, whether it had been a vibrant Pinot Noir, a tangy Sangiovese or a fruity Merlot.

And now, all that was left of him were ashes and bones. That and memories, photos, books, and articles he'd written. Henry hadn't just been her father, but her mentor and closest friend. Usually, she called him by his first name, only occasionally had she referred to him as "Dad." Aunt Emma, Henry's sister, who'd raised Sofia after her mother's death, always called him Henry and so Sofia picked up the habit from childhood. He became "Dad" whenever Sofia commented on one of his odd ways, usually with a rolling of the eyes. Because Henry had been somewhat eccentric.

He had degrees in microbiology and biochemistry and had tinkered with making and blending wine already as a student. He'd told Sofia a few stories of his first experiments with grapes and other types of fruit. While other boys were watching TV or playing video games, Henry and a friend made wine in the old shack behind his parents' house. Sofia remembered the photo of him as a youngster. Even then he'd been tall and sturdy, with wild hair and a handsome face.

Sofia inherited his enthusiasm for the art of winemaking. As a child, she'd sometimes watched him for hours at their former home along the Russian River. She still remembered the earthy smell of the cellars and the beautiful oak barrels. After her mother's tragic death from a drug overdose—Sofia had been twelve years old—Henry and Sofia moved to Santa Monica to live with Emma. In their new home, the cellar with the wine barrels and the steel tanks had been replaced by an office where Henry studied and wrote about winemaking. He also taught winemaking at different colleges. In the fall, he would travel to Tuscany where he worked with Italian wine aficionados on some joint project, the exact nature of which Sofia never really understood. A few times, when she was still a child, he'd taken her along on a trip to Italy and they'd visited Florence, Siena, and the surrounding areas.

Letting her eyes wander over the well-kept grounds of the cemetery, its clean gravestones, the mausoleum in the background, and the flowers and bushes, Sofia found some solace in the fact that her father would rest in good company. Famous people were buried here. One of the gravestones belonged to the German author, Heinrich Mann, the brother of Thomas Mann, whom her father had greatly admired.

4

Only a few people were standing around the grave before the official memorial service in the cemetery's chapel. Emma, Henry's sister, stood next to Sofia with her arm around her niece's waist. John Wagner, her father's lawyer, and his wife were there as well as Henry's parents, Lydia and Bernard Laverne, and on the other side of the grave a few close friends of the family had gathered.

"I think they're starting the ceremony." Emma's words woke Sofia from her musing.

"Let's go," Sofia said. She took Emma's arm and led her across the lawn to the chapel. She shivered in the cool breeze coming from the ocean. It was June in Santa Monica; fog blanketed the coastline and it smelled musty. It'd been foggy in the mornings for a few weeks, a typical sign of June gloom as it was called by the locals. It would warm up later, once the sun burned away the mist.

Inside the chapel, it was warm. The smell of moist grass was replaced by the sweet scent of jasmine. The ceremony was held by a friend of the family, a young Methodist minister. Henry, Emma, and Sofia had gone to church occasionally on Sundays, more for social reasons than for any kind of strong religious convictions. They'd met their friends there and often joined them for breakfast at one of the coffee shops after church.

The minister gave a short sermon and there was music and a prayer. Sofia, however, couldn't concentrate on the ceremony. Her mind strayed to the past. She thought of her childhood; when her mother was still alive.

Suffering from bipolar disorder, Cleo had become unpredictable in her moods whenever she went off her medication. Memories of her mother were confusing. There were times she'd been kind and they'd had fun together. But more often than not, Cleo had been distant and absent, both emotionally

5

and physically, when she'd been recovering from bouts of insanity in mental institutions.

During that time, it was mainly her father who gave her the love and attention she needed. During Henry's stays in Europe, she lived with her aunt Emma in Santa Monica. She loved those vacations. Emma was single and an adventurous woman. They spent the time swimming in the ocean, backpacking and camping in the Santa Monica Mountains. They took trips to Disneyland and the San Diego Animal Park.

Sofia felt an arm on her shoulder. Emma smiled at her through tears. They got up and joined the other mourners. As they walked out of the chapel, Sofia's eyes fell on a young man standing outside and her heart clenched.

Chapter 2

It was James, the man she'd been married to for two short and painful years. She hadn't seen him inside; he must have arrived late. Tall, slender, and handsome, he was a favorite with women, Sofia remembered with a pang of pain. He was wearing a dark-blue suit, his curly red-brown hair reaching the collar. It was longer than the last time she'd seen him.

After Henry's heart attack, Sofia had called her former in-laws to give them the news. Although she'd not been in touch with her ex-husband after the divorce, except for legal matters, she'd maintained a loose connection to the family. However, Sofia had not expected that anybody would show up, least of all James. Seeing him triggered a range of mixed feelings. James had been a student of Henry's in the winemaking program at UC Davis and they'd been friends, although they hadn't kept in touch after Sofia and James split up. On the one hand, Sofia felt it was kind of James to make an appearance, but at the same time, she wished she didn't have to face him during this already emotional time.

He walked up to her and they hugged. James murmured his condolences and hugged Emma as well. The situation felt awkward. James seemed uncomfortable and kept looking around. Out of politeness, Sofia invited him to come to lunch with them, which he accepted.

"My parents send their love. They're sorry they couldn't make it," he said to Sofia.

Sofia nodded. "Thanks for coming." He walked with them to the exit of the cemetery and Sofia told him how to get to the restaurant.

They had lunch at an elegant place down at the boardwalk in Santa Monica. It was a luxury hotel along the ocean where Henry had taken Sofia and Emma for special occasions such as birthdays or other celebrations. Sofia felt he would have appreciated having his farewell lunch there. In a reserved area with a beautiful view of the Pacific Ocean, mourners and guests gathered for lunch. Sofia and Emma were sitting next to John and his wife, and James.

The atmosphere in this beautiful place was more light-hearted than in the chapel. The conversation centered around Henry and his love of wine. James talked about what a great teacher he'd been.

"Everybody loved him," he said. "And we all enjoyed the private wine tasting parties he had at his house." James smiled at Sofia, who became sad as she remembered. During those gatherings she'd first met and fallen in love with James. How hopeful she'd been. Why did it all turn sour in the end?

The next moment, however, it became clear to her what had gone wrong. In honor of Henry, Sofia and Emma had ordered wine for everybody. The restaurant was known for its delicious food and fine wines and one of the reasons Henry had frequented it was their wine menu. The waiter came to their table, showed them the bottle, and asked who would like to taste the wine. Sofia motioned at James. "He's a vintner and winemaker and probably the expert at this table." She wanted to say something nice to him, since he'd come all the way for the funeral.

James smiled back at her and gave a demonstration of wine tasting. Everybody watched him as the waiter poured the Pinot Noir and James tilted the glass, swirled the wine, sniffed it, and took a sip. Sofia felt he exaggerated the whole procedure but John and his wife observed him fascinated.

James closed his eyes, seemingly savoring the taste, then opened them and stared at the waiter. "Too young; too cold."

Sofia was shocked. Even if it were true, it wasn't the right place and time for such a criticism. The waiter looked stunned and offered to bring them another bottle.

"May I try?" Sofia said. James glared at her but nodded and handed her the glass. Sofia tried the wine without making a big production. As far as she could tell the temperature was fine and she liked the taste. Not wanting to offend James outright but trying to keep the waiter from bringing a new bottle, she put down her glass and smiled.

"I have to admit I love it. I may not be a connoisseur but to me the wine tastes fine." She turned to the waiter. "Why don't you let the other people try it as well? We'll vote on it."

"I don't mind bringing a new bottle," the waiter said in a flustered tone.

"Let's all try it," John offered. Everybody got a glass and tried the wine. John shrugged. "It tastes perfect to me, but what do I know?"

Emma and John's wife, Jeanie, took small sips and nodded approvingly and so did Henry's parents.

"I'm afraid you're overruled, James," John said. "Your taste buds are just too refined for everyday wine drinkers like us."

James made a face and shrugged. "Suit yourself."

"If you want to order something else, James, go ahead. I didn't mean to force you to drink this one if you don't like it," Sofia tried to appease him.

"I'm fine with this one. It's not up to my standards. After all, you asked for my opinion. But it's okay."

After everybody had their glass filled and plates of food began to arrive, the little episode was soon forgotten by the other guests. The near fiasco, however, reminded Sofia why their marriage hadn't worked out. She remembered how often James had made her feel inadequate.

Of course, Sofia hadn't had much experience in the winemaking business when she first met James, who was six years her senior. Her knowledge had been mainly theoretical. She'd taken a few classes and learned from her father. In the beginning of their marriage, she mainly worked in the office of the vineyard, which belonged to James's family. When her in-laws and owners of the business were semi-retired, James took over control of the vineyard. Sofia wanted to learn as much as possible about the actual work with wine but James didn't encourage or support her. She was responsible for the office and that was the way he liked it.

However, as she became more independent and knowledgeable, she began to make some suggestions of how to improve the daily work at the vineyard. Unfortunately, she soon realized James was not about to give up control over the way the business was run. It belonged to his family and Sofia had always been made to feel like an outsider. It had hurt her deeply.

And then James's affairs with other women began. No, Sofia didn't regret not being married to him anymore. James almost managed to kill her love of vineyards and the art of winemaking. After the divorce and after she'd moved back to Santa Monica to live with her father, it was mainly Henry who'd encouraged her to study the subject in more depth. He helped her get a job with a reputable wine, food and travel magazine, where she was the junior editor for the wine section and wrote articles for their blog.

The rest of lunch passed amiably although James's feathers had been ruffled and he was quiet and almost morose during the meal. Shortly before dessert, he left because he had to drive back to northern California.

10

Relieved that he was gone, Sofia was able to enjoy her cup of coffee and strawberry cake and relax among her friends and family.

After lunch, Emma and Sofia drove Henry's parents to the airport. They lived in a retirement community in Brattleboro, Vermont, and had come out for the funeral. Sofia hadn't seen much of her grandparents since Bernard and Lydia lived across the country. They encouraged her to keep in touch.

"Don't become a stranger," Lydia said with tears in her eyes as she kissed Sofia and Emma good-bye. "We have a guest room. You're always welcome."

Sofia and Emma promised to visit them soon.

Chapter 3

A few days later, Sofia and Emma were sitting in John Wagner's office in a small business complex on Fourth Street in Santa Monica. Sofia had been there a couple of times as a child with her father. She still remembered the piles of papers and folders stacked on the lawyer's desk and not much seemed to have changed since that time.

"How can you find anything in this mess?" Emma asked with a chuckle as John shuffled through the folders on the desk, opening and closing them.

"Ah," he said, lifting an eyebrow. "You'd be surprised. This is an organized mess." He picked up another folder and opened it. "See, here it is," he said with a quick smile. He began to sort through some papers.

Sofia didn't know how old John Wagner was but she figured he was about her father's age, in his fifties. He was of medium height, somewhat overweight, and had gray curly hair and a reddish face, which Sofia felt pointed to high blood pressure. How ironic, she thought. John was much more of a heart attack candidate than her father had been and yet it had been her father who had died from it. A feeling of sadness flooded her. Taking a few deep breaths, she suppressed the tears that gathered in her eyes.

"Well, then," John said and cleared his throat. "This should be fairly straight forward, at least most of it." He gave Sofia and Emma a quick, measuring look. "I assume you know that Henry made a living trust, which means this should go through the legal process fairly quickly, since there won't be any probate." He brushed his hand through his hair.

"Yes, Henry mentioned a living trust but that was quite a while ago," Emma said. "I don't know the details though."

John glanced at them. "He didn't mention the fact that he updated the trust recently?"

"No," Emma said. "Not that I know of." She glanced at Sofia. "Did he mention anything to you?"

Sofia shook her head. "No, nothing."

"Oh, boy." John's forehead got even more crinkled. He took off his reading glasses, rubbed his eyes, then faced them with a worried look. "Does that mean you know nothing about the property in Tuscany?"

Sofia and Emma stared at each other, then back at John. "Property in Tuscany?" Emma said stunned.

John nodded, then shook his head. "Henry promised he would tell you. We talked about it several times and again just a few days before ... well, I guess he didn't get around to it. Oh, dear."

"What?" Sofia's heart picked up speed. "What's going on?"

"Darn it, Henry," John said as if talking to himself. Then he sat straight. "I guess it's up to me now to inform you." He fidgeted on his chair and glanced at the two women then lowered his gaze.

"Well, this news may surprise or rather shock you. But you have to believe me; Henry was going to tell you. At least that was his intention when I last talked to him." John shuffled through his papers again.

"Come on, John, don't drag it out like this," Emma said. "It couldn't be that bad, could it?"

"Okay, here it is." He faced Sofia. "Many years ago, when your mother was still alive, Henry went to Tuscany a lot, as you may still remember."

Sofia nodded.

"He studied Italian winemaking methods and did some business there, which you know as well," John continued.

"Yes, but that's not the shocking news, is it?" Emma prodded.

John looked down at a piece of paper. "No. Anyway, Henry spent a lot of time at one particular vineyard near a town called Vignaverde. He got to know the owners quite well. It was an extended family business. At the time, the vineyard had financial problems and Henry helped them out and invested some of his own money in the business and became part owner." John glanced at them again.

"He owned part of a vineyard in Tuscany?" Sofia couldn't believe what she heard. "But ... I never knew about this." She looked at Emma, but Emma shook her head.

"No, that's news to me, too. What in heaven?"

"Well, there's more to this story," John said. "And the 'more' is the reason Henry didn't tell you, although I encouraged him many times to finally be honest with his family." John cleared his throat. "While he was there, he fell in love with a woman, the daughter of the owner. According to Henry, it was at a time there were a lot of problems in his marriage." John glanced at Sofia. "You know the mental problems your mother had put a real strain on their relationship. I'm sure you're aware of this." John hesitated.

Sofia stared at him. "Yes," she whispered.

"The relationship with the woman didn't last but it had consequences. Luisa Santucci, that's the woman's name, became pregnant and had a baby, a girl. Her name is Julietta."

Chapter 4

Stunned silence lingered in the room. A feeling of nausea came over Sofia and she felt her world fall apart. Her father, the man she loved and admired and considered her closest friend, didn't feel close anymore. Now, he wasn't only gone physically but the emotional and spiritual bond between them had been shattered. "That's not possible," she whispered. "Why? Why didn't he tell us?"

John rubbed his forehead. "I think the main reason was that he was ashamed. At first, he couldn't tell anyone because he was still married. And later, he never found the right moment. As I said, we had a long talk and Henry had decided to let you know, to tell you everything."

"Why didn't *you* tell us?" Sofia asked, then shrugged. She knew John couldn't have told them without Henry's approval.

"I wish I could have," John said. "But that was impossible. Henry wasn't just my friend, he was my client."

Sofia nodded. "I know." Her mind felt like a beehive and her heart was racing. She couldn't focus on anything she'd just heard. Tuscany, vineyard, affair. Finally, a thought began to crystallize. She looked up and stared at John and Emma. "I have a sister," she whispered.

At home in Henry's house on Alta Street in Santa Monica, which now belonged to Sofia, Emma prepared a light dinner but Sofia was barely able to eat. Emma, who lived nearby, offered to spend the night again. She'd been staying with

Sofia most of the time since Henry's death.

"I'll just pick up a few things at home and come back," Emma said.

Sofia told her she was going to be okay alone. "I have a headache and just need a good night's sleep and digest what I heard today ... at least somewhat."

"Are you sure? Don't you want to talk?"

Sofia forced a smile. "Not tonight. Thanks Emma. Don't worry, I'll be okay."

Emma hugged her and gently touched her cheek. "If you need me, please call."

"I will, thanks."

"I'll be back tomorrow." Emma kissed her and left.

Sofia got ready for bed, but she doubted she'd be able to sleep. Being alone, the shocking news of her father's secret life began to overwhelm her.

When her father unexpectedly died, it had been terrible. But at least they'd still been connected to each other through a shared history and loving memories. But now, she felt like she didn't know him anymore. He'd become a complete stranger. Sofia felt rootless and abandoned.

Unable to fall asleep, she got up, made herself a cup of herbal tea, and took an aspirin for the headache. However, not even the hot liquid was able to soothe her heart. She was torn between utter sadness about the loss of her father and anger about his betrayal.

A sister, a fourteen year-old sister, she'd never met, somewhere in Italy. A vineyard, what did it all mean? For fourteen years, her father had spent several weeks each year in Tuscany with his other daughter, while Sofia believed that he'd been there on business.

"How could you do this to me, you bastard." She knocked down the framed photo of Henry from her nightstand, then

16

fell to her knees and hugged the picture to her chest. Painful sobs rocked her. What should she do now? She'd inherited a piece of property. At least her father had the decency to leave her something from his double-life. No, that wasn't fair. From what she'd been told by John, he'd been more than generous with her, as far as money and property was concerned. But what did money and property matter when he had deprived her of her sister?

Exhausted from crying, she finally fell into a fitful sleep but kept waking up with the same sad thought in mind and a hollow ache inside her chest. She'd lost her father; he was gone.

The following morning, Emma came by with a bag of fresh croissants. While she prepared tea for breakfast, Sofia was pacing the living room. "I still can't believe it," she said. She sat down on the sofa, then got up again and continued to walk around. She brushed over her eyes, which felt scratchy from crying and lack of sleep. "Why didn't Dad tell me? I can understand that he didn't tell me about the affair when I was a child. But I'm an adult. He could've told me a long time ago. Why did he have so little trust in me? I wouldn't have blamed him for the relationship. This really hurts me." Her voice broke.

Emma came back from the kitchen, carrying a tray with a pot of tea and two cups, which she put on the coffee table. She sat down and motioned Sofia to sit next to her. She put her arm around her niece. "He wanted to tell us. He was getting ready to and then the heart attack happened."

"But why did he wait so long? Fourteen years, Emma. He knew I always wanted a sister or a brother. This is so cruel."

Emma sighed. "I know, it wasn't right. But try to understand Henry a little. At first, he was probably ashamed of his affair with this Italian woman. You know he always felt guilty for not having been able to save your mother. I know he couldn't have done anything more for her. He tried everything, but I know he felt in part responsible for her death. And after your mother died, he probably didn't want to upset you even more. It was enough trying to make you understand what had happened to her."

"Yes, but that was a long time ago. He could've told me years ago," Sofia said, anger surging through her again.

Emma poured the tea and gave a cup to Sofia. "I know." She shook her head. "Perhaps it was because he'd hidden it for some many years and the longer he waited, the more difficult it became to confess."

Sofia took a little sip of tea, then put the cup down. She glanced at the garden through the window. Her eyes lingered on the bougainvillea with its red and yellow blossoms and the blooming jacaranda tree in the front yard. "Still, it's going to take me a while to get over this. One thing is for sure, I want to go and meet my sister. I wonder if she even wants to see me. And her mother, my father's girlfriend. Oh, this is so confusing." Sofia covered her face with her hands.

"From what John told us, Julietta is eager to get to know you," Emma said thoughtfully. "You know I just remembered something Henry said right before he … passed away." Emma glanced at Sofia.

Emma had been the one to find Henry lying on the floor in his study. She'd come by while Sofia was at work.

"What?" Sofia peered at Emma.

"I wanted to tell you before, but there was so much confusion and all the rush with the doctor and everything and I forgot."

"What is it?"

"Before Henry died, he tried to tell me something. It

didn't make sense then and I was so upset and afraid I didn't pay much attention to it." Emma put her hand over her eyes. "He slurred the words and I could barely understand him but now I think he said 'Tuscany' and something about a journal."

"Journal?" Sofia mused. "I know Henry wrote in a journal in the mornings. It must be among his things in the study. Perhaps we'll find something that will shed some light."

They went into Henry's room that was still as cluttered as it had been when he was alive. Sofia hadn't had the heart to go through his things and clean up. She pulled out the drawers on his desk, but didn't see anything that resembled his journal.

"Could this be it?" Emma asked. She lifted a black notebook from the bookshelf.

"Yes, that's probably it," Sofia said as Emma handed her the book.

They sat on Henry's old sofa and Sofia began to page through the journal. Henry's handwriting was difficult to read and it took Sofia some time to sort through the short paragraphs of writing about wine interspersed with comments about things to do, notes to himself, and even a few shopping lists. One of the entries, however, began with a comment that made Sofia's heartbeat speed up. "Here's something," she said and began to decipher her father's scribbles.

Sofia read hesitantly. "I went to talk to John and gave him the last change to the trust. He's going to clarify it with our lawyer in Florence. Now, the distribution of the property is finally settled. I should have done it a long time ago. I am such a coward. I need to tell Sofia, and Emma, of course. I want to take Sofia to Vignaverde to meet Julietta. I hope Sofia will forgive me for not telling her sooner. I really want my two girls to meet and get along. I think that was one of the reasons I waited so long. I was always afraid there would be animosity, but Sofia has a kind heart and I'm sure she'll accept her sister. And Julietta has asked me about my family in California several times. How could I have withheld the truth for so long? Well, it will be over soon. Whatever their reaction is going to be, I'll have to bear it."

That was it. Sofia paged through the journal some more to see if he'd written anything else about it, but after a few pages, she stopped. She handed the journal to Emma who read the entry. Sofia stared at her hands and felt tears drop on them. "Oh, Henry ... Dad, why *did* you wait so long?"

"Well, at least now we know a little more about his intentions," Emma said. "He was wrong not telling us, not telling you, but he sounds truly contrite. Please, Sofia, don't condemn him. He made a big mistake but he loved you dearly." Emma put her arm around Sofia's shoulder.

Sofia nodded. "Yes, I know. I just wish ... it would be so wonderful if he could've taken me and introduced me to the family. Now, I have to do it by myself. I need to go to Tuscany and find out what this is all about. A sister, Emma. I have a sister." Sofia felt a smile tickle her lips.

"Yes, and a vineyard, or at least part of it. Perhaps this will make up a little for the loss of the vineyard up north," Emma said. "I wish I could come along, but you know I have to start teaching again in late August. And I'm sure you don't want to wait until Christmas break." Emma taught elementary school in Santa Monica.

Sofia was nervous about going by herself, terrified in fact, but she didn't think she could wait that long. "I'd love to be there during the grape harvest. It would also give me an opportunity to write about winemaking in Tuscany. I just hope the family is okay with me coming."

20

"I'm sure they are. John said he would inform them of your plans. He has a lawyer friend there who will help you." Emma got up. "We have travel guides on Tuscany. Let's see where Vignaverde is."

Sofia went to her father's study to get a map. She spread it out on her father's desk. When they found the small village, her heartbeat accelerated. A mixture of fear and excitement flooded her, fear of the unknown and excitement about a great adventure waiting for her.

PART TWO: TUSCANY

Chapter 5

After Sofia had taken leave of Emma at the Los Angeles International Airport and sat by herself, waiting to board the plane, fear and despair overwhelmed her again. Her plan to visit this Italian family she didn't know seemed insane now. She'd been to Italy with her father years before, but this journey she was undertaking now was not a pleasure trip. It was scary and Sofia was almost ready to bolt, go back through security, and stay in her familiar environment. But for that, it was too late.

What had she been thinking when she decided to spend three months in a country she didn't know, staying with a family she'd never met? What if her sister was mean and arrogant, a spoiled teenager? What if the family hated her? And what should she do with the vineyards she inherited? John assured her that his lawyer friend, who had taken care of her father's business in Tuscany, would help her. But still, it was all so unreal.

At home, her confusion and pain about the death of her father and his secret life had slowly given way to cautious excitement about her upcoming adventure. But now, being alone, she felt homesick for Emma and frightened.

"No," she said to herself, as she wiped away a tear, "I can't be a coward. It will be all right." She took a deep breath and forced a smile.

The flight from Los Angeles to Florence was long and tiring. The plane left in the afternoon on its way to Frankfurt,

Germany, where it had a stopover of two hours before going on to Florence. After dinner and a glass of wine, which, to Sofia's disgust, was served in a plastic cup, most passengers either watched the movie, listened to music, or went to sleep. Sofia paged through her travel guide on Florence and Tuscany for a while, watched a film she wasn't much interested in, and turned the monitor off halfway through. She tried to sleep but she was too nervous. Her snoring neighbor and the rather uncomfortable airplane seat didn't help.

Sofia thought of the days ahead. John told her that his lawyer friend would pick her up at the airport and take care of her. He knew about Sofia's case and, according to John, spoke fluent English. This was a great relief to Sofia, whose Italian was almost non-existent.

"Had I known of a sister in Italy, I would've learned to speak Italian," Sofia said to John before leaving. "I won't even be able to speak to Julietta." John, however, assured her that Julietta spoke English. Henry had told him once that he'd arranged for Julietta to take English classes from an early age on. "He'd always planned to get you two together one day."

When Sofia woke from the scent of coffee that came from the kitchen cubicle on the plane, she realized that she'd fallen asleep after all. The flight attendant distributed hot towels and soon breakfast was served. To Sofia's surprise, the coffee tasted quite good.

In Frankfurt, Sofia waited in the airport coffee shop for her flight to Florence. She had another cup of coffee and read her travel guide. For the first time since her departure, excitement about her adventure was stronger than her fears and uncertainties. She looked forward to spending a day in Florence before going on to Vignaverde. It had been at least ten years since she'd been there last with her father. Hopefully, John's friend was waiting for her at the airport. She wouldn't know what to do if she missed him. She also worried about her suitcase making it to Florence. She'd heard all kinds of horror stories about lost luggage on airplanes.

The flight to Florence was short. To Sofia's relief her luggage was on the baggage carousel. She grabbed it and walked into the waiting area where family and friends picked up the passengers. She scanned the waving and smiling crowd, realizing she had no idea what the lawyer looked like. She tried to swallow, but her mouth felt dry as fear began to spread from the pit of her stomach to her chest.

Just as she was about to lose all courage again, she saw her name on a sign held up by an elegantly dressed man who was scanning the arriving people with piercing dark eyes. Her fears somewhat allayed, Sofia walked toward him and waved. When his eyes came to rest on her, they changed from a scrutinizing glare to a short questioning expression and then to a warm, soft gaze. He smiled and motioned her around the cordoned off area to the exit where he met her.

His name was Adriano Gori as Sofia remembered. He was an attractive man, somewhat stocky without being fat, only slightly taller than Sofia. He had tanned skin and thick, black hair.

"*Signorina* Laverne, welcome to Firenze." He shook her hand and took her suitcase.

"Mr. Gori, thank you for picking me up," Sofia said.

"Call me Adriano, please," he said as they walked outside to the parking lot.

"Sofia," she said.

"Beautiful name." He smiled.

It was mid afternoon and quite hot in Florence. Adriano pulled a white handkerchief out of the pocket of his jacket and wiped his forehead. Sofia wondered why he was dressed so formally in this warm weather, then remembered that he might have come from work. He was a lawyer. Perhaps he had been at court.

"It's warm here," she said as they walked to a shiny, metallic gray car. Adriano pointed his key at the lock, which gave a slight beep.

"Yes, it is quite hot today," he said. He opened the car door, took off his jacket, and put it on the back seat, then stripped off his tie and tossed it on top of it. He opened the trunk and stowed Sofia's suitcase in it.

"Did you come directly from the office?" Sofia asked. He looked at her surprised. "Just because you're dressed ...," she tried to find the right word, not wanting to sound nosy.

"Ah, yes, I did not have time to change," he said. "Too much work."

"I'm so grateful you're taking the time to bring me to Vignaverde. I'd be lost by myself," Sofia said as they sat in the car.

"It is my pleasure to help you." Adriano gave her a quick smile. "I shall drive you to your hotel." He reached for a piece of notebook paper on the dashboard and glanced at it. "This is it, is it not?" He showed her the paper.

Sofia was relieved he spoke English fluently. His way of expressing himself was a little formal, as if he had studied it at the university, and he spoke with an accent. But his friendly and warm behavior soothed her frazzled nerves somewhat.

"Yes, that's it," Sofia said, pointing at the note. "I think it's right in the center of Florence. Do you know where it is?"

"Yes, it is in the center."

"Do you think it's a decent place? I found it on the Internet."

"I do not know the hotel but it is in a good area," Adriano said. "Very convenient."

"Perhaps I can do a little sightseeing tomorrow," Sofia said. "I have a day before we go to Vignaverde."

"Have you ever been to Firenze, Sofia?" he asked.

"Yes, but a long time ago."

"It is a very busy city, lots of tourists," Adriano said. "Too many tourists, crazy." He sounded irritated and waved his hand as if he wanted to chase away some imaginary people. He seemed to have the typical love-hate relationship many people living in tourist-mobbed places had. They resented the intrusion of the outsiders but loved the money they brought.

"Florence is a wonderful city, though, from what I remember when I was here last with my father. So much art, so much to see."

"Yes, Firenze is a very interesting city," Adriano agreed. He gave her a quick glance, then focused on the road again when they reached the *autostrada* or freeway.

"*Mi dispiace*," he said. "I would like to express my condolences on the death of your father. Forgive me for not thinking of it before."

"Oh, that's quite all right," Sofia said. "But thank you."

"He ... died suddenly, your papa, no?"

The informal term *papa* and Adriano's gentle, warm voice brought tears to Sofia's eyes. She blinked and nodded. "Yes, a heart attack."

"I'm very sorry," he said.

Sofia turned to him. "Did you know my father well?"

"I knew him a little," Adriano said. "We always met when he was in Italy, of course, since I took care of his finances and checked the accounting of his vineyards. And I also went to the estate with him a few times." He paused. "He was a very nice man, your papa. Very passionate about wine. And very generous. It is sad that he died so young."

"I know. I miss him terribly." Sofia swallowed, feeling a lump in her throat.

Adriano nodded. It was quiet for a while, then he cleared his throat. "And now you have come to claim your property." It was the voice of the lawyer now.

"I guess you could call it that," Sofia said with a wistful smile. Then in a more serious tone. "Until a few weeks ago I didn't even know I owned property here … I don't know how much you know, how familiar you are with the circumstances."

Adriano gave her a quick glance. "Giovanni told me. I am quite familiar with the circumstances. He had to tell me, because I am representing you." He sounded apologetic.

It took Sofia a moment to realize he meant John. "Oh, I'm glad you know. I'm so grateful for your help. I wouldn't know what to do. This is all very new for me."

"I shall help you with all the legal matters and I shall introduce you to the family … *idiota,*" he yelled, as a car passed them at high speed and cut them off.

Sofia flinched. Adriano slapped the steering wheel, changed the lane and passed the car, honking and staring at the driver, his now fiery dark eyes shooting daggers. He took a deep breath and glanced at Sofia. "*Scusami,*" he murmured. The smile was back.

He stepped on the gas. Sofia tried to see the speedometer but it was in kilometers. She figured he must be driving at least eighty. *He is Italian,* she thought. *Gentle and warm one moment, furious the next.*

They approached the center of the city and Adriano slowed down as they drove through the narrow streets. Sofia took a deep breath. She was grateful not having to drive herself in this mess of small cars, motorcycles, scooters, and tourists crossing the streets without checking for cars.

"Will you be able to park near the hotel?" Sofia asked. "I read in my travel guide that you can't park in the center."

"This is correct, yes, but I have a permit, since I often work in the city," Adriano said. "It is difficult to park though, even with a permit, but I hope we shall be lucky."

At the hotel, which was close to Casa di Dante, the house where the poet allegedly had lived, Adriano stopped the car on the sidewalk. They got out and walked to the hotel lobby. Adriano waited until Sofia had checked in and got the key to her room.

"Go and inspect the room and come back to let me know if it is to your liking," he told her.

The room was small but clean and quiet, away from the busy streets. Sofia dropped off her baggage and came back to the lobby. Adriano was talking to the receptionist and a man standing next to her. He introduced Sofia to the man, who turned out to be the manager of the hotel.

"If you have any questions and need help tomorrow with sightseeing, just ask at the desk," Adriano said.

"I recommend making reservations if you want to visit the Uffizi gallery and other places tomorrow. We can do that for you." The manager gave her a big smile.

Sofia was grateful for the help and the friendly reception. After accompanying Adriano to his car, they shook hands.

"I am sorry I cannot take care of you during the day tomorrow because I am very busy at work. But I hope I may have the privilege of inviting you to dinner tomorrow evening. We can talk some more about Vignaverde and the *famiglia*," Adriano said.

"I'd love to have dinner with you. I hope I'm not taking up too much of your time," Sofia said.

"Not at all. It will be a pleasure." He smiled and gently

31

touched her arm. "Have a good time sightseeing tomorrow. And if you need anything, ask the receptionist. And here is my business card. I shall not be in Florence directly during the day but if you have a problem ..." He pulled out a card from his wallet and gave it to her.

"Don't worry, I'll be fine," she said. "But thanks."

When Sofia was alone, she walked back to the hotel, feeling very tired all of a sudden. Not having slept much during the night on the plane as well as the few nights before her departure had caught up with her. She wanted to call Emma before going to sleep but she'd forgotten to recharge her cell phone and she didn't know how to work the phone in her hotel room. It would have to wait until the next day. She missed Emma but was too exhausted to feel sad. The minute she put her head on the pillow, she fell asleep.

Chapter 6

The next morning after a quick breakfast of coffee, orange juice, and rolls with butter and jam, Sofia grabbed her camera and headed out. She was refreshed and ready to tackle the tourists and the art. She had a Firenze card, which the receptionist at the hotel had obtained for her. It would let her see some of the sights, including the Duomo and the Uffizi gallery, without having to wait in line for two to three hours. Seeing the long lines, she was glad she'd bought this somewhat pricey pass. She walked the short distance to the Arno River and crossed the famous Ponte Vecchio with its jewelry stores and carts, then headed back to the Uffizi.

One of her favorite painters in the Uffizi was Sandro Botticelli. She spent some time admiring the playful depiction of springtime with its mixture of idealized and realistic faces of the pagan characters in his paintings. There was so much to see at the gallery but after a few hours, Sofia was getting tired from taking in all these works of art. She would come back later during her stay in Tuscany and see more of the paintings. It was almost noon and she decided to look for a place to eat before the lunchtime crowd headed to the restaurants.

Outside, the sun, which had been hiding behind clouds in the early morning, was out and lit up the beautiful Renaissance and medieval buildings. It was August and it would be getting hot in the afternoon. Sofia decided to buy a sandwich somewhere and have a picnic lunch. She remembered from her former visit with her father that they had bought sandwiches and eaten in a small park at Oltrarno, the old part of Florence south of the Arno River. Trying to remember where it had been, she walked across one of the bridges and made her way through the cobblestone streets. Inhaling the different smells coming from the restaurants, coffee shops, and small corner grocery stores made her aware of how hungry she was. In one of the stores, she bought a couple of rolls, prosciutto, and cheese along with fruit and a bottle of mineral water.

There were signs pointing toward the Boboli Gardens where she had been with her father as well. She would have loved to visit the beautiful grounds full of works of art again, but that would have taken another few hours.

As she strolled through this quaint and less touristy neighborhood with its small shops and art galleries, memories of her father flooded her. He'd been in this city many times and twice she had accompanied him. How wonderful would it be if they could've been here together now? Why did he have to die so soon and why hadn't he confided in her? All of a sudden, this beautiful city made her feel lonely. Tears rose to her eyes and she took a deep breath, trying to soothe the ache in her chest. When she turned the corner, she saw a church she recognized. It was the Santo Spirito church her father had taken her to. She remembered that the interior had been designed by Brunelleschi who had also constructed the dome of the Duomo. There were a few artworks by Michelangelo inside, too.

After a quick walk through the church, Sofia sat on a bench on the Piazza Santa Spirito and unpacked her lunch. Taking a bite of the fresh bread, topped with tasty prosciutto, she smiled. Sitting in that peaceful spot, she felt more content again.

She was so grateful having found the entry in Henry's

journal. At least she knew now that he felt sorry for what he'd done. Still she couldn't help remembering all these years she'd trusted him unconditionally only to realize now that this trust had not been mutual. How could he have misjudged her so terribly? Did he know his own daughter so little that he was afraid she would reject him when she learned the truth? She'd read the journal entry over and over again. It was like a conversation he'd begun, which had been cut short by his death. She was still too confused and angry at him, but eventually, it would be up to her to continue the conversation. Meeting her sister was a first step.

On her way back to the Duomo after lunch, Sofia stopped at one of the many cafeterias for an espresso. In the afternoon, she had planned a stroll through the Duomo. As with the Uffizi gallery, her Firenze pass allowed her to go inside without waiting in the long line. The Duomo with its marvelous dome by Filippo Brunelleschi, the Baptistery with its bronze doors, designed by Ghiberti, and the Campanile— the bell tower or Giotto's Tower—took up the rest of the afternoon. The beauty of the artworks dispersed her feeling of melancholy. In spite of all the turmoil, it was exciting to be here. Perhaps she would even move here one day. She could ask Mr. Gori about the legal requirements. As a lawyer, he might know.

Adriano Gori picked Sofia up at eight o'clock. By then she was starved. She hadn't eaten anything since her light lunch and she wasn't used to the late dinner hours of the Italians. Adriano met her in the lobby. He'd parked his car in one of the public lots and had walked to the hotel.

Sofia had put on one of the few dresses she'd packed, a sundress with a blue-and-purple pattern that matched the color of her eyes and flattered her light-brown hair with the blond highlights. She hadn't expected to need to dress up, living on a vineyard in Tuscany, but she didn't want to give the impression of a sloppy tourist, in case Adriano was wearing a suit again. To her relief, he was dressed in slacks and a lightweight sports jacket.

"You look very pretty," he said with a smile as he opened the hotel door for her.

"Thank you," she said, feeling her face flush.

"We shall walk to the restaurant. It is right down the street," Adriano said. He glanced at her shoes. She was wearing sandals with a small heel.

"Yes, that's fine," Sofia said. "They're comfortable," she added, motioning at her shoes.

"Good, you never know with young ladies." He chuckled.

"Do you have children, Adriano?" Sofia remembered John telling her that Adriano was married.

He nodded. "Oh, yes, two of them, a girl and a boy, well, the boy is a young man now. He must be about your age." His face stretched into a smile. "Lucia is sixteen and Marcello is twenty-two."

"I'm twenty-four," Sofia said.

Adriano shrugged. "Almost the same."

They walked a short block along Via de Alighieri to the *ristorante* Paoli. "They serve typical Tuscan food and it is also well-known by tourists, so I made reservations," Adriano said. "Did you have a nice time sightseeing today?" he asked.

"Yes, I did. There is so much to see. I'll have to come back," Sofia said.

"You will be here for a few months. Perhaps you can come back to Firenze another time."

Sofia nodded. "That's what I'm planning to do."

When they entered the restaurant, Sofia gasped. It was a

spectacular place with high, decorated, vaulted ceilings and walls full of paintings and photos. It looked more like a church than a restaurant. The atmosphere, however, was anything but contemplative. Friendly, jovial waiters greeted them and led them to the reserved table. One of the waiters produced two large, impressive-looking menus. There was a lot of laughter and cheer from both the guests and the people who worked there. A delicious smell of roasted meat and all kinds of other food and spices wafted from the kitchen.

"Wow," Sofia said. "This is quite a place."

Adriano smiled at her. "Do you like it?"

"Yes. Do you come here often?"

Adriano laughed out loud, which seemed at odds with his otherwise mild-mannered demeanor. "No, usually not. I prefer the more quiet places. But I wanted to show you something of the ... how do you say ... flashy side of Firenze. And the food is very good here."

"Well, this is certainly a wonderful place to have dinner. Thank you for taking me here." Sofia looked around at the many energetic waiters who served the meals with a flourish.

"Also, one of your presidents ate here." Adriano pointed at a bust on the wall.

"Who is it?" Sofia asked. "I don't even recognize him. Oh, wait, here it says." She pointed at the menu. "Woodrow Wilson, the twenty-eighth president of the United States. I didn't know this."

"Well, that is good company, no?" Adriano said as he studied the menu, then looked up. "What would you like to eat?"

Sofia sighed. "Too many choices."

Adriano perused the menu. "I can make a suggestion. If that is all right with you?"

Sofia nodded. "Yes, please."

"However, you have to help me with the wine. You are probably an expert," Adriano said.

"Oh, no." Sofia laughed. "My father was the expert. I love wine, particularly red wine, but I don't know too much about Tuscan wine, since I was here before I was allowed to drink."

When their enthusiastic waiter came back, Adriano asked him to recommend a wine. That led to a lively exchange between the two men in rapid Italian, of which Sofia understood hardly anything. After they seemed to have made a decision, Adriano told her that the waiter recommended a Sangiovese and Merlot blend, a so-called Super Tuscan.

"These are the same grapes that grow on your vineyard," he said.

"Oh, well, then it must be good." Sofia chuckled.

They decided to start with a salad, which to Sofia's amusement was elaborately prepared at the table. While Adriano ordered a steak, which was served with a side of mashed potatoes, Sofia decided on a smaller piece of meat, a veal chop with truffles and vegetables. They skipped the traditional pasta after the salad and went right to the main menu.

After a few bites of her tender chop and the savory vegetables, Sofia sighed with pleasure. "This is the first solid meal I've had since I came here and it's wonderful."

Adriano seemed relieved. "I am happy you like it."

"Tell me," Sofia said after taking a sip of wine, "do you know what I'd have to do if I decided to stay in Tuscany permanently? I mean live here."

Adriano gave her a measured look. "It depends. Immigration is not my specialty but I can find out for you. You think you may want to stay here?"

Sofia shrugged. "I've been thinking about it. It all depends, of course, how I feel once I get to Vignaverde. I love

Italy, but ... it's probably a pipe dream. I really don't know."

"You will have time to decide," Adriano said. "You should wait until you meet the *famiglia*. I wanted to tell you a little about them. We can have dessert and an espresso and talk."

Sofia nodded. She felt Adriano looked concerned. Just then, the waiter pushing the dessert trolley stopped at their table and pointed at a display of delicious-looking pastries. Sofia wasn't exactly hungry anymore but she couldn't resist and chose the fresh strawberries with cream. Adriano picked a small *profiterole* or cream puff. They ordered espresso and Adriano encouraged her to order a *digestivo*, an after-dinner drink, but Sofia declined.

"The wine was just enough for me, thank you," she said. "I'm not used to a lot of alcohol."

Adriano smiled. "But you are the daughter of an *amante del vino*, no?"

"Yes, but believe me, my father was a very moderate drinker, in spite of the fact that he loved wine. He drank little but he enjoyed it very much." Sofia looked down at her hands, feeling emotional again. She felt Adriano's hand on her arm and looked up.

"We should talk about Vignaverde," he said, his face serious. He cleared his throat. "I do not want to make you feel worried but I must tell you. Some members of the family are a little ... shall we say ... upset about the situation. You know Italian families are very close ... how do you say ... knitted together?"

"You mean close-knit?" Sofia interjected.

"*Si*, yes, and some of the people are not happy that somebody from abroad now owns part of their property."

Chapter 7

Sofia stared at Adriano. "But ... my father was a foreigner, too. Did they resent him?"

"I think they had no choice but to accept him. They needed the money." Adriano shrugged. "When I talked with them about your papa's trust, they had hoped that after his death his two fields would go to his Italian daughter, to Julietta, and therefore back to the family. You know there are two parts to your property. You inherited your father's house and his vineyards. They don't seem to care about the house but they would have liked the vineyards back."

"Oh, gee, I didn't know there would be problems," Sofia said. She felt her heart sink.

"Do not worry," Adriano continued. "They have no legal rights. The trust is very clear and it is in accordance with Italian law. Besides, they have other vineyards and Julietta will inherit part of those. And your papa was a very generous man. He saved the estate. He gave money to the family when they had financial problems. He also provided very well for your sister. Part of the profit from your papa's vineyards, from the grapes and the wine went into an account for her. She will get the money when she is eighteen. Now, the property is yours and you can decide what to do with it."

"Oh, I would love to continue to give some of the profit to my sister. That should stay the same."

"*Bene*, that is kind of you."

Sofia sighed. "I just hope they don't see me as the enemy. Which members are unhappy about the inheritance? Julietta's mother? Her name is Luisa, right?"

Adriano nodded then waved his hand in his typical dismissive gesture. "I am not sure how *signora* Santucci feels about it. She does not seem to have an opinion. She defers to her brother Edoardo. He and his father, Silvio Santucci, are the ones who seem to be unhappy about the situation."

"Why?"

Another shrug. "It is a complicated family story. See Edoardo and Luisa are half-siblings. They have the same mother but a different father. Luisa's father died and her mother married *il dottore* Santucci. Edoardo is Luisa's younger brother and the old Santucci's son. Unfortunately, the *dottore* is quite greedy and he did not like the fact that your father had acquired part of the estate. But he could not do anything about it. He no longer owned it. He had gifted the property to Luisa and Edoardo in equal shares. He must have regretted it later."

"Why? What's wrong with giving it to his children?" Sofia asked.

"See, this happened before *signora* Santucci became involved with your father and before your father bought part of the property. When *dottore* Santucci found out, he was quite upset. He is a real hardcore, old Italian. He believes that only Italians can produce good wine and the land belongs to the family and not to outsiders. I think, too, that he has mental problems." Adriano finished his espresso.

"There is also a son from Luisa Santucci's former marriage, a Guido Berlusconi. He is a very unsavory character. He had an interest in the two fields that belonged to your papa. He called me once and was very rude. But I told him he had absolutely no right in the property."

Sofia sighed. "Oh, wonderful. This looks like it's going to be a family soap opera."

"Soap opera? What is this? Oh, you mean a *telenovela*?"
"Yes."

"Do not worry about it. Your property is safe."

"It's not so much the property I'm worried about, but if the people hate me, it will be very unpleasant. You mentioned Edoardo, Luisa's brother. What kind of a person is he?"

"Edoardo is … how shall I say it? … a little weak. I mean his character. He is not a bad person but I think he is still afraid of upsetting his father." Adriano waved his hand. "This is just my opinion and I may be wrong."

Sofia sighed. "I wonder how Luisa feels about me."

"It is difficult to say. Perhaps she feels a little guilty. She was your papa's mistress."

Sofia laughed. "Mistress? That sounds so old-fashioned."

"What would you call it?" Adriano asked.

"Well, girlfriend, maybe?"

Adriano raised an eyebrow. "It was just a temporary affair, from what Giovanni told me."

"Yes, but my father sure felt guilty about it. I guess that's why he never told anyone."

"But it was just an affair, no?"

Sofia looked at Adriano surprised. "Well, perhaps Italian men think differently about having affairs when they are married. But I think my father was quite puritanical about it."

"Perhaps you are right. In Italy, it is not such a big deal."

"But that isn't very nice for the women, the wives, I mean?" Sofia couldn't help but wonder how Adriano felt about this. He looked like a happily married man. Had she misjudged him?

He seemed to have guessed her thoughts. "No, it is not nice for the wives. And it is not good for the family. I do not believe in having affairs." He shrugged. "But it happens, no?"

"I guess so." Sofia took a deep breath. "I'm already more

than nervous about meeting Julietta and the family. This news doesn't make it any easier."

Adriano put his hand on hers again. "I am so sorry. I did not want to worry you. I just wanted you to know the situation. And you do not have to worry about Julietta. She likes you. She is looking forward to meeting you."

"You know her? How is she?" Sofia asked eagerly.

"I met her a few times when I was there with your papa. She is a teenager, you know. Strong opinions. A little rebellious. But a nice young girl." He smiled. "She reminds me of my own daughter."

"I hope we'll get along," Sofia said quietly.

"I am sure you will be very good friends. She asked me a lot of questions about you. Unfortunately, I could not tell her much, since I did not know you. But she looks forward to meeting you. And she wants to go to California, to Hollywood." Adriano raised his eyebrow and laughed. "The dream of all young girls, no?"

Sofia nodded. "I guess so." Then after a short pause. "You know, Adriano, the property isn't the most important thing. I mean, I'd love to own a vineyard in Tuscany, but having a family or friends is more important to me. So, if they insist on having the grape fields back, I may consider letting them have them. I would be happy just to own the house and perhaps help with the harvest and the winemaking and all that."

"*Bene*," Adriano said, then measured her with a stern expression. "This is of course your decision. But, please, do not tell them anything or do anything without consulting with me first. Do not sign anything." He was all lawyer now. "I cannot represent you if you make deals without telling me. You do not know the laws here and you may regret it later."

Sofia hurried to appease Adriano. "Don't worry, I

wouldn't do anything behind your back. Of course, I'll talk to you first." Although she felt a little miffed that he treated her like an uncooperative child, she could understand his concerns. As John had told her, Adriano was getting paid out of her father's trust for representing her and he seemed to feel responsible for her actions and her well-being in Italy. She liked the fatherly feelings he expressed toward her. It felt good and alleviated the pain of losing her own father and soothed her anxiety a little bit.

"I would also like you to continue taking care of the finances like you did for my father," Sofia continued. "I won't be here all the time and I would like to know that someone represents my interests here. Would you do this?"

Adriano nodded. "If you wish, certainly. I thank you for your trust in me. We can talk about the details later."

"Well, my father trusted you and John trusts you." Sofia hesitated, then went on. "John said you are one of the few lawyers he really trusts." She left out the fact that he'd said "Italian lawyers," not wanting to hurt Adriano's possible national pride.

Adriano laughed. "He must know lawyers very well. He is one himself." Then more seriously: "I will always keep your interests at heart."

In the meantime, it had gotten late and Sofia, who was still suffering from jet lag, was getting tired. She tried unsuccessfully to suppress a yawn. Adriano, seeming to notice she was fading, waved over the waiter and asked for the check.

"Thank you, again, for the wonderful dinner," Sofia said.

He gave a quick smile. "I shall take you back to your hotel, so you can rest. If it is okay with you, I would like to leave early tomorrow, right after rush hour. Perhaps at nine o'clock?"

"That's fine," Sofia said. "How far is it to Vignaverde?"

"If traffic is not bad, approximately one hour or a little more," Adriano said.

"I also have to look into renting a car there, so I can get around."

Adriano hesitated. "I do not think there is a rental agency in Vignaverde but there should be one nearby. We will find out. Do not worry."

Before going to bed, Sofia called Emma to let her know how she was doing. They chatted for a while. The weather in California had gotten quite hot and Emma had been busy watering the lawn and the plants at Sofia's home.

"And guess what?" Emma said. "My friend Bertha up north just told me that your ex is no longer working for his parents' estate. He went back to school to study law or finance, something in that area."

After hanging up, Sofia thought about this interesting piece of news. She wasn't that surprised. She always felt that James had mainly worked at the vineyard because his father expected it, but his heart hadn't been in it. He wasn't the right person for this business. All the other grape growers or winemakers Sofia had met shared common traits: they were passionate about winemaking; they were supportive of each other, even if they were competitors. They shared rather than hid their knowledge. James lacked those qualities. He was too competitive and too much into himself.

In spite of being tired, Sofia didn't sleep well that night. Her talk with Adriano about the attitude of the family toward her intensified her worries. She woke up in the middle of the night, hearing voices outside. She'd left the windows open to get some of the evening breeze after the sweltering heat of the day. In the courtyard downstairs, a few young people were laughing and talking. It smelled of cigarette smoke. After a while, someone upstairs hissed *"silenzio."* More giggling, then a clanking sound, as if someone was kicking a steel bucket around, and finally it got quiet again. Sofia went back to bed but couldn't fall asleep for quite a while.

Chapter 8

Sofia woke up with a headache the following morning. She groaned as she got out of bed and stumbled into the bathroom. After a quick shower, she ate a leftover roll from the day before and downed an aspirin. The sun was just above the horizon and the sky was clear except for a few purple clouds to the east. It would be a pleasant day. After packing her suitcase and bag for the drive to Vignaverde, she decided she needed a slightly more substantial breakfast to prepare her for the adventure of the day—meeting her *famiglia* and the *padrino* Santucci, as she called Edoardo and his father after the character depiction she had received from Adriano.

Since the hotel breakfast room wasn't ready yet, Sofia walked to the cafeteria at the corner where she ordered a cappuccino and a few rolls. The fragrance and taste of the coffee and the lightly sweet, crunchy bread put a smile on her face. The aspirin seemed to be doing its job and her head felt clear again. Outside, a golden glow enveloped the dome of the main cathedral. It was impossible not to be content in this beautiful city.

Back at the hotel, she paid her bill and waited at the entrance for Adriano so he wouldn't have to find parking. A few minutes later, his silver Lancia came driving through the narrow street. He stopped, got out, and gave her a bright smile. *"Buongiorno*, Sofia, how are you?"

"Nervous," she said. "I didn't sleep well last night. Otherwise I'm fine."

He grabbed her suitcase and put it in the trunk. "Nervous about meeting your sister?"

"Yes, that, and the rest of the family."

"I understand," he continued as they sat in the car. "Meeting your sister will be very emotional," he stated. "But also very happy."

"I hope so, yes," Sofia said with a sigh.

He started the car and drove it slowly through the narrow streets to the wider road leading out of Florence. "Have you had breakfast?"

"Yes, thank you. What about you?" Sofia asked.

He shrugged. "Just some coffee."

"We can stop on the way," Sofia suggested. "If you're hungry."

"This will not be necessary. It is not a very long drive. And we will be having lunch with the family," Adriano said.

"Oh?" Sofia looked at him. "How do you know?"

Another shrug. "This is the way it is done here. They know we are coming."

Sofia had to smile at Adriano's logic, but he was probably right. This was Italy after all, a country known for its hospitality.

"We shall take our time, so you can enjoy the country-side," Adriano said.

"That would be great." Sofia didn't mind having a little extra time before meeting the people she would be staying with. At the thought of these complete strangers, she felt a tightening in her chest.

As they left the city of Florence and headed south, Sofia gazed at the charming countryside, the meadows, and the rolling hills. They passed occasional ocher-colored stone farmhouses and a few lonely cows and horses. The clouds sailing across the sky tossed large patches of shadows on the fields, darkening the landscape for a few seconds and giving it an almost menacing feeling. As soon as the clouds had passed, the sun bathed the brown and deep green fields in a friendly golden glow.

Sofia took a deep breath and pulled her camera out of her purse.

Adriano glanced at her. "Would you like to take pictures? We can stop somewhere."

"Yes, please," Sofia said.

They drove on for a while, then turned off the main road and drove up the hill to a small town that looked like a fortress with walls surrounding it. Adriano parked the car outside the city walls of San Donato.

"It is a hill town like Siena but not so full of tourists," Adriano said as they got out of the car. "But it is very pretty and you can take photos."

It was a lovely town with the typical features of the Tuscan hill towns Sofia remembered from her former trip to Siena. They took a stroll through the narrow streets, admiring the village square, the central piazza surrounded by old Tuscan buildings with natural stonewalls, a beautiful old *palazzo* that was now a hotel. Everywhere blooming purple vines drooped from the walls and arches. From the old Etruscan defensive walls surrounding the town, they had a wide view of meadows full of rust-colored and purple plants, and of small paths winding around olive groves and past vineyards.

"Doesn't this look a little like Vignaverde?" Sofia asked, as they were sitting in front of a small bar, drinking coffee.

"Yes, a little. All of the hill towns here in the Toscana share similarities. Vignaverde does not have that many tourists either." Adriano downed his espresso in one gulp. "Shall we go?"

They drove back to the main road and continued. The rest of the way to Vignaverde presented the same picture. Meadows with sunflowers in full bloom took turns with other wild flowers, the ever-present olive groves, and the fields with their symmetrical rows of vines.

They came to a crossroad and circled a roundabout, then continued. "We shall be in Vignaverde in half an hour," Adriano said and Sofia's heart began to beat faster.

Soon they had the first view of the city. Vignaverde, like many of the hill towns in Tuscany, was surrounded by Etruscan walls. An impressive-looking fortress greeted them from above a wooded hill of stone pines. Adriano parked the car at the entrance of the town. "The estate is nearby, but I want to inquire about car rentals here. There is a tourist office at the central plaza. We can ask there."

They got out of the car and walked through the arched stone gate into the town. Vignaverde was another one of the vibrant Tuscan cities of about five to six thousand inhabitants who lived in the town itself as Adriano mentioned. But unlike Siena, it was pleasantly quiet and devoid of tourist mobs. Sofia inhaled the slightly musty scent in the narrow streets leading to the center of town. They entered the Piazza San Francesco, the central religious square. It was surrounded by impressive-looking medieval buildings. Vignaverde was founded back in Roman times.

Adriano motioned at the chapel in the square. On its facade, they could see a sculpture of a human skull with two wings, one on each side. "This is the symbol of the human soul," he said. "Bones are what is left of us when we die. The wings symbolize the soul, that which survives." He turned around and pointed at the different buildings. "In fact, you can see the cycle of Christian life here. There is the baptistery, which means birth, then the cathedral, which signifies life. And here was the hospital where we end up, and finally the cemetery, death. The hospital and the cemetery were moved outside of the city walls in modern times. These buildings are more or less in every central square in Tuscan towns."

"Fascinating," Sofia said. "I didn't know any of this."

Adriano put his hand on her shoulder. "Well, this is now your hometown as well, so you need to know."

Sofia nodded, then added with a sigh, "I hope I can make it my home. At least my second home."

"You will," Adriano said. "But let us go to the tourist office."

Inside the small building, they met an older woman who told them that the closest rental car agency was in Cecina near the coast.

"We shall go there after meeting the family. It is not very far from here," Adriano said. He glanced at his watch. "We have time to walk through the town, if you wish."

"Yes, let's do that," Sofia said.

They strolled leisurely through the narrow cobblestone streets with its small shops, a bakery here and there, and a rustic restaurant next to homes. It smelled of coffee and some kind of herb, was it basil or oregano? The sounds of laughter and talking gave the town a lively atmosphere. Most of the people appeared to be locals, young and old women and men. Children were running through the streets playing. They all seemed to know each other, there were constant greetings of "*ciao*." Sofia asked herself if she would ever be accepted as one of them.

They'd just turned a corner when she heard a young voice calling "*signor* Gori." Adriano and Sofia turned around and Sofia's breath caught. A young girl waved and came hurrying toward them. She had long wavy chestnut-colored hair and wore a dark-pink skirt and black top.

"It is Julietta," Adriano said. He touched Sofia's back lightly as if to reassure her. But he didn't need to tell her who it was.

PART THREE: THE ITALIAN SISTER

Chapter 9

Sofia recognized the girl right away. She was a younger version of herself. As soon as Julietta noticed Sofia, she stopped short, stared at her, then her face lit up and she cried "Sofia." She began to run again, then flung herself at Sofia and threw her arms around her. She greeted her with a gush of Italian words, of which Sofia only understood the term *mia sorella*, my sister.

Julietta's enthusiastic embrace almost made Sofia stumble. Overwhelmed by her half-sister's exuberant welcome, she hugged her as well, then stepped back a little. Searching for a few words of Italian to greet her new sister, all she could think of was "*Ciao*, Julietta." On the one hand, she was relieved that Julietta seemed genuinely happy to meet her. At the same time, she couldn't muster the same joyful excitement yet. It was all too much, too soon, and confusing.

Julietta seemed to feel Sofia's reluctance. She let go of her and the two sisters looked at each other quietly for a few seconds. Like Sofia, her sister had inherited most of Henry's facial features—his firm chin, his wide open face, and his purple-blue eyes. She seemed to also have the tall figure of the Laverne side of the family. She was a little bustier than Sofia and her hips were a little rounder. The most noticeable difference was her darker skin color and her long chestnut hair that flowed in waves down her back. She must have inherited the reddish-brown hair color from her mother's side whereas Sofia had her father's light-brown hair, streaked with blond.

These thoughts tumbled in bits and pieces through Sofia's mind. The next moment, Julietta's eyes filled with tears. "I wish Papa was here. I miss him so much."

The shock of hearing Julietta referring to Henry as her papa and the girl's sadness brought back the pain of his passing and the turmoil his secret life had created. Sofia felt tears flooding her eyes and she searched her purse for a tissue. A cloth handkerchief appeared before her face and as she grabbed it and looked up, she saw Adriano's face and his kind and now misty eyes. Julietta hugged her again, gentler this time, and Sofia inhaled a light jasmine scent.

She felt hands gently tapping her back and realized that a small group of men and women had gathered around them. Some of them seemed to know Julietta. They hugged her and laughed, then hugged Sofia and murmured *"benvenuta, welcome."* They motioned at a small bar and coffee shop nearby where someone was waving. Still half-dazed, Sofia felt herself being led into a room where it smelled of coffee and freshly baked goods.

They sat at a small table and cups of coffee appeared in front of them as well as a cup of hot chocolate for Julietta. Tears had dried and Sofia had somewhat recovered from the shock of meeting her sister so unexpectedly. She took a deep breath and listened to the enthusiastic voices around her. She understood very little but she couldn't help being affected by the joyful atmosphere.

It was a happy occasion after all, *un' occasione di festa,* as everybody seemed to call it. Two sisters meeting for the first time. Sofia was moved by the warmth of the people around her. They didn't know her but seemed to accept her as one of them. She was the long-awaited American sister of Julietta, of the girl whom many in this small town seemed to know and love.

The Italian Sister

Now Sofia was able to look at Julietta more closely. Her sister was an attractive young girl, not pretty in the girlish sense, but strong and striking. She would be a beautiful woman. Sofia wished she had a little more of Julietta's roundness in the right places. She always felt she was too thin.

A lively conversation in both Italian and English developed and Sofia was surprised how many of the people spoke at least a little English. She felt embarrassed for her lack of Italian and decided to take the time to study the language. Perhaps Julietta, who seemed fluent in both, would teach her.

Half an hour later, Adriano called the waiter. Sofia wanted to pay but someone had already taken care of the bill. *"Grazie mille,"* Sofia said, nodding at everybody, *"molto gentile."* It was one of the few Italian phrases she knew. They all acknowledged her with a smile.

"You can drive with us," Adriano said to Julietta as they got ready to leave.

"I have my *bicicletta* with me," Julietta said.

Adriano shrugged. "This is no problem. We can put it in the trunk."

He put Sofia's suitcase on the backseat, lifted Julietta's bright-red bike into the trunk and secured the lid with a rope. They got into the car and drove the fifteen minutes on a small country road to the estate.

"Did you have a good trip?" Julietta asked Sofia.

Sofia nodded and smiled. "Yes, thank you." She glanced over her shoulder at her lively sister. For a few seconds, nobody said anything, but Julietta was obviously not the quiet type. She and Adriano began to converse in rapid Italian with each other.

As they drove around a corner, Sofia saw a sign with the

name Podere Francesco Ginori. Before her and to the left and right, the vineyards with their neat, parallel lines of vines stretched into the distance and a cluster of small and medium-sized orange and yellow stone houses stood on top of a small hill. At the bottom of the hill was a group of larger buildings that looked like barns, storage sheds, and a stone building Sofia assumed was the winery. The houses were flanked by Italian stone pines and cypress trees.

"Is this it?" Sofia asked.

"Yes, we are here," Adriano said. He drove his car up the hill to a fairly large house and parked in the driveway.

As soon as the car stopped, Julietta jumped out and rushed toward the house. As Sofia got out of the car, she saw a woman step outside who had the same longish, wavy, chestnut-colored hair as Julietta. Sofia guessed it must be Luisa. Julietta grabbed the woman's hand and pulled her toward the car. The woman said something to the girl and followed her. She faced Sofia with a measured look. "*Signorina* Laverne?"

Sofia nodded, then added quickly. "Please call me Sofia. I'm pleased to meet you."

"My name is Luisa," the woman said with a quick smile as they shook hands. "Did you have a pleasant journey?"

"Yes, thank you." Sofia didn't know what to make of Luisa. She was soft-spoken and friendly but lacked the warmth of her daughter. Then again, Sofia couldn't expect the same kind of enthusiasm from her father's former girlfriend as she experienced from her sister.

Adriano and Luisa greeted each other with the formal *signora* and *signor*. Their behavior toward each other was polite and formal. Sofia noticed with relief that Luisa, too, spoke fluent English.

"Please come inside." Luisa waved them toward the

house, an old but beautiful Tuscan stone building with ocher walls. It was a two-story house with green shutters and a gray stone roof. Inside, it was pleasantly cool; the thick stonewalls seemed to protect the interior from the summer heat that had become quite intense by then.

Sofia had to adjust her eyes to the dark hallway that led to a staircase. The smell of cooking and the clatter of dishes told Sofia that the kitchen was close-by. Luisa opened the door to a large living room with solid wood furniture and a huge fireplace. The windows in the room were quite small but a floor-length glass door led to what looked like a patio. It was closed now and the shutter was half-way down, probably to keep out the midday heat. Near the glass door was a group of heavy easy chairs and a coffee table.

Luisa motioned them to take a seat, then said something to Julietta who left the room and came back a few minutes later with a big jar of what looked like lemonade. She was followed by an old woman, dressed in a longish black skirt, her gray hair covered by an embroidered black scarf. She looked like a woman out of an old-fashioned Italian movie. She carried a tray with sturdy-looking glasses, which she put on the coffee table, then glanced at Adriano and Sofia and murmured something that sounded like a greeting.

"My mother," Luisa said, introducing the woman. Adriano, who had gotten up when the woman entered, greeted her politely with a *"Buongiorno, signora."* The woman nodded but didn't say anything and left the room, followed by Julietta.

"She can't hear very well," Luisa said, apparently trying to explain her mother's unfriendly demeanor. She poured each of them glasses of lemonade, which Sofia gratefully accepted. Although there was no ice in it, it tasted cool, sweet, and refreshing. They sat for a while in a somewhat uncomfortable silence, which was interrupted when Julietta came back in, carrying a plate with an Italian pastry.

"I love these," Sofia said as she picked one up. "They're called *biscotti* right?"

"*Cantucci*," Julietta said and sat down next to Sofia.

"*Biscotti* is the ... how do you say?" Luisa wrinkled her forehead. "The general term for cookies which are baked twice. *Cantucci* is a type of *biscotti* with almonds in it. We usually eat them with *vin santo*, a sweet red wine," Luisa said with a smile. "I thought you would be thirsty after your trip, so lemonade is better."

Sofia nodded. She noticed that Luisa seemed to warm up to her a little. "I love your lemonade."

"My mother made it," Luisa said.

I hope she didn't poison it. The thought made Sofia want to laugh out loud, but she was afraid she wouldn't be able to stop laughing.

Adriano, who had taken a sip of lemonade, got up and walked toward the fireplace, which he seemed to study with intensity. After a while, he sat down again, took another sip of lemonade, then turned to Sofia. "Would you like to see your house? It is next door."

"Ah, yes," Luisa hurried to say. "Julietta can show you. We will eat in about half an hour, if this is okay with you?"

Sofia got up. "That would be great. I feel like freshening up a little."

"I shall unload your suitcase for you," Adriano said and followed Sofia and Julietta outside.

When she stepped into the courtyard, Sofia breathed a sigh of relief. It was hot outside but it was a welcome reprieve from the somewhat strained atmosphere in the house. Sofia wasn't sure if the tension was mainly her own, but while Luisa was somewhat cool but pleasant, her mother had acted less than friendly. Perhaps the old woman was just a little odd, and her being somewhat hard of hearing may add to her behavior.

Adriano lifted Sofia's luggage out of the car. He insisted on carrying her suitcase while Julietta grabbed her travel bag.

"We can walk. It is right around the corner." Adriano pointed at a second house that became visible as they walked the short path past a small and what looked like old olive grove with its typical gnarled branches. The house next to a few stone pines was built in the same style as the main house, but it was smaller.

"Papa's house," Julietta said in a somber tone. "Now it belongs to you," she added matter-of-factly.

Sofia glanced at Julietta. Did it bother her sister that Sofia owned it now? Julietta looked serious but not angry.

The house was lovely. The front door was solid wood topped by a stone arch. At the side of the house, the roof extended over a patio that was surrounded by a garden with sun flowers, a patch of dark-blue freesia, of red and yellow snap dragons, and a magnolia bush with white and pink blossoms.

"How beautiful," Sofia exclaimed.

"It is very nice, indeed," said Adriano.

"Who kept it up while my father wasn't here?" Sofia asked as Julietta pulled out a large set of keys from her skirt pockets.

"I watered the plants inside and Alfonso works in the garden." Julietta unlocked the door and pushed it open. "Alfonso is our gardener and he also helps with the grape harvest."

They stepped into a small hallway with a wardrobe. Sofia's heart clenched when she saw a jacket and a pair of boots that had obviously belonged to Henry. Once again, she was overwhelmed by the strangeness of her situation. Here she was, six thousand miles away from home, in a house she hadn't known about that had belonged to her father.

The living room resembled the one in the main house, except it was smaller and the windows were larger. The house in general looked newer and had obviously been built later than the main house. There was a fireplace, a coffee table, brown and orange patterned easy chairs and a couch. Julietta opened a glass door and the shutter in front of it that led onto a patio. The sun shining into the room gave it a cheery feeling. An open doorway connected the living room with a modern kitchen. Next to a vaulted doorway was a dining table with a few high back wicker chairs Sofia had seen in some of the Italian restaurants. On the table was a large glass bowl full of fruit, a bottle of red wine, a jug of what looked like lemonade and a basket with bread, a hunk of cheese, a salami sausage, and a jar with olives. Next to it stood a vase with a colorful bouquet of flowers, seemingly from the garden.

"Wow," Sofia said. "How nice. What a delicious spread and such beautiful flowers."

Julietta smiled. "Mamma and I prepared it, to welcome you."

"This is so kind. Thank you very much." Sofia was pleased to learn that Luisa seemed to have made an effort to make her feel at home. Perhaps they could become friends after all.

Sofia immediately fell in love with the house. All the floors downstairs were made of irregular stone slabs of different colors, ranging from yellow to gray, light orange, and white, which gave the floors a mosaic-like quality. The stones in front of the fireplace were granite with flecks of mica.

The Italian Sister

While Adriano waited downstairs, Sofia and Julietta climbed the stairs to the first floor. There were four rooms upstairs—two bedrooms, and a room with a desk and a sofa-bed that looked like a study as well as a bathroom. The larger bedroom contained a queen size bed, a small table by the window, two chairs, an antique-looking chest of drawers, and a few lamps. Sofia felt a stab of pain in her chest again when she saw what appeared to be a men's woolen sweater hanging at the closet door. It had obviously been her father's bedroom.

The smaller bedroom looked like a child's or young girl's room. The bed was covered with a colorful bedspread and there were a few plush animals leaning against the headboard.

"This was my bedroom when Papa was visiting," Julietta said. Her voice trembled and tears formed in the corner of her eyes.

Sofia felt sorry for her sister. It must be so hard for Julietta to have lost her father and now have her foreign sister take over. That's why she had been surprised when Julietta welcomed her so warmly. Perhaps that had been a sign of her Italian temperament. Then again, she seemed a genuinely warm person. Sofia gently touched her arm. "It can still be your bedroom, if you want to."

"Mamma wants me to stay in the main house, so you have privacy," Julietta said with a shrug.

Sofia was just about to offer to talk to her mother to let her stay, then changed her mind. There would still be time, once they got to know each other a little better. Sofia wanted to be close to her sister but for right now, she indeed needed some privacy.

They went downstairs and joined Adriano who was sitting on one of the iron garden chairs on the patio. He got up and smiled at them. "You like the house?" he asked Sofia.

"It's wonderful. I love it and look at the view." In front of them and all around, the green hills, woods, and the fields of Vignaverde stretched into the distance.

"Well, I will leave you now so you can relax. Do not forget we will have lunch in about twenty minutes. Afterward, Julietta and I can show you your vineyards. And perhaps tomorrow, we can drive to Cecina and ask about the rental car."

"That's great. Thank you. So you're going to spend the night here?" Sofia was happy to hear that Adriano wasn't driving back the same day. She needed his presence. He was the only calming factor in this emotional upheaval.

"Not here, but nearby," he said. "I have a friend in the next village whom I am going to visit."

After Adriano and Julietta had left, Sofia took a deep breath and looked around the house again. She sat down in the living room by the open door that led to the patio and gazed at the landscape in front of her. It was quiet, no birds singing in the midday heat. There was a humming sound from far away, perhaps some agricultural machine. It smelled of dry grass and a mixture of jasmine from the outside and a scent of fruit from the bowl on the table. Sofia got up and put some of the perishable things, the cheese and the sausage, into the refrigerator, then took another stroll through the house. She carried her luggage upstairs, then stopped in front of the master bedroom.

"I guess that's where I'm going to stay," she said quietly, her voice slightly echoing in the empty house. It all felt so strange and familiar at once. Her father's presence seemed to be everywhere—his sweater at the door, a bathrobe and some other clothes and underwear in the closet, shaving utensils in the bathroom. It was if he would step into the room at any moment.

In California, Sofia had taken leave of her father during and after the funeral, but here in Tuscany where he'd lived his secret and second life he was still present. Nobody seemed to have moved his things, as if the family still expected him rather than his American daughter.

"Dad?" Sofia's voice broke. No, she couldn't go there now. If she started to cry now, she wouldn't be able to stop. She pushed her pain down, opened the suitcase, and took out her cosmetic bag. In the bathroom she washed her face, combed her hair, and put on lipstick. She left her cosmetic bag on the chair and decided to remove her father's old cosmetics later.

At the door she wondered if she needed to lock the house. It seemed like such a safe and peaceful environment. Perhaps it wasn't necessary, but Sofia had money and a few valuables in her travel bag. Used to locking doors in California, she stuck the large old-fashioned key into the keyhole and turned it, smiling at the squeaky sound.

Chapter 10

Back in the main house, Julietta was busy setting the large dining table with rustic-looking plates and bowls, some plain white and others with a blue-and-white pattern. Sofia counted seven place mats. From the kitchen came a delicious smell of meat and Sofia felt her stomach growl. The glass door to the patio was open now and Adriano stood outside next to a fairly tall and very slim man with curly black hair and a short beard. He and Adriano seemed to be engaged in a lively discussion underscoring their points with hand gestures.

When Sofia stepped outside, both men turned to her. Adriano gave her a quick smile. "Ah, Sofia, please meet *signor* Santucci, *signora* Santucci's brother."

The man stared at her with piercing dark eyes. The corners of his thin lips pointed downward, which made his scowl even more pronounced. For a moment Sofia didn't know what to do, then she walked up to him and stretched out her hand. "I'm pleased to meet you."

He gave her what appeared to be a disapproving look and hesitated. Sofia wondered if she'd made a mistake, but Europeans shook hands, didn't they? He finally responded, but his handshake was limp. "*Benvenuta, signora,*" he said but in a tone that sounded less than welcoming. He continued to stare at her, more questioning now than disapproving.

"Please call me Sofia," she said, trying for a friendlier atmosphere.

He nodded, then after a slight hesitation: "Edoardo." He

turned back to Adriano and said something in Italian. They two men continued their discussion and Sofia felt out of place. She finally went inside and asked Julietta if she needed help.

"*No, grazie,* everything is ready," Julietta said. She went into the hallway and took a few steps on the stairs, then called "*Nonno, mangiare.*" After a few more calls, a door opened upstairs with a squeaky sound and someone responded in a grumbling voice. Julietta smiled at Sofia and lifted an eyebrow.

The door to the kitchen opened and Luisa brought in a large steaming bowl of soup, minestrone from the looks of it. She was followed by her mother whose name Sofia didn't know yet. As before, she gave Sofia a look of suspicion but then seemed to make an effort to be civil. She motioned her to be seated. Julietta brought in a jug of water. After putting it on the table, she sat next to Sofia. Adriano and Edoardo came inside. Adriano sat across from Sofia, and Edoardo picked up a bottle of red wine that was sitting on the table and got ready to open it. He looked at Sofia and pointed at the bottle.

"It is from your vineyards," he said in clear English.

Strangely enough the man who was least friendly to her, aside from the old woman, was the first one to officially acknowledge Sofia as the owner of the vineyards. Everybody else so far had referred to the fields as Henry's property.

While Luisa was ladling out soup, the door opened with a bang and an old man stepped into the room. Sofia detected right away that he must be Edoardo's father. He was skinny like his son. His face was lined with age but he still had a full head of black hair with very little gray or white. He was supporting himself with a cane. As he approached the table, Adriano rose and greeted him with a respectful "*Buongiorno dottore.*" The old man glanced at him and nodded but didn't return the greeting. His lack of courtesy didn't seem to surprise or bother Adriano. He sat down again and smiled at Sofia.

While watching *dottore* Santucci shuffle to the table, Sofia asked herself what kind of a doctor he might be. It was only now that the old man noticed her. He stopped short and stared at her. The way he glared at Sofia made his son's initial disapproving demeanor seem almost friendly. The piercing eyes of the old Santucci were outright hostile. Then, as if her host remembered that he owed her at least some civility, he bowed his head slightly. "*Buongiorno, signora,*" he said briefly, then sat down, not paying attention to her anymore.

Sofia didn't make any attempt to ask him to call her by her first name. His behavior toward her certainly didn't encourage any familiarity.

They began to eat and after Sofia's frazzled nerves from the encounter with the old Santucci had calmed a little, she was able to taste the admittedly delicious food. Lunch seemed to be the main meal here. After the soup was finished, plates with chicken, fish, and several kinds of vegetables, among others eggplant, tomatoes, and different kinds of zucchini squash appeared, carried in by the old Mrs. Santucci and Luisa. Edoardo poured the wine. Everybody raised their glasses and toasted each other, everybody except for the old people. The old Mrs. Santucci was quiet and kept to herself. Her husband glared at Sofia as well as at everyone else occasionally. At least he didn't single her out anymore, Sofia thought, somewhat more at ease. Besides, she probably wouldn't have to deal with him much, since he was old and retired. Luisa and Edoardo were in charge of the estate.

To Sofia's relief, the grandparents left after lunch. Adriano, Sofia, and Edoardo sat in the living room, drinking espresso while Julietta and Luisa cleared the table and cleaned up in the kitchen. Sofia offered to help but Luisa told her to relax and entertain the gentlemen. Sofia had smiled at the proposition. Obviously Edoardo and Adriano didn't need to be entertained. They were soon again engaged in a lively discussion and from the little Sofia understood, it was about politics. Not being able to follow the talk in Italian and feeling tired from the heat, the wine, and the filling lunch, she had a difficult time keeping her eyes open.

"Would you like to have a *riposo*?" she heard someone say and realized that she had nodded off. Adriano looked at her amused.

"Sorry," she said, feeling embarrassed.

"No need to apologize," Edoardo said in an unusually friendly tone. "It is the heat and the food. We all take a break after lunch."

"Would it be possible to show Sofia her property a little later?" Adriano asked Edoardo.

Edoardo's face puckered as if he had bitten into a lemon. However, he nodded. "Yes, once it is a little cooler. Would this be all right?" He gave Sofia a questioning look.

"Oh, yes, great," she assured him.

"*Bene*," Adriano said. "I will visit my friend in the next town but I shall be back later in the afternoon." He turned to Sofia. "Perhaps you can take a nap?"

"That would be great. I am a little tired." Sofia got up, eager to have some time to herself. She walked the short path to her house. The sun was at its hottest and Sofia was relieved to notice that it was pleasantly cool inside the house even without air conditioning. She poured herself a glass of lemonade and went upstairs to lie down on the bed. After drinking the refreshing liquid, she fell asleep almost instantly.

Chapter 11

A shadowy figure walked toward her. As it came closer, Sofia thought she recognized Julietta or perhaps her mother. The figure smiled at Sofia and moved her mouth as if she was talking but there was no sound. When she was right in front of Sofia, the smiling face turned into an ugly mask. The skin peeled off and fangs protruded from her mouth. Sofia was paralyzed and something or someone was choking her. She heard a scream and woke up, realizing it was she who screamed. She was panting and sweat poured down her face. She looked around the room. It was empty. Sliding to the edge of the bed, she lowered her feet to the floor.

"What a nightmare," she whispered. She couldn't remember ever having had such a shocking dream. It must be her anxiety, which had been building for weeks. She shook her head, then waited until her heartbeat felt normal again. Brushing her tangled hair out of her face, she looked at the clock on the night stand. It was five in the afternoon. She must have slept for three solid hours. She got up and opened the shutters all the way. Outside, dark clouds had formed on the horizon and a breeze kicked up. It felt like a thunderstorm was brewing, which might also explain her headache.

In the bathroom, Sofia washed her face, then went downstairs. She drank another glass of lemonade and stepped outside on the patio. There was definitely a change in the weather. The temperature had dropped. She heard someone at the front door. She went to open but realized she hadn't locked the door. Julietta came inside.

"*Signor* Gori is here," she said after giving Sofia a quick hug. "*Zio* Edoardo wants to take us to your vineyards, now that it is a little cooler."

Sofia touched her forehead. "I have a headache. It feels like before a thunderstorm."

Julietta nodded. "Yes, we think there will be rain." She motioned Sofia to sit down. "I will do a ... what do you call it? A *massaggio*."

"Thank you. It's called a massage." Sofia sat down. She flinched when she felt Julietta's hands on her neck, thinking back to her nightmare.

"Hold still," Julietta said. "It is not going to hurt." She gently rubbed Sofia's shoulders. After a while, Sofia was able to relax enough to feel the tension lessen.

"That's wonderful," she said. "You're an expert."

"I do it for Mamma sometimes," Julietta said. "When she has a headache."

After a while, Juliette stopped and Sofia got up. "I feel much better. Thank you." Sofia looked outside where the sky had darkened with clouds. "I hope the storm won't damage the vines."

"The rain will make it cooler and that is good for the grapes. As long as there is no hail. Hail can do a lot of damage," Julietta said.

Sofia nodded. "You're right. Let's go and join the others."

When they stepped outside, a gust of wind greeted them. They walked over to the main house where Edoardo and Adriano were waiting outside. Edoardo glanced at them with his usual scowl, then motioned at an old van. They climbed inside and he drove along the path past Sofia's house. After a few minutes he stopped the car at the side of the road. They got out and Edoardo led them to a large field that stretched along a hill. From the position of the sun that occasionally peaked through the now increasingly thick clouds, Sofia recognized that the hill was facing the west and southwest.

"This is one of your vineyards," Edoardo said. "The other field is right on the other side of the road."

"They are in an ideal spot," Sofia said.

Edoardo glowered at her. "Do you know anything about vineyards?"

Sofia stared at him, getting irritated at his seemingly patronizing question. "I'm not an expert but I used to work on a vineyard in California a few years ago with my ex-husband and even earlier with my father. I know a little something. I know for instance that the sea, meaning the Mediterranean, is to the west here, which means the vines will get the sea breeze in the afternoon. I also see that the vines are planted in horizontal rows along the slope, which makes for good drainage but prevents erosion. Perhaps you don't think Californians know anything about growing grapes and making wine, but they do." Her face felt flushed.

Edoardo held up his hands. "I apologize. I did not mean to question your knowledge. California wine has a very good reputation. Your father always brought a few bottles and they were excellent."

Sofia was embarrassed at her angry outburst. "Yes, there are good winemakers in my country. But I would love to learn more about the way wine is grown and made here. I would like to help with the work."

Edoardo's face softened somewhat. "We would appreciate your help. We are always shorthanded, especially during harvest time and even now during *inviatura*, how do you call it?"

"Veraison," Sofia said. "The time of ripening."

"Yes, it is somewhat late this year because spring and even early summer have been unusually cold."

The Italian Sister

The tension that had been growing between them was diffused, at least for the moment. They all walked along the edge of the vineyard and Sofia got excited when she saw the beautiful grapes that were a mixture of deep blue and purple next to the green ones that weren't ripe yet.

"Are these Sangiovese grapes?" she asked.

"Yes," Edoardo said and pointed to the other field. "And these are Merlot grapes. There the soil has too much clay for good Sangiovese grapes. But it is perfect for Merlot. Your father's wine is a blend of Merlot and Sangiovese."

Sofia sighed. "Yes, Henry had shipped bottles of it to California. It is an excellent wine. I just didn't know it was from his own vineyard."

There was a moment of silence. To change the topic Sofia asked if she could taste one of the grapes. Edoardo nodded and pulled off a small cluster of the ripe berries and handed it to Sofia. The grapes weren't too sweet yet. They had thick skins and lots of seeds and a puckery taste.

"They'll make perfect wine," Sofia said with a smile.

"They sure do," Adriano said. "I love the wine from these fields and from the estate in general." He smiled at Edoardo who acknowledged the compliment with a nod.

Just as they were heading back to the car, Sofia saw the old Santucci stand at the edge of the field, staring at them with his usual angry look. Edoardo waved to him but the old man didn't wave back. He merely kept on walking along the path, hitting the ground with his cane and seemingly muttering something.

"Shall we give a*l dottore* a ride back?" Adriano asked.

Adriano is too polite. Sofia sighed inwardly. She wasn't eager having to ride back with the rude old man in the car.

"He has his own car," Edoardo said to her relief and pointed at an old beat-up Fiat, which was parked near their van.

After their visit to the vineyards, Adriano went to stay with his friend for the night. Sofia turned down Luisa's invitation to have supper with them. She was tired and worn-out from the day and wanted to be alone for a while. And she was in no mood to endure more of the old Santucci's hostile eyes.

"Besides," Sofia said. "I want to try the wonderful food in the welcome basket."

Luisa seemed to understand her wish to relax alone in her home. "Your father sometimes had lunch with us but made his own supper," she said. "There is a nice grocery story in town and Julietta can show it to you one of the next days. You can use our car. I want to give you some coffee for tomorrow morning. And if there is anything else you need, let me know."

Luisa seemed to be making an effort to make Sofia feel more at home here. Sofia told her that Adriano would take her to Cecina to rent a car. She gratefully accepted the tin of coffee and went back to her place.

In the meantime, the wind had picked up even more. Just as Sofia reached her house, the first raindrops were beginning to fall. She closed the glass door to the patio and the windows upstairs, then sat down and prepared herself a light meal of cheese, salami, and bread. She drank a glass of wine from one of her father's bottles. It was delicious, fragrant, smooth, with a light touch of tannin and Sofia savored each drop of the rich and flavorful wine.

After finishing her meal, she poured herself another glass and sat in the living room, watching the stormy scene outside. The rain had stopped again, but the heaps of dark clouds still looked ominous. Tired from the wine, the food, and the emotional day, Sofia went to bed early.

Chapter 12

In the middle of the night, Sofia was awakened by loud thunder and the sound of heavy rain. The window she'd left open was swinging back and forth and she got up to close it. Outside, lightning lit up the landscape, and thunder and lightning happened almost at the same time, which scared Sofia. It meant that the lightning was very close, too close for comfort.

She tried to turn on the lamp on the bedside table. Electricity must be off and Sofia didn't have a flash light or candles. Another raucous thunderclap made her heart jump. She looked outside again, where another streak of lightning lit up the landscape. She thought she saw someone standing outside in the garden, someone with a cane.

No, that wasn't possible. Certainly the old Santucci wouldn't be outside during this pandemonium. She waited for another lightning strike and again she thought she saw a figure but a fierce gale tossed rainwater against the window and she couldn't see anything clearly. More thunderous noise but now it seemed to come from downstairs. Was someone at the door? Nobody in his or her right mind would be outside, but then the old Santucci didn't seem to be in his right mind to begin with. But the door was on the other side of the house and not where she had seen the figure. When she thought she heard pounding at the door, she grabbed her robe and went downstairs. She crept toward the entrance hall with her hand on the wall, trying to orient herself in the dark. Now she heard the knocking on the door clearly.

"Who is it?" she called, afraid to open the door, in case it was the old man after all. She was relieved when she recognized Edoardo's voice and opened the door. Another gust of wind almost knocked it out of her hand.

Edoardo stood there, wrapped in what looked like a black rain slicker. He stepped inside, water dripping from his coat and collecting in puddles on the stone floor. He reached under the coat and pulled out a wrapped package. "Two flashlights and candles," he said.

"Oh, thank you," Sofia said. "But I'm so sorry you had to walk through this storm."

Edoardo pulled down his hood and wiped his face with his hand. "This is not a problem. We thought you might be scared. Do not be scared. We have rainstorms like this occasionally. It will clear up soon."

"Thank you." Sofia was surprised by his concern. "What about the vines, though?"

Edoardo shook his head. "The rain cools the air and this is good. There is no hail and the vineyards have natural protection from the hills and the rows of trees. We will have a little damage but not serious. See? It is almost over."

The wind had diminished, the thunder sounded farther away, and the rain was steady and all this within a few seconds after one of the wildest storms Sofia had ever experienced.

"Thank God," she said. "To be honest, I was a little worried. So thank you for checking on me." At that moment, the light came back on and the refrigerator began to hum in the kitchen.

Edoardo gave a barely perceptible smile. "You are welcome."

Sofia remembered the figure she thought she had seen earlier. "Was your father outside, by any chance?" she asked.

Edoardo's eyes narrowed. "No, of course not. He is at home. Why do you ask?"

"I thought I saw someone from my bedroom window, someone with a cane."

Edoardo's facial expression darkened. "This is not possible. Why would my father be outside in the middle of the night during such a storm?"

Why indeed? Sofia mused.

"You must have seen something else," Edoardo said.

Sofia nodded. She began to doubt herself. "It was probably just the wind or a shadow."

"Are you all right now or do you need anything else?" Edoardo asked, his voice stern now. Had she insulted him by suspecting that his father had been outside?

"No, I'm fine and thank you very much for coming out here during such weather. I really appreciate it."

Edoardo gave a quick nod, pulled up his hood, opened the door, and left. Sofia watched him in the glare of the now functioning lantern along the path. She closed the door and went inside.

Upstairs she glanced outside the window again. It was still raining a little and there were some remaining flashes of lightning far away but the wind had died down. There seemed to be nobody outside, so perhaps the figure had been a figment of her imagination.

Back in bed, she tried to fall asleep but couldn't settle down. She kept thinking about the figure with the cane. She'd never suffered from hallucinations and in spite of all the reasons that spoke against it—he was old and had no business being out in a rainstorm and Edoardo claimed that he was at home—she was convinced she had seen the old Santucci.

Sofia fell back to sleep but kept waking up. When her

travel clock showed five in the morning, she got up and went downstairs. There was an espresso machine in the kitchen. She filled it with water and added some of the coffee Luisa had given her. Waiting for the water to heat up, she opened the door to the patio and stepped outside. It was still dark but the rain had stopped and it was quiet. It smelled of wet grass, some kind of herbs and the sweet aroma of flowers from the garden.

The patio was covered with leaves, twigs, and a few small tree branches from the storm. She also found a dead bird right in front of the door, probably another victim of the storm, Sofia thought. *Poor thing.* She bent down to look at it more closely. It was fairly large and black and could have been a crow. Its head was twisted and the dead open eyes stared at her. Her breath caught; a chill shot down her spine. It looked as if someone had wrung the bird's neck. But that wasn't possible, was it? Who would do such a thing and put the bird in front of her door? Did someone want to scare her? She thought of Adriano's words about the family's resentment toward her.

The nightmare of the previous day, the figure with the cane she thought she'd seen during the night and now the dead bird filled her with dread. She stood up and took deep breaths. But no, she told herself. She couldn't get all crazy. The nightmare had just been that … a nightmare, nothing real. The bird probably flew against the wall or the window during the storm and broke its neck. The shape she had seen at night had probably just been a shadow of something. Sofia went inside and got the dustpan from the kitchen. She carefully lifted the bird and placed it under a bush next to the patio. She would bury it once she came back.

Back inside, it smelled of coffee. She poured herself a cup and carried it to the easy chair in the living room. In the meantime, the sun was about to rise, filling the hills with light and shadows. The deep bronze of the meadows turned golden and hues of pink and purple colored the horizon. Now, in the light of day, the Tuscan landscape looked and felt reassuring and benign again. Sofia sipped the fragrant, slightly bitter brew and felt the fears of the night slowly fade.

PART FOUR: REAL OR IMAGINARY DANGERS

Chapter 13

A few hours later after showering and dressing, Sofia stepped outside just as Adriano's car entered the driveway of the main house. The air was fresh and smelled clean from the rain and the sky was a deep blue again. Birds whistling and singing greeted the day.

"That was quite a storm last night," Sofia said as they were driving along the highway westward in the direction of the Mediterranean.

Adriano glanced at her. "Yes, fortunately, it did not last very long. Did the electricity go out here, too?"

"Yes, for a short while," Sofia said. "I was scared with all the lightning. I didn't know if the house had a lightning rod or something."

"These storms happen quite often here, more in autumn though. But the houses are protected and there are hills and high trees away from the property. So they get hit first. The storm did not harm the vineyards, I hope?"

"No, fortunately not. That's what Edoardo said." Sofia told him that Luisa's brother had come over to check on her.

"Oh? This is considerate, is it not?"

"Yes, I was surprised. Perhaps he is nicer than I thought at first." Sofia hesitated. "I really think his father is the one who hates me. I think he was outside my house last night, watching it."

Adriano gave her a questioning look. "What do you mean?"

Sofia told him about the figure of an old man with a cane

she thought she had seen. "Edoardo told me it was impossible, but I know I saw him ... or someone who looked like him."

"This is strange," Adriano said. "But why would he be out there in such a storm? And how could you see him in the dark?"

"I saw him when lightning lit up the meadow in the back of the house."

"And you are absolutely sure it was him you saw?" Adriano's voice sounded doubtful.

Sofia sighed. *He must think I'm nuts.* "I'm not sure. One minute I'm convinced it was him, but then I think again that perhaps it was a shadow or something."

Adriano was quiet for a while, then cleared his throat. "Perhaps you were scared of the storm and I think you are a little scared of the *dottore* because of his behavior. He looks angry a lot, and I think he is a little ... how do you say? *Matto*." He twirled his finger around his temple.

"Crazy?" Sofia said.

"Yes." Adriano nodded. "Do not worry. He is old and stubborn but he will get used to you after a while."

"Probably," Sofia said, but she wasn't convinced. She wanted to tell him about the dead bird, but decided not to. Claiming that someone had twisted its neck and put it in front of her door might really qualify her for the loony bin.

Cecina was a small town along the Tuscan coastline. They had no trouble finding the rental agency. What was more difficult, however, was renting a car with an automatic transmission and Sofia didn't know how to drive a stick shift. The assistant at the agency told them that usually you had to reserve an automatic three months in advance. Luckily, the only car with an automatic transmission they did have available at this time would be returned around lunchtime. Sofia filled out the paperwork and they were told to come back at around one o'clock.

They took a walk through town. Along the boardwalk, the breeze was pleasantly cool. Sofia inhaled the scent of salt from the sea and the occasional whiff of suntan lotion from the sunbathers on the beach. The tourists seemed to be mainly Italians on their summer vacation. At one of the restaurants, they ordered lemonade and an assortment of sandwiches, made of *ciabatta* bread, spread with pesto paste and topped with roasted eggplant, green peppers, and tomatoes. They were delicious.

"Food is too good here, I'm going to get fat during the next few months," Sofia said.

Adriano chortled, then coughed and apologized. He gave her an amused look. "There is no fat on you whatsoever. Even if you gained a few kilos, you would still be thin."

"I know I'm too thin. I wouldn't mind gaining some weight but you know what happens. The pounds go to the wrong places." She laughed. It was relaxing being here with Adriano, away from the Santuccis and the tensions.

Adriano shook his head. "I did not mean to say that you are too thin. You are just right."

Always the gentleman, Sofia thought.

After lunch, they went back to the rental agency and to Sofia's relief, a blue Honda civic with automatic transmission was waiting for her. After signing the rental contract and getting the keys, Sofia got into the car and adjusted the seat and the mirrors.

"Do you remember how to get back?" Adriano asked.

Sofia hesitated. "I think so."

"I will drive ahead of you. Just follow me." Adriano got into his car. On the way back, Sofia was careful to pay attention to the directions. Tomorrow she would be alone, without Adriano's helpful and comfortable presence. She better get used to it. Sofia decided not to let the old Santucci's hostility toward her ruin her experience. She wanted to work in her vineyards as much as possible. It was the first chance she had after her divorce to help with veraison and be present during the grape harvest.

When they arrived at the estate in the late afternoon, Adriano wanted to say good-bye but there was only the old Mrs. Santucci in the house. Everybody else was working in the fields. Adriano told her to give his regards to the family, which the old woman acknowledged with a nod.

"I will see you in about two months. Edoardo invited me to the harvest celebration in October," Adriano said to Sofia. "Or, in case you come to Firenze in the meantime, let me know."

"I certainly will," Sofia said. She hated to see him leave but she knew he'd taken a lot of time away from his work and his family to get her settled.

"Thank you very much for all your help. I'm really grateful." They shook hands.

"It is my pleasure. I wish you a very good time. You will see, most of the people here are kind. And if you need help or have questions, you have my telephone number. You can call me anytime." He got into the car and waved at her.

Sofia watched with an aching heart as his silver Lancia drove slowly along the gravel path toward the highway. Feeling lonely by herself, she considered joining the people who worked at the vineyards, then decided to start working the following day. Halfway back at her house, she saw the old man again. Mr. Santucci was walking past her home toward the fields, his cane clinking whenever it hit a stone on the road. Sofia slunk behind a tree to hide from him but he didn't pay any attention and kept on walking.

Why am I afraid of him? He was just a grumbling old coot. Inside the house, she breathed a sigh of relief. She would have to get over her fears. She couldn't panic every time she saw him. Perhaps Adriano was right and he would learn to accept her. Even if they wouldn't become close friends, at least he would get used to her.

She opened the door to the patio. It was still strewn with leaves and blossoms from the storm. She went to check for the dead bird, but it was gone. *How strange.* Had she imagined it in the morning? No, of course not. The bird had been removed, but by whom? Or by what? It could have been an animal. That must be it, Sofia thought. A dog or some other animal could have dragged it away. If people wanted to scare her with the bird, they probably wouldn't have removed it, would they? *Stop it, Sofia. Stop the stupid fears.* She couldn't go nuts over a dead bird, for heaven's sake.

There was a wooden shed next to the house. The door was halfway open and Sofia discovered some garden tools in there and a broom. She began to sweep the granite floor of the patio and wiped the iron garden chairs.

Afterward, sitting outside, she inhaled the scents of the summer evening, the sweetness of the flowers. She recognized a few but several of them were foreign to her. Her father had been an encyclopedia when it came to plant and flower names. Sofia wondered if he'd planted the garden himself. Perhaps Julietta helped him. She almost saw him, his tall frame, his wild hair. Did he kneel in the dirt and plant the seedlings as he'd done at home? At his other home. Which of his houses had he considered his first home? Which of his lives was his true life? She wished so much he was here. She had so many questions.

They would sit together at this shaky old garden table,

drinking wine. Perhaps Julietta would sit with them, a glass of grape juice in her hands. Or did she already drink wine? She was only fourteen but Sofia remembered that in Europe young people were allowed to drink alcohol earlier than in the States. But fourteen was young, so it must be grape juice. Luisa might join them. Would she and Henry smile at each other? From what John told her, it had been a short fling not a serious relationship. Still, they had a child together; they were parents. But none of this was real. Henry was dead and Luisa and her family didn't feel close to her yet.

She missed her father more than ever now. If he were here, he would have a perfect explanation for all the stupid incidences of the past night, the dead bird, the shadow of the man. She felt the familiar ache in her chest and her eyes filled with tears.

There was a knock at the door. Sofia realized she had locked it after seeing old Santucci. She wiped her eyes, got up, and opened.

Julietta stood outside, a basket with strawberries in her hand. "From Mamma," she said. Seeing the smiling face of her sister, Sofia felt her sadness and fears fade.

They sat on the now clean patio, eating the berries. They were sweet and juicy, fresh from the garden. It was quiet, just the occasional munching sound. Sofia wanted to start a conversation but felt oddly inhibited. It irritated her that she couldn't feel completely relaxed around her sister. Julietta seemed so kind and easygoing. But then she remembered the nightmare. Had it been a warning after all? Was Julietta's kindness pretense? How did her sister really feel about her? If it weren't for Sofia, Julietta would have inherited her two vineyards. She must be resentful. But Julietta didn't seem to harbor any hard feelings.

Sofia had to stop feeling so distrustful. She came here to

bond with her sister. She was family after all, almost the only family she had left, aside from Emma and her grandparents.

She felt Julietta's eyes on her. Sofia glanced at her and smiled. "They are really good." She pointed at the empty basket.

Julietta nodded, then got up. "Mamma said you should have dinner with us tonight. Tomorrow, I can take you shopping for groceries if you want to have dinner here. Papa usually had lunch with us and dinner here. Sometimes he ate all his meals with us. Mamma said you are always welcome."

"That's very kind of you. I wouldn't mind having lunch with you. Did you have dinner with Papa here?" Sofia asked.

"Sometimes, yes. Sometimes I helped him cook."

Sofia hesitated. "Are your grandparents eating with you tonight?"

"No, not today. They are eating with *zio* Edoardo and *zia* Gina."

Sofia was relieved. "Don't they normally eat with you?"

"They have lunch with us. Sometimes, they eat at Uncle Edoardo's place. Sometimes they eat upstairs, when they are tired. They have a kitchen upstairs. Mamma and I buy groceries for Nonna."

I guess there would be no way avoiding the old people all together, Sofia thought. But at least she wouldn't have to deal with them tonight. Besides, being together with Luisa and Julietta would help her get closer to them. She wanted to make a real effort to get to know them better.

Chapter 14

Sofia woke early to another hot summer day. She showered, had a quick breakfast of coffee and rolls, and got ready to work in the vineyard. It was still veraison, the time of ripening of the grapes when the berries changed color from green to various shades of blue or purple depending on the variety. Sofia remembered from her work in the vineyard in Northern California that this was a critical stage in the process leading up to the actual *vendemmia* or harvest. Much of the canopy work such as trimming of the vines to give the grapes as much air and sunshine as possible had begun during past months. Now, it was time to cut back the suckers and remove poorly developed clusters to encourage the growth of the more vigorous ones. All of this was important for a balanced crop and the best possible fruit.

Sofia dressed in loose pants, a long-sleeve light shirt that wasn't too warm but prevented her arms from being burned by the sun. When she heard someone knock, she put on her sun hat, grabbed a bottle of water and the work gloves, and opened the door. Julietta was outside, dressed in dungarees and sturdy boots, wearing a fedora sun hat. She was on vacation from school and liked to help with the work on the estate.

"Are you ready?" Julietta pointed at her water bottle. "You do not need this. We have water at the vineyard."

The two stepped outside. It was still dark, but a fine line of silver on the horizon was the first sign of approaching dawn. During the hot summer months, work in the vineyards began before the sun was up and lasted until around noon, when it got too hot for the workers.

Sofia figured it was going to be at least in the nineties Fahrenheit or around thirty centigrade as she saw on the European thermometer that day. Fortunately for the grapes, the temperature dropped during the nights to the twenties centigrade which was the equivalent of the seventies in Fahrenheit. The high temperatures helped the ripening process and the cooler nights prevented them from ripening too fast or drying out.

"We have to walk," Julietta said. "Uncle Edoardo and the others are already there."

It was a short distance to the vineyards. As they came close to the fields, dawn was spreading and Sofia saw that quite a few people were at work already. Edoardo's van was parked nearby. A trimming machine was slowly driving through the rows in between the vines, removing dense foliage at the top of the vines to continue to give sun and air to the ripening grapes. As they approached the field with the Sangiovese grapes, Edoardo stepped out of the vineyard and gave Sofia a quick look-over. He nodded and said something in Italian to Julietta.

"Uncle Edoardo wants us to work in the Merlot field." She pointed at the field next to the one they stood at. "They have enough workers here."

"Is this in order with you?" Edoardo turned to Sofia.

"Of course, wherever you need help." Sofia was surprised at his politeness. "It doesn't have to be one of my fields. I can help everywhere."

Edoardo gave one of his rare smiles. "We will work all the vineyards the next few weeks. Do not worry, there will be plenty of things to take care of." He removed his hat and wiped his forehead. "There is a young man from your

91

country working over there. He is here to learn about Italian wines and winemaking. He has been helping us last year as well."

"Oh, good," Sofia said, wondering who he was.

"He is really cute, a hottie." Julietta pushed Sofia a little with her elbow and wiggled her eyebrows.

Edoardo glared at her and said something in Italian that sounded like an admonishment. When he turned his back, Julietta stuck out her tongue at him and grinned. Sofia remembered Adriano's remarks about Julietta being the rebellious teenager. She smiled and followed her as they crossed the gravel path to the next field. A few people, Luisa among them, were checking the grape clusters and cutting off the less developed or weak ones. Luisa's hair was tied back and wrapped in a yellow scarf. She was wearing jeans and a yellow top. With her suntanned skin and the vivid dark eyes, she was still an attractive woman.

No wonder her father had fallen in love with her. Sofia tried to imagine how Henry, Luisa, and Julietta had worked together in the vineyard, snipping off clusters of grapes, perhaps smiling at each other, taking a break occasionally and sipping water from the huge bottles that were standing in the shade of the cypress trees next to the vineyards. A wave of pain spread through her chest and regret filled her heart. Why had she been excluded from this for so long? Sofia shook the thoughts from her mind. After all, she didn't even know what kind of a relationship Luisa and Henry had had. They might not have been that friendly anymore or even worked together.

A shuffling sound behind her woke Sofia from her musing. Luisa smiled at her, perhaps wondering what she was daydreaming about. Sofia took a deep breath and grabbed the shears Luisa handed her. She told her to work together with Julietta.

Sofia and Julietta worked in rows next to each other. The workers in the vineyard were spread out evenly so all the vines and clusters got checked. It took Sofia a while to get into the swing of things, adjusting to the speed of the other workers and still being able to concentrate enough on her work. Still, after a while, someone in the next row caught up with her. She first detected him out of the corner of her eyes. When she looked more closely, a fairly tall and very handsome young man with wavy blond hair and dark-brown eyes nodded and smiled at her, then said something in Italian.

"Sorry?" Sofia asked.

The young man stopped working and smiled more broadly. "Are you the American sister?" She recognized the American accent and realized that this must be the young man from the United States.

"Yes, I am, and I guess you are the American vintner. Which part are you from?" They both stopped working for a moment.

"California, just like you." He motioned with his head to Julietta. "She mentioned you." He gave her a questioning look. "Last year, your father was here. I'm sorry to hear of his passing. Juliette told me when I got here. A heart-attack, right?"

Sofia nodded.

"At first, I couldn't believe it. Last time I saw him, he looked so healthy and vibrant. What a loss. I'm so sorry."

"Thanks, yes, I still can't believe it either sometimes." Sofia took a deep breath.

"I worked with him last year," the young man continued. "You weren't here though."

"No, I wasn't. I didn't even know about this place."

"No?" He stared at her.

Sofia immediately regretted having mentioned her ignorance about Vignaverde. Her family history wasn't any of his business. She didn't even know him. "It's a long story. But we better continue our work. They're catching up with us." She motioned to the workers in the rows next to them who were progressing quite fast.

"True," the young man said. "By the way, I'm Nicholas."

"I'm Sofia. Pleased to meet you."

He nodded and continued with his work. Sofia went back to checking the clusters of grapes. It was quiet and peaceful. Everybody was busy working. There was an occasional exchange of words or someone laughed. After a while, Sofia found her own rhythm and experienced once again the satisfaction of working with her hands.

Sofia had always liked working in the vineyards. She'd done it sometimes together with her father when she'd been a child and they still had their vineyard at the Russian River. Later, at her in-law's place, she had taken time off from her office work and helped out during veraison or the harvest. These had been her favorite times. She enjoyed the earthy smell of the soil, the variety of colors from the light green of the vines to the blues and different shades of purple of the grapes next to the green ones. A vineyard to her was a feast for the senses. She also liked the camaraderie among the vintners and helpers, the feeling of harmony, of working toward a common goal—tending the vines and giving the grapes the best chance for a bountiful harvest. She enjoyed writing about winemaking but the hands-on work in the vineyard energized her. It was something she missed when she'd moved to Santa Monica after her divorce. Now, she was able to do it again, and in her own vineyards. A feeling of pride and gratitude flooded her.

The Italian Sister

Sofia stopped for a moment, rose and stretched, massaging her by now aching back with her hands. In the meantime, the sun had begun to rise on the horizon.

An older woman in a row next to hers had caught up with her. She had a wrinkled face and a few strands of curly gray hair had escaped the dark-blue scarf on her head. Her hands, however, worked as nimbly as those of the young people. She glanced at Sofia and gave her a quick smile then continued to work.

Chapter 15

In the afternoon, Sofia decided to check out the cellar on the way to her house. Edoardo had given her a quick tour on one of the first days, but she wanted to have a closer look at the barrels with her father's wine. The cellar was built into the hill, so it was mainly underground. There were two entrances, one from above by means of a staircase and one on even ground next to the winery where the necessary equipment such as connecting hoses between the fermentation tanks and barrels could be brought in.

Sofia descended the stairs to the lower level and entered the large room where the long rows of barrels from the past harvest were waiting to be bottled. Down here, the temperature dropped several degrees. She shivered lightly, feeling the sweat on her forehead and body cool. She inhaled the musty and slightly sour smell. It always reminded her of the childhood when she played in the cellar while her father worked.

The estate of the Santucci family was of medium size and all the barrels were stored in the same cellar. They were stacked in racks lying on their sides, four barrels high, all through the room.

In the back of the cellar, she heard a noise. She saw someone working a forklift, moving some of the barrels. It was an older man she'd seen a couple of times on the estate. He looked in her direction and nodded. Sofia pointed to the back of the cellar to let him know where she was heading. He nodded again.

The Italian Sister

The worker began hoisting a barrel down from the top row and depositing it somewhere else. Sofia was careful not to get close to the machine, so she wouldn't be in the way. She walked slowly toward the part of the cellar where she remembered having seen the barrels with the wine from her Merlot and Sangiovese grapes. She looked at them with a mixture of pride and sadness. They were part of her father's double-life and now belonged to her. She was happy to be able to continue the care of her father's cherished grapes and his love of winemaking, but seeing the barrels once again made her realize how much she missed him, how this estate and its people still felt unreal to her. It was as if her father had assumed a different identity here in Tuscany. He was someone she didn't really know and she wouldn't have the opportunity to ever know. She shook her head, trying to chase the thoughts and sadness away. What good did it do to linger on something she couldn't change?

Turning back, she saw that the forklift had moved and the man was working at a stack of barrels closer to her. She was getting ready to move away when he hoisted another barrel. The forklift swung around in her direction and the barrel ended up above her head. She stepped back quickly and at the same time, someone pulled her away. There was a loud shout and the next thing she witnessed was the barrel dropping to the floor with a loud crash right where she had stood just a few seconds ago.

She inhaled sharply, her knees wobbled under her, and her heart was racing. The old man slid down from the forklift and stared at her with wide-open, terror-filled eyes. She turned to look at the person who pulled her to safety. It was Nicholas.

"My God, that was close," he said. His face looked white in the dim light of the cellar. "Are you okay?"

Sofia was shaking. "I ... I think so. I can't believe this. I thought I was standing far away from the forklift and he knew I was here. So what ...?"

"I don't know what happened. I just came in when the forklift turned. You're not supposed to turn that fast. It's very dangerous. Umberto obviously lost control of the forklift. I know forklifts are dangerous but he should know better."

"Who is Umberto?" Sofia asked, her heart still beating fast.

"He lives on the property. I'm not sure what his function is. But I know he drinks too much."

"*Cosa c'è?* What's happening?" she heard a voice from the entrance. It was Edoardo. He came in and stared at them, then at the old man who stood next to the forklift.

Nicholas told him briefly what had happened.

"He should not work the forklift," Edoardo said. He walked over to the man and talked to him in a loud and angry voice in Italian.

"What are they talking about?" Sofia asked. She couldn't understand anything.

"Edoardo told Umberto he had no business being in the cellar and working the forklift."

Edoardo threw up his hands and turned around. He came up to Sofia. "Are you all right?"

Sofia nodded. "Yes, thanks to Nicholas who pulled me away."

Edoardo stared at the barrel lying on the floor. It didn't seem to be damaged.

"Umberto should not work this machine," he said. "He is too old and ... well. I am very sorry this happened. But be careful in the cellar with the forklift. Accidents do happen, so make sure to stay away from any of the machines."

Sofia was getting irritated. It seemed Edoardo put some of

the blame on her. "I was watching very carefully."

Edoardo nodded. "Let's get out of here. Thank God, nothing happened."

"I just wanted to have a look at the barrels with my wine," Sofia said. She hated Edoardo's patronizing ways. It wasn't her fault that they employed incompetent workers.

At that moment, Umberto came up to them.

"*Scusami, ho sbagliato,*" he said. It sounded like an apology. He trembled and looked really shaken.

"It's okay. Fortunately nothing happened," Sofia said, feeling a little sorry for him.

Edoardo and Umberto left the cellar with Edoardo still talking in an angry voice admonishing Umberto who shuffled along, his shoulders slumped. Nicholas and Sofia followed behind.

Outside, the sun was low on the sky and the heat had diminished a little. Sofia was still in shock from the incident with the barrel. "Thank God, you were there," she said to Nicholas. "You saved my life."

He smiled. "Not quite. You stepped back just in time. But yes, I don't even want to think about what could've happened. These barrels are heavy."

"Anyway, thanks for being there," Sofia said. They slowly walked the small path uphill toward Sofia's house. Sofia stopped halfway, shaking her head. The longer she thought about the near-accident, the less sense it made. "I don't understand how this could've happened," she said. "He saw me. He nodded at me. I was in a different area of the cellar than he was working at. And then all of a sudden the forklift was next to me and the barrel over my head. It's almost as if he did it on purpose." Sofia glanced at Nicholas.

Nicholas narrowed his eyes. "This doesn't make sense. Why would he want to do this?"

Sofia shrugged. She felt sorry having expressed her suspicions. Nicholas didn't know anything about her situation, about the fact that the family may resent her for having inherited her father's vineyards. But he was right. It wouldn't make sense.

"Never mind," she said. "So many things have happened within the past few months with my father's death and all that. I see ghosts everywhere."

"I understand but I really think he was drunk. He lost control of the forklift. I bet they'll never let him work it again. They better not," Nicholas said, giving Sofia a pensive look. She was struck by his warm brown eyes.

They continued on their way and separated in front of Sofia's place. Nicholas walked in the direction of a cottage where he stayed with some other workers during his time at the estate.

Chapter 16

It was just around sunset. Sofia was sitting on the patio, drinking lemonade and watching the spectacular display of color as the sun was lowering itself behind the horizon, filling the hills and meadows with purples and different shades of brown and yellow. It was peaceful in the evenings but Sofia felt frazzled after almost having been crushed by a barrel of wine. How odd. The incident gave the idea of death by alcohol a whole new meaning. She still couldn't understand why it happened. It really didn't make sense. Even if Umberto had been drunk, why did he drive the forklift over to where she stood?

Sofia thought she heard a knock at the door and got up to open it. Julietta was outside, handing her a basket with vegetables from her family's garden.

"Thank you," Sofia said with a smile and waved her inside.

"*Zio* Edoardo told me what almost happened to you in the cellar," Julietta said. "Are you okay?"

Sofia shrugged. "Yes, I'm still alive. My nerves are shot though."

They both went outside and sat on the patio. "Want some lemonade?" Sofia asked.

Julietta nodded. "I'll get another glass," she said, got up, and went into the kitchen. Sofia realized that Julietta knew her way around the house better than she did. She had practically lived here when Henry was with her. Sofia felt a pang of jealousy in her chest. She hated feeling resentful toward her sister. It wasn't her fault after all.

Julietta came back, poured herself a glass of lemonade and sat down. "This stupid Umberto," she said, after taking a sip. "I don't know why Nonno keeps him around. He drinks too much and he doesn't do any work."

"Nonno keeps him around?" Sofia asked.

"Well, actually, everybody does. He is just an old friend of Nonno's but the two argue all the time."

Sofia gazed at the darkening fields in front of her. "I think he did it on purpose." She didn't know if it was true, but it kept bothering her.

Julietta looked at her dumbfounded. "Why?"

Sofia shrugged and sighed. "I don't know. I just have a feeling. I'm probably wrong."

"But why would he do something like this? This does not make sense."

Sofia thought about the figure she had seen during the storm, the dead bird with its twisted neck. "Perhaps someone wants me gone."

Julietta stared at her and seemed genuinely stunned. "Why?"

Sofia didn't want to tell her about her discussion with Adriano Gori about the family. She felt he had told her in private. "What if the family is upset that I inherited the two vineyards from my father? If I wasn't here, they would go to you. Don't you feel unhappy about this?" Sofia challenged her.

Julietta still looked at her with unbelieving eyes. "Why should I?"

"Well, doesn't your family feel I'm an intruder?" Sofia prodded.

Julietta shook her head. "You really think I want to take your vineyards away from you? Is that why you are so ... so distrustful of me? I don't want your stupid vineyards. I don't want any vineyards at all." A sob escaped her and she glared at Sofia.

Sofia was taken aback by her sister's outburst. "I'm sorry. I don't mean to be distrustful. But look at it from my point of view. I had no idea that this existed." Sofia swept her arm in an arc taking in the fields around her. "I didn't know about you. I didn't know I had a sister. It was such a shock. It still is. I always wanted a sister and when I found out Henry had kept you hidden from me for so long ..." Sofia's voice broke.

Julietta wiped a tear from her cheek. "I do not know why Papa never told you. Perhaps he was ashamed of me."

"Oh, no, I don't think so. He was ashamed about getting involved with your mother when my mother was still alive. And then, he didn't have the courage to tell me. He loved you." Sofia now regretted her feelings of resentment toward Julietta. She seemed to suffer as much under the situation as Sofia did.

"He said he would tell you about me and bring you here next time he was visiting. But then he died," Julietta said in a low sad voice.

"I know. I wish so much he was still here with us," Sofia said. She took a deep breath. "Anyway, let's not talk about the vineyards anymore. I don't want them to drive a wedge between us. I'm really happy to have you as my sister."

Julietta shrugged. She didn't seem to believe her.

"I really do," Sofia said. She gently touched Julietta's arm. Julietta flinched a little but didn't pull away.

They sat quietly for a while. Sofia poured them both another glass of lemonade. "It's so beautiful here," Sofia said.

Julietta gave a quick smile. "Yes." She took a deep breath. "Perhaps I can visit California once. I always wanted to see where Papa was from."

"That would be wonderful," Sofia said. "I'd love to have you." She turned to Julietta. "You said you didn't want any vineyards. Wouldn't you like to work together with your mother and your uncle once you're through with school?"

Julietta shook her head, then shrugged. "I am not sure. Perhaps I want to do something else."

"What do you have in mind?"

Another shrug. "I don't know yet."

Sofia nodded. A cautious truce had been established again and Sofia didn't want to endanger it by asking too many questions.

Chapter 17

It was time to pick the white grapes for the Pinot Grigio. The Sangiovese grapes for the red wine would take another few weeks to fully ripen. Sofia, Julietta, Luisa, Edoardo and all the helpers and volunteers were busy all day long, picking grapes, putting them into plastic crates along the rows of vines. The workers carried the full crates to the flatbed trucks, where other volunteers stacked them on top of one another in such a way that the grapes in the crates underneath didn't get smashed. This prevented them from splitting and collecting unwanted yeasts and molds before they were crushed at the winery. The seasoned workers were doing the picking and eliminating of the spoiled or unsuitable grapes and the younger and agile ones were walking back and forth, carrying the full crates to the truck. It was an extremely busy time, since all the picked grapes of a field had to be crushed the same day.

After a day of hard work, Julietta and Sofia relaxed with glasses of lemonade on the patio, watching the sun set behind the hills. Sofia noticed that Julietta had been unusually quiet the whole day. Sofia wondered if her sister was still upset about the talk they had about the inheritance and the situation with their father.

"Is everything all right? You seem kind of gloomy today?" To Sofia's dismay, Julietta burst into tears.

"What's the matter?" Sofia put her arm around her sister.

"My birthday is soon and ... Papa isn't here to celebrate with me," she sobbed. She got up and went inside, then came out again with a box of Kleenex.

At the mention of her father, Sofia was overcome by sadness. She'd brought her sister some gifts from California, a couple of T-shirts, one with the logo of Hollywood on it. She found out that Julietta had a birthday in September and had decided to give her the presents then. She'd also packed two necklaces her father had given her. She could give them to Julietta for her birthday, as a gift from her father.

"It is the first birthday he is not here with me," Julietta said sadly. She pulled a tissue out of the box and wiped her face.

Sofia remembered that for the past years, Henry had always been in Tuscany during fall. She thought it was for business reasons and now she realized that the real purpose had been to see his daughter and to be present on her birthday and for the harvest of his grapes. She felt ashamed for her feelings of jealousy. After all, she'd had her father during the whole year and not just for a couple of months.

"You are lucky you lived so close to him," Julietta echoed Sofia's feelings. She got up and walked to the end of the patio, then turned back. "You know I was always jealous of you when he left again. Sometimes ... sometimes I even hated you. You had him all to yourself." A sob escaped her. "I'm sorry ..." She started to cry again, covering her face with her hands.

I guess I'm not the only one who is jealous. Sofia got up and hugged her sister. "I'm sorry, too. I wish I had known. We could've been together. If only he'd been with both of us more." She picked up a strand of Julietta's hair and brushed it behind her ear. "Did Papa do anything special for your birthday?"

Julietta pulled out another Kleenex from the box and brushed her tears away. "We celebrated with the family, but he always made me a real American chocolate cake with nuts in it and lots of frosting on top, in different colors. And candles of course."

"I could make you a chocolate cake. I know it's not the same as if Papa made it, but at least it's something to remember him by," Sofia said.

Julietta looked at her with hopeful eyes. "You know how to make it?"

Sofia chuckled. "He made me the same cake when I was younger. It's the only cake he knew how to make."

"Perhaps we can make the cake together," Julietta suggested. "I know where to get the ingredients. Papa always took me along shopping for them." She hesitated, then gave a little smile. "It will be fun. The recipe must still be around here somewhere." They went inside and Julietta browsed through one of the drawers in the kitchen cabinet. She pulled out a sheet of paper and held it up. "Here it is."

"Okay, good, we'll go shopping on Saturday." Sofia began to feel excited. "Perhaps, we can take a day off from work and go to the beach. A little birthday outing."

Julietta nodded. "I will ask Mamma. I am sure she will allow it. Come on."

The two walked over to the main house. Julietta found her mother in the living room and overwhelmed her with a flood of Italian. Sofia, who had learned some Italian since she got here a month before, understood the gist of it. Julietta told her mother about their cake-making project and to Sofia's surprise, Luisa's serious face broke into a smile. She nodded. "Thank you," she said, facing Sofia. "This is very kind of you."

Chapter 18

In the evening after working in one of the vineyards, Sofia took a quick shower. A knock at the door made her pause. She'd left the door unlocked, thinking that Julietta would join her. She put on her bathrobe and went to open the door. To her surprise, Nicholas was outside. She was embarrassed that her hair was dripping wet and she wrapped her robe tightly around herself.

"I'm sorry," he said, as he gave her a quick look-over. "I didn't realize ... this probably isn't a good time, but I wondered if, perhaps, you wanted to join me for dinner tonight. There's a nice place in town I sometimes go to. I'd like to invite you. It would be fun to speak English once again," he added with a chuckle.

Sofia hesitated, surprised at the invitation. But an evening out sounded like fun. She'd only been to town a couple of times with Julietta to buy groceries since her arrival at Vignaverde. "Yes, why not? Sounds good. Thank you."

"Great." Nicholas smiled. "Would eight o'clock be okay?"

"Sure, I'll be ready." Sofia saw Julietta walk up to the house. She smiled at Nicholas and the two exchanged a few words in Italian. Juliette watched, as Nicholas walked away.

"Did he invite you?" she asked Sofia.

"Yes, he did. How did you know?"

Julietta shrugged. "I think he likes you."

Sofia raised an eyebrow. "He doesn't know me. We only just met."

"Well, I just noticed. And he invited you."

"Yes, but that's because we're from the same country." Sofia smiled. Her sister was at an age where boys and being in love were all-important."

"I bet he likes you." Julietta winked at Sofia.

"I think you read much more into this," Sofia said.

"He is charming," Julietta said, thoughtfully.

Sofia studied her. "*You* seem to like him?"

"Yes, he is nice, but he is too old for me." Julietta shrugged. "But he would be perfect for you."

"Will you stop?" Sofia shook her head. "This is not my intention at all. In fact, that's the last thing I need. Getting involved with another winemaker from California. I've had enough from the last one."

"Oh? Why?"

"I'll tell you some other time. I have to get some clothes on and get ready." Sofia started climbing the stairs.

"Wear your purple dress. It brings out the color of your eyes. Have fun. See you later." Julietta laughed.

Sofia shook her head and chortled. *Clothes and boys.* It reminded her of her own favorite things as a teen. In front of her closet, she perused her somewhat limited wardrobe. She pulled out the blue-and-purple dress Julietta mentioned, put it back in again, grabbed a blouse to go with her slacks, then hesitated. Going out in the evening was actually the only time she could wear a dress rather than her daily dungarees. She took the dress out again, put it on, dried and brushed her hair until it was silky, and put on some eye shadow and lipstick. She checked her appearance in the mirror, hoping she wasn't overdressed, shrugged, and grabbed a light jacket. Although it was hot during the day, it tended to cool off in the evenings. Downstairs, she poured herself a glass of water and sat outside on the patio to wait for Nicholas.

He came to pick her up a little before eight. He was

109

dressed casually in black jeans and a green-and-yellow patterned shirt. Sofia had to admit, he was good-looking with his athletic figure, wavy blond hair, suntanned skin, and dark expressive eyes. *California beach boy, except for the eyes,* she thought when she greeted him.

They drove the short way to the village in Nicholas's rental car, which he'd gotten at the same place in Cecina where Sofia had rented hers. His, however, was a stick shift, which he obviously knew how to drive. Sofia told him about her experience at the rental agency, when she came close to having to learn to drive a stick shift.

"It's not really that difficult," Nicholas said. "I'm used to it because of the farm machines I drive in California."

"Where do you work in California?" Sofia asked.

"Right now, I work on my grandfather's fields, helping him out, since he's getting a little too old for doing the work all by himself," he said. "Eventually, I want to have my own vineyard and winery."

"Oh, so you'll be an independent entrepreneur," Sofia said.

"Yes, that's been my dream all along. Right now, I'm just getting started," Nicholas said.

In the meantime, they had arrived at the parking lot outside Vignaverde. Nicholas parked his car and they walked through the gate under the Etruscan arch into town. Nicholas had picked a small family-run trattoria for dinner, which served typical Tuscan food. As was often the case in the Tuscan restaurants, the walls of the dining room were of irregular natural stones and an arched ceiling covered the place. The starched light-pink tablecloths and napkins gave the rustic interior a touch of elegance. A young waiter brought them the menus and told them about the specialties for the evening. After ordering some appetizers, mineral water, and wine, Sofia and Nicholas studied the menu. Aside from the meat and fish, it listed several dishes of pasta.

"So, what made you come to Vignaverde?" Sofia asked as she put the menu aside and took a sip of mineral water.

"Well, actually, I guess indirectly your father. That was a few years ago. Another winemaker mentioned your father and the fact that he was doing some business with vintners in Tuscany. I called Mr. Laverne one day and he gave me a couple of addresses, one being Podere Francesco Ginori."

Sofia stared at him. "Who was it? Who told you about him?"

"James Antonini."

"What?" Sofia's heart lurched.

"What's wrong?" Nicholas asked. He put down his menu and gave her a puzzled look.

Sofia leaned her head into her hands, looked up and shook her head. "James Antonini is my ex-husband. I can't believe he knew about the vineyard. This is all so upsetting. I seemed to be the only one who didn't know."

"James never mentioned that your father owned a vineyard. He just told me he had dealings in Tuscany because he traveled there so often. I'm sorry, I didn't mean to upset you." Nicholas's eyes expressed concern.

Sofia shook her head. "I don't mean to blame you. It's just … so much has happened with my father's death and then I found out about his secret life."

"I understand. I didn't realize James was your husband. We weren't close. I met him at some wine function and we got to talking. It must have been after your divorce, because now I remember he mentioned Henry Laverne as his former father-in-law."

Sofia shrugged. "It's not your fault that my family history is such a disaster. I'm just stunned that here I am so far away from California and I run into someone who not only knows my ex-husband but who knew my father and the vineyard I knew nothing about. It's just unnerving."

"I really don't know much about your background. I met your father, yes, and I found out from Julietta that her sister from California was coming to visit. That's about it. The rest I'm finding out in bits and pieces."

"I'm sorry I'm making a big deal out of it. I owe you an explanation about the whole thing," Sofia said just as the waiter came with two plates of delicious looking pasta, gnocchi for Sofia and a dish of spaghetti al pesto for Nicholas.

Nicholas smiled at her. "I don't mean to pry, but, yes, to be honest, now you've made me curious about your family history. It sounds like some kind of fiction. But let's enjoy the meal first. You know, it isn't good talking about disturbing things while eating. That's at least what my grandfather always tells me."

"You're right. Let's eat. This looks delicious." Sofia took a deep breath. The news about her family had upset her, but after a few bites of the delicious meal and some more wine, her mood improved again.

After finishing a lovely dessert of ice cream topped with hot chocolate sauce and while drinking a cup of espresso, Sofia wanted to give Nicholas an abbreviated version of her background. But once she began, the story about her troubled childhood with her mother, her father's love, his untimely death and the story of his life in Tuscany began pouring out of her. Halfway through, she stopped for a moment. Why was she doing this? She barely knew Nicholas but he exuded a kindness and trust that made her talk. *I'll regret this later on*, she felt at one point, but couldn't stop herself. She took a deep breath and looked at him embarrassed.

"I'm sorry, I hope I'm not boring you."

"Boring me? No way, this is a fascinating story." Then after a pause: "How do you feel about your father now? Are you still angry with him?"

Sofia shrugged. "It comes and goes. He was such a wonderful father. I really loved him ... still do. But I just can't understand why he kept all this hidden for so long. Then I feel again like I don't know him at all."

Nicholas nodded. "What are you planning to do now? I mean, you now have a vineyard here, two fields of grapes, and a sister. Are you planning to stay?"

"I don't know. I want to but I don't feel completely welcome here. And I guess I might get homesick for California and Emma. But I'll be here a lot, I think."

"You say, you don't feel completely welcome?" Nicholas waved at the waiter and ordered another espresso for the both of them.

Sofia hesitated. She didn't want to tell him about the family's supposed resentment toward her for inheriting the vineyards. She had already told him more than she had wanted.

"You know, it's difficult for both sides. They must feel somewhat weary of me, not knowing me. And I don't fully trust them either."

"Yes, I understand," Nicholas said. "From what I learned during the past two seasons I was here, the fields that belong to you are some of the prime fields of the estate." He lifted a shoulder. "Perhaps they were afraid of what you were going to do with them. You could sell them and that would be a real loss for the estate and the family."

Sofia glanced at him. She hadn't even thought of that possibility. "Did anybody say anything to that extent?"

"Oh, no, it's just a thought. I mean, if it was me, and I found out that someone I didn't know would all of a sudden

113

own an important part of my property, I'd be worried, too. Don't you think so?"

Sofia nodded. "You're right. Of course, I have no intention of selling the fields. If at all, I'd sell them to the family or give them back or something."

"I think once they know you better and know your intentions, they'll be much more accepting."

"You're probably right." Sofia smiled. "Well having a sister like Julietta does make the whole thing worthwhile, I think. And being able to really work in a vineyard again. It's quite satisfying."

"You're very lucky. Owning part of a beautiful estate in Vignaverde is quite something. I'm jealous," Nicholas said.

"I hope you'll be able to have your own vineyard in California, too," Sofia said.

"It will happen, eventually," Nicholas said. "Then I can import some of your wine. Or we can do it together. Wine from this vineyard would be a great addition." He emptied his cup of espresso and winked at her.

Sofia gave a quick smile, wondering if he meant it or if it was just one of those non-committal suggestions one makes after a pleasant evening.

Nicholas dropped her off at the main house. As she stepped out of the car and walked toward her home, she saw something in front of her door. She couldn't see what it was in the half-dark. It looked like a small bundle and she wondered if someone had left something for her. When she got closer, she stopped short, then approached slowly, holding her breath. It was another animal, a rabbit. She came closer and almost choked at the gruesome sight. The rabbit was lying on its side and its head was covered with crusted blood. Sofia gave a terrified shriek, then turned around and ran to the main house.

Chapter 19

Sofia banged on the door, then turned the knob. It wasn't locked.

She found Luisa and Edoardo in the living room. "Somebody is leaving dead animals at my place," she blurted out, her heart racing.

"What do you mean?" Luisa said. She and Edoardo got up and stared at her.

"The other day, I found a dead bird and now, there's a rabbit at my door steps." Her voice was shaking.

The door opened and Julietta came inside. "What's the matter?"

"I don't know what's going on," Sofia said.

Edoardo stared at her. "Show us."

They all walked over to Sofia's house. Julietta put her arm around Sofia. "Don't be scared."

Fortunately, the rabbit was still there. What if it had disappeared like the bird? Then they would have really taken her for a mental case.

Edoardo bent down and turned the dead rabbit around, checking it. "Aha." He stood up again. "It was shot," he said.

"Who would do something like this?" Sofia's voice cracked. "And why in front of my door?"

"Ah, no." Edoardo shook his head. "It was not shot here. Hunting season just started on Sunday. I am sure the rabbit was shot out in the fields or the woods. I heard several gunshots today. It probably was not killed properly and ran away. And by chance, it ended up here and died. This happens sometimes. Do not worry. I will get rid of it."

Luisa touched Sofia's arm. "I'm sorry. No wonder you were scared."

"But then what about the bird?" Sofia asked. Their explanation sounded reasonable but she wasn't convinced yet. "It looked like it had its neck twisted. And then it disappeared."

"When did this happen?" Edoardo asked Sofia.

"It was right after the storm. First I thought it was because of the storm, but now, there's a dead rabbit. I don't know what to think anymore."

Edoardo gave her what Sofia felt was an indulgent look, as if he needed to calm a frightened child. "I am sure the bird died because of the storm. Every time we have a storm, I find one or two dead birds. And you said you did not bury it right away. You left it outside?"

Sofia nodded.

"An animal may have dragged it off. Perhaps a dog. There are some wild dogs around," Luisa said.

"*Esatto.*" Edoardo nodded. "I will get a shovel."

"There is one in the shed behind the house," Sofia said. They all waited while Edoardo went to get the shovel.

"I'm sorry. You must think I'm crazy. But it really frightened me. It was as if someone wanted to scare me."

Luisa shook her head. "No, I'm sure this is not the case. You are just not used yet to our wild ... what do you call it?"

"Wild West?" Julietta said, laughing.

Luisa smiled. "Something like this. If you are scared to be by yourself tonight, you can stay with us. Or Julietta can sleep here."

A few days before, after the emotional exchange with Julietta, Sofia had asked Luisa if her sister could spend the night at her place once in a while, so they could get to know

117

each other better. Luisa had agreed.

"I'm sorry, I'm making such a fuss," Sofia said. She was embarrassed and now felt she had overreacted. But she was grateful for Julietta's company.

After Edoardo got rid of the dead rabbit and he and Luisa had gone home, Julietta and Sofia sat in the living room, drinking a cup of hot tea.

"How was dinner with Nicholas?" Julietta asked her.

Sofia smiled. "We had a good time. He is very nice," she said.

"Are you going to see him again?" Julietta asked.

"Perhaps," Sofia shrugged, smiling at her sister's eagerness. She got up and opened the patio door.

They stepped outside. Sofia inhaled the scent of flowers in the garden. Warmed up from the sun during the day, they gave off an intense fragrance. The moon lit the rolling hills in the distance. "No more dead animals, thank God," she said.

"I would have been scared, too," Julietta said. She hugged Sofia.

Julietta went to bed and Sofia checked the doors to make sure they were locked. The sensible explanation Luisa and Edoardo had given her for the dead animals sounded true, but a certain unease remained. It still seemed a strange occurrence that in the space of a couple of weeks, she had found two dead animals on her property. She thought of the figure behind the house she'd seen during the storm. And what about the wine barrel that almost crushed her?

Coincidences? Or did someone want to scare or even harm her? If so, they'd succeeded. The image of the twisted neck of the bird and the dead rabbit with its bloody head made her shudder.

Chapter 20

The following Saturday, Sofia and Julietta went shopping for Julietta's birthday cake. They drove to Vignaverde to one of the few *alimentari* or grocery stores where they got the ingredients—flour, baking soda, dark chocolate, nuts, butter, eggs, and sugar. They also picked up cocoa powder, confectioner sugar, and vanilla extract for the frosting. In a different store, they bought colorful candles, cake decorations, and some balloons.

"Might as well go all out," Sofia said, getting excited about the birthday celebration. Julietta, too, seemed to have overcome her disappointment about her father not being present and insisted on buying some funny hats for the party.

As they walked through town, Sofia stopped at a shop window that displayed beautiful alabaster artwork. "Let's check it out," she said to Julietta.

They went inside and looked at the display of bowls, vases, and all kinds of small sculptures. Sofia carefully lifted an alabaster vase, turning it around and admiring its brown-and-white texture. In her guidebook, Sofia had read that alabaster was plentiful in Vignaverde. There was a museum and many of the stores sold art objects and souvenirs made of alabaster. The carving of this translucent stone went back to Etruscan times. Sofia decided to buy a few things as presents for Emma and her friends in California.

"Beautiful," she said and brushed her finger lightly over the fine carvings. She bought several of them and the sales girl wrapped them carefully in bubble wrap paper.

"*Ciao*, Julietta," someone called as they stepped out of the store. They turned around and Julietta smiled and waved at a young man who came walking down the street.

"*Ciao*, Marco."

Sofia noticed, amused, that Julietta's face was flushed and her eyes sparkled. She realized why. The young man who sauntered toward them was stunningly handsome with wavy dark hair, green eyes, and a trim figure. He hugged Julietta and gave her a kiss on the cheek. She introduced Sofia as "*mia sorella d'America.*"

"I am very pleased to meet you. Julietta told me a lot about you." Marco spoke English with the usual accent.

"Marco is in my English class," Julietta said.

Since Julietta's English was more advanced than that of her classmates, she attended lessons for older students at her school.

Marco hugged her. "Yes, and Julietta always helps me with my homework. I would not know what to do without her."

Julietta blushed again and gave him a playful slap on the arm. "You exaggerate as usual."

"What are you doing here?" Marco asked.

"Getting stuff for the birthday party," Julietta said. "You are going to come, right?"

"I would not miss it … how do you say? … for the world." His handsome face stretched into a smile. "Listen, I would love to invite you for a cup of coffee, but unfortunately, I have a dental appointment in ten minutes." He looked at his watch. "But some other time, okay?"

"Yes, thank you. You have to go to the dentist?" Julietta asked.

"Just cleaning," Marco said, showing a row of perfectly aligned, white teeth. "Anyway, it was nice meeting you." He turned to Sofia. "You will be at the party, too, I hope."

"Oh, yes," Julietta said eagerly and put her arm around Sofia. "We are going to make the birthday cake today."

"Fantastic. I look forward to it." Another charming smile. "Well, I am on my way. See you tomorrow then." Marco waved and walked off.

"Isn't he cute?" Julietta grabbed Sofia's arm and squeezed it hard.

"Ouch." Sofia chuckled and rubbed her arm. "He sure is and you're swooning."

"Ah, yes." Julietta sighed. "But I think he has a girlfriend. I am not sure. Anyway, he will be at the party by himself. I told him he could bring a guest, but he said he would be alone. So, who knows, perhaps he is not dating anyone."

Sofia laughed. "Come on, you lovebird. Let's go home and make the cake."

At Sofia's home, they put the ingredients away. Sofia studied the recipe again. She wasn't exactly an experienced baker, but neither had her father been and so the recipe was very detailed and easy to follow. They had to collect a few utensils from the main house, since Henry obviously hadn't done a lot of baking while in Tuscany. Sofia, however, found a mixer. She mixed and beat the batter while Julietta turned on the oven. After the cake was in the oven, they sat around the kitchen table, licking the utensils with the leftover-batter. Soon the scent of chocolate permeated the kitchen. Sofia was relieved when she saw the batter rising nicely in the pan. It had been some time since she had made a cake from scratch. After the allotted time, they took the cake out and admired its nice shape.

"It looks even better than when Papa made it," Julietta said. "His always came out a little crooked, but with the frosting it was okay."

Sofia was happy Julietta seemed to have gotten over her sadness about her father's absence. "It'll look perfect with the decoration," she said. "We'll put the frosting on when the cake has cooled a little."

Julietta mixed the ingredients for the frosting—butter, cacao powder, confectioner sugar, and a dash of vanilla extract. They applied the frosting together and then licked the spoons clean.

"I'm going to have a sugar high before I even taste the cake," Sofia said.

"What is a sugar high?" Julietta asked.

"Oh, you know, when you get all jittery and excited from too much sugar."

Julietta nodded, then pointed at the cake. "What about the decorations?"

"We'll put those on tomorrow before the party," Sofia suggested.

The birthday celebration would take place the following day at lunch, and in the afternoon, a few of Julietta's friends from school would join them for ice cream and cake and a little party.

"It will be fun," Julietta said and her eyes sparkled. "Perhaps Papa will celebrate with us."

"We'll save him a piece of cake," Sofia said. The two sisters giggled.

Ever since their talk about their father and the inheritance, the air between them had cleared. Sofia felt more relaxed around Julietta and Julietta had become her old bubbly self again.

"I wanted to give you something for your birthday," Sofia said. "I know it's a day early, but anyway, here it is." Sofia handed Julietta the packages.

Julietta opened the box with the Hollywood T-shirt first and screamed with excitement. She put it on and it fit perfectly. She turned around in front of the mirror, admiring the logo and the picture on it.

"And here is something from Papa," Sofia said and handed her the package with the jewelry.

When Julietta opened the box, she looked at the necklaces with wide-open eyes and turned them around slowly without saying anything. For a brief moment, Sofia was afraid she didn't like them. One was a simple gold chain with a teardrop-shaped stone. And the other one was more modern, a long chain with a mixture of real pearls and other types of semi-precious stones.

Julietta's eyes filled with tears. "They are beautiful," she whispered with a sob. "Oh, my God, they are wonderful." She hugged Sofia, then stepped back and put one of the necklaces on. "Thank you so much. I love them. And thank you, Papa." Tears were streaming down her face and she smiled at the same time.

Sofia felt they had truly bonded.

Chapter 21

As Julietta had hoped, the birthday was a success. They had a good lunch of her favorite food: pizza *quattro stagioni* or four-season pizza, which Luisa made from scratch, and salad. To Sofia's pleasant surprise, they had invited Nicholas as well. For dessert and as an accompaniment to the cake, Edoardo's wife, Gina, had prepared homemade blackberry and raspberry ice cream.

Sofia had met Edoardo's wife a few times during the work in the vineyard. She was a pleasant woman, livelier than her husband. Unfortunately, she didn't speak English as well as the other people, so they didn't talk much to each other. But Gina was friendly and polite and didn't seem to harbor any resentment toward Sofia.

In the afternoon, a few of Julietta's friends from school as well as Edoardo's and Gina's children, a ten-year old boy by the name of Francesco and a girl of about seven, called Diana, came in time for the cake ceremony. Besides boys and girls from Julietta's class, there were a couple of older students at the party, Marco, the handsome young man Sofia had met the day before, and two girls from Julietta's advanced English class.

Marco had brought Julietta a present, a lovely pair of earrings, which, as if by design, fit the new necklace she was wearing. He hugged and kissed Juliette who blushed deeply. She surreptitiously glanced at her mother who was busy setting the table with paper plates and napkins and didn't notice the exchange.

The Italian Sister

Sofia went inside where Gina was spooning ice cream into dessert bowls. Sofia carried the decorated cake with the fifteen candles outside. Everyone was seated at a long wooden table under a canopy of colorful paper streamers Luisa and Edoardo had put up.

It was a cheerful party and even Edoardo smiled more than usual. The highpoint for Sofia, however, was the fact that the old Santucci was not present. He was gone for a few days, supposedly visiting a friend. Without the old man, the atmosphere was lighthearted and pleasant, and his wife Donna, Julietta's grandmother, was more relaxed and surprisingly chatty.

Julietta blew out the candles. When she cut the cake, she set aside one piece. "For Papa."

Luisa nodded. "We'll save it for him," she said quietly.

Sofia who sat next to Julietta put her arm around her when she collided with Marco who sat on the other side and was trying to do the same. They looked at each other and Marco smiled and pulled his arm back. "*Mi dispiace,*" he said, "I'm sorry."

Out of the corner of her eyes, Sofia saw Edoardo watch him with a scowl. *The concerned uncle,* she thought.

Marco and Julietta, however, gave no further indication of intimacy. After the cake and ice cream was finished, Marco spent most of the time talking to one of the older girls from the English class and Julietta entertained her girlfriends from school.

The celebration lasted until sunset. Julietta's friends began to leave, and Marco got up, and he and Julietta went over to Luisa. Marco and Luisa shook hands and the two talked for a while. Luisa smiled and shook his hand again as he was getting ready to leave. He gave Julietta a friendly pat on the back and left.

125

Christa Polkinhorn

After the last guests had gone, Sofia, Luisa, and Gina cleaned up while Francesco and Diana helped their father carry the tables and chairs inside. After cake and ice cream, nobody was hungry for dinner anymore. Edoardo, Gina and their children walked over to their place and Sofia and Julietta helped Luisa put the dishes away.

"Can I stay at Sofia's tonight?" Julietta asked her mother.

Luisa glanced at her. "Yes, but I want to talk to you first."

Sofia felt Luisa wanted to be alone with Julietta. "I'll see you guys later."

"Thank you for helping with the birthday party and for the cake and the beautiful presents. This was really nice, wasn't it, Julietta?" Luisa said.

"Yes, thank you, Sofia. Papa would have loved it," Julietta said and hugged Sofia, who was touched by the display of gratitude.

Half an hour later, Sofia pulled some laundry out of the dryer. Her father had had the foresight to have a washer and dryer installed in the house which was a godsend when working in the fields. Sweaty T-shirts and dirty overalls piled up fast in this hot weather. The following day would be another working day at the estate.

While Sofia was folding shirts and underwear, Julietta came in, carrying a cloth bag with her clothes for the morning. She dropped the bag by the door and plopped herself on the sofa, watching Sofia fold laundry. She looked troubled.

"What's the matter?" Sofia asked.

Julietta sighed. "You have to help me with something."

"Oh? What is it?"

"You have to help me convince Mamma to let me go to Marco's party." Julietta jumped up from the sofa and threw

126

her arms around Sofia. "Please, please."

Sofia pushed Julietta back a little and held her by the arms. "Which party?"

"Marco has one every year at the end of the summer holiday for his classmates and friends. And since I am in his English class, he invited me as well and asked me to bring a friend, so I invited Monica. Marco asked Mamma for permission. Isn't he cool? He is such a gentleman."

"Okay," Sofia said slowly. "So what did your mother say?"

Julietta groaned. "She thinks I am too young to go to a party with older guys."

Sofia hesitated. "I can't really blame her. He is quite a bit older than you are and so are most likely the guys in his class who will be at the party. They may have different ideas what kind of entertainment they like."

"What do you mean? And he is only three years older." Julietta kicked her clothes bag away.

Sofia chuckled. "Well, you know what I mean. Boys his age usually want more than just dancing and having a good time. There may be alcohol and—"

"I never drink alcohol. And I am not a child anymore. I am fifteen today." Julietta's eyes flashed and she glared at Sofia.

Sofia sighed. "I believe you. You wouldn't intentionally do anything you're not supposed to. But I also know at a party with a lot of people and with a guy you really like, it is easy to lose control. It has happened to many young girls that they forget themselves and end up pregnant—"

Julietta groaned. "Oh, please. You are even worse than Mamma. It is a party. I am with a friend. And besides, Marco's parents are going to be there. So I do not think we are going to have an orgy with his parents there." Julietta gave a dismissive snort.

Sofia had to laugh. "Well, let's see what your mother is going to decide. If his parents are there, perhaps it will be all right. When is the party anyway?"

"In a week. Please you have to help me."

Oh, no. Sofia sighed when Julietta looked at her with her purple-blue puppy-eyes. The last thing she wanted was to get into a tug of war with her sister holding the rope on one end and Luisa pulling at the other end and Sofia being stuck in the middle. She could easily identify with Julietta's desire for independence but she also understood and shared Luisa's concerns.

Chapter 22

The Monday after Julietta's birthday party was another day of work at Podere Francesco Ginori. As Luisa had told Sofia, the estate was named after one of the ancestors of her family who had started a small vineyard over two centuries ago.

Edoardo who had tested the ripeness of the grapes had announced that Sofia's field with the Merlot varietal was ready for picking. Everybody was in the field, working. They started at sunrise to get as much of the heavy work done in the cool early morning hours. By now, Sofia was familiar with the working routine.

The workers were evenly spread out throughout the field, cutting the clusters of fruit and putting them into plastic containers along the rows of vines, carefully removing any damaged fruit. Later, at the winery, the workers put the grapes on a conveyor belt and checked them again for anything unsuitable. The grapes were tossed into a machine, a destemmer and crusher, and fed into the fermentation tanks, where yeast and sulfites were added. And now, the grapes sat "on the skins," meaning the fruit including skins, pulp, and grape seeds were beginning to ferment. The shining huge steel fermentation tanks where the grapes sizzled and bubbled and did their magic always reminded Sofia of a modern version of a witch's cauldron.

The harvest was one of Sofia's favorite times in the vineyard. Months of preparation and testing, of caring for the vines and grapes came to fruition on those days. A spirit of excitement permeated the whole estate. Picking the grapes was hard and sticky work but the joy of seeing the fruit ripened to perfection almost lets the vintners forget their aching arms, shoulders, and backs and the sweat pouring down their faces.

In the evening, the workers often gathered around a fire to relax, talk, and have a good time. This evening, Sofia went home to take a shower before joining the other workers. Just as she was about to go out, someone knocked. Expecting Julietta, she was surprised when Luisa stood in front of the door.

"You worked so hard today," she said with a smile. "Perhaps we can share some wine from one of the past *vendemmia*. It is from your fields." Luisa held up a bottle of red wine.

It was the first time Luisa had come to Sofia's place for a friendly visit. Usually they met at the main house or she would come by to bring something or give Sofia a message.

Sofia invited her inside. "Let's sit on the patio. It's pleasant in the evening." She went to get a corkscrew and two glasses. Luisa opened the bottle and poured the apple-red Sangiovese wine into the glasses. They swirled the wine a little, then put the glass down to let the wine mingle with the air or "breathe."

They sat quietly for a while, glancing at the yellow and green fields in front of them that turned golden in the early evening light. Finally, Sofia lifted the glass and smelled the wine. "Interesting," she said. She hesitated, smelled it again. "Reminds me of flowers. But I couldn't tell you what kind." She laughed and inhaled the aroma again. "Complex."

"Yes. Enrico used to say that, too ... I mean Henry. I used to call him by his Italian name sometimes." Luisa gave a quick smile. She held the glass against her nose as well.

Sofia nodded. She took a sip and let it stay in her mouth.

"Spicy. I like the slightly tangy taste. Good tannin." She took another sip and hesitated. "A touch of berry, from the Merlot?"

Luisa nodded. "Yes, you have a good palate."

"Thank you. My father and I used to do it as a past time, taste different wines. He taught me a lot." She gave a wistful smile and took another sip. "I love this wine."

Luisa nodded. "Yes, it is one of my favorite estate wines. Henry tried out several blends of Sangiovese and Merlot."

Both women were quiet for a while. By then, the sun was about to set with its typical colorful display. Birds, which had mainly been silent in the heat of the afternoon, began to sing and twitter. It smelled of dry grass and sage.

Sofia sighed. "It's so beautiful here. No wonder Dad fell in love with this place." She turned to Luisa who looked straight ahead, then glanced at Sofia. She looked thoughtful, almost sad.

"How did you meet my father?" It was a question Sofia had wanted to ask for a while but had always been reluctant to. Relaxed from the wine and the warm early fall evening, she finally had the courage to touch this delicate subject.

Luisa glanced at her, then looked down at her hands. "It was a long time ago," she began. She cleared her throat and took another sip of wine.

"A friend of ours from Siena brought him here and introduced him. Henry was looking for Tuscan wine to import for his own estate in California, to add to his own *portafoglio* ... how do you say it?"

"Portfolio," Sofia said.

"Yes. He worked for a vineyard then, right?"

Sofia nodded. "Yes, that was when my mother was still alive. We lived near the Russian River and Henry and some of his colleagues had a vineyard together."

Luisa swirled the wine and looked at it thoughtfully. "I am sorry, this must be difficult for you … about your mother, and Henry and I."

Sofia shook her head. "Don't worry. My mother and father had a difficult marriage and my mother was never really present. I'm not angry at my father or at you. I just wish my father had had the courage to tell me about it. It was such a shock when I found out." Sofia's hand shook a little as she lifted her glass.

"I know," Luisa said. "I asked him many times why he would not tell you."

"What did he say?" Sofia asked.

Luisa shrugged. "At first, he said he could not tell anyone. Then later and during the last visit, he said he would tell you and your aunt about me and Julietta. He would bring you here to meet your sister."

"Yes, but then it was too late." Sofia brushed a strand of hair out of her face.

"Yes," Luisa said. "It was such a shock when we heard that he died. It was terrible for Julietta. She loved and adored her father and she was sad that she could not see him more often. And now, she will not be able to see him at all anymore. She still wakes up at night crying."

Sofia's eyes filled with tears. "I know. I feel the same way. But in a way it must even be worse for Julietta."

"I think it is good you are here," Luisa continued. "It seems to help her. You are like a connection to him. You know what I mean?"

Sofia nodded. "Yes, I feel the same way about Julietta. When we are together I feel Henry's presence somehow. It's difficult to explain."

Luisa nodded and poured them each another glass of wine. Sofia noticed that they had drunk about half the bottle and she began to feel the effect.

"Henry must have been happy here," Sofia mused.

"He was ... at first. He was very excited about the vineyard. Then we had a terrible year, such bad weather. We lost almost the whole harvest. And we had debts." Luisa sighed. "My stepfather made bad investments. He wanted to grow the estate too much. We thought we had to sell everything."

"Your stepfather? You mean the old Mr. Santucci?" Sofia remembered that Adriano had told her about the family relationship and that Luisa's real father had died.

"Yes." Luisa gave her a furtive glance. "My own father passed away long ago and my mother remarried. Unfortunately the wrong man. But that is another story." She waved her hand in a dismissive gesture.

Sofia was both surprised and a little relieved. Obviously, she wasn't the only one who didn't much care for the old man and the fact that Luisa had misgivings about her stepfather made Sofia feel closer to her.

"The old Mr. Santucci seems to hate me."

"Do not take it personal," Luisa said. "He does not like Americans. And the fact that an American owns part of the estate really bothers him. Although it is not even his property anymore, he still feels he is in charge."

"What does he have against Americans?"

"Something happened during the war, the Second World War. I do not know the details. It was long before he met my mother and my family, sometime in 1943 I think. He was a boy then, but his father and uncle were in the Italian army. They were captured by the American forces and became prisoners and allegedly they were shot in cold blood by the Americans. There was a scandal about it because according to the law, prisoners of war have to be treated humanely." Luisa shrugged. "It was war and I guess laws were not always followed. But the officers in charge of the killing were punished afterward. This is what Edoardo told me.

"Losing his father and uncle like that really hurt my stepfather and supposedly created a real hardship for the family. As a result of this, his mother became ill and died shortly afterward. I guess it was a really tough time. He never seemed to have gotten over it and ever since then, he does not like Americans much."

"Boy, he must have hated my father, too, considering he ended up owning part of the estate."

"Yes. Had he known that Henry would end up being a partner, he would never have handed over the estate to us," Luisa said and gave a little snort. "See, because he mismanaged the estate so badly, the bank refused to give us another loan. The only way they would consider it was if someone more reputable was in charge. So he decided to hand over the property to Edoardo and me. Also, at the time, he had some problems with his health and was not able to work much anymore. Anyway, he made one good decision in this whole mess and signed the estate over to the descendants."

"That must have been hard for him, giving up all the power," Sofia said.

"Yes, it was. But he figured he would rather give it to his children than lose it to the bank. The loan we got, however, was not enough to pay all the debts and support the estate. Then Henry offered to invest some of his own money and take over two of the fields. He had been visiting us for several years and bought some of our wine. He loved the estate and he particularly loved the Sangiovese and the Merlot vineyards." Luisa stopped and gave a dreamy smile.

"Anyway," she continued. "Henry really saved us. It was

134

thanks to him that we survived and that the estate is profitable again."

"So, what was Mr. Santucci's reaction when he found out that my father owned two of the fields?" Sofia asked.

Luisa smirked. "He was not too happy about it, as you can imagine."

"Jesus, I'm beginning to feel sorry for him," Sofia said thoughtfully.

Luisa shrugged. "I used to feel sorry for him, too, but he was so power-hungry, he brought it on himself. If he had not wanted to be the most powerful winemaker in Tuscany, this would never have happened." Luisa poured them both another glass of wine. "Anyway, during that time, Henry and I became very close." Luisa glanced at Sofia, then averted her eyes and looked out onto the now darkened fields. "That is when I became pregnant." A pause. "But then after your mother died, Henry wanted to end it. He felt guilty; he felt he was somehow responsible for her death, that he did not do enough for your mamma." She shrugged. "We began to quarrel. I wanted him to come here and live here. He said he could not." She paused, picked up her glass again and drank the rest.

"When we met we were both unhappy in our marriage. My husband had left me and Henry had problems with his wife, too. But later our love ... Henry's love for me was not strong enough."

Sofia turned her wine glass in her hand, then glanced at Luisa. "What about you? Your feelings?"

Luisa shrugged. "I loved him more. I was really in love with him. But he became like far away ... distant, I think this is the word. Eventually, my feelings for him cooled as well but we remained good friends. And he always loved and supported Julietta." Luisa put her hand on Sofia's arm. "Do not be angry with him. He was a good man. And it was my fault too, that we became involved."

Sofia, touched by Luisa's sudden warmth toward her, shook her head. "You don't need to apologize or feel guilty. What happened between you and my father is not for me to judge. I only regret I didn't know earlier. It would have been so wonderful if we could have all sat here together. You, Julietta, Henry and I." Sofia's voice broke.

Luisa nodded and Sofia saw tears in her eyes. She took a deep breath. "Well, I'm glad we talked about this." Then pointing at the bottle. "We drank the whole thing. I don't think I can walk anymore."

Luisa laughed and Sofia realized that it was the first time she heard the woman laugh out loud.

"Oh, by the way. Julietta asked me to help convince you to let her go to Marco's party. Please don't tell her I told you." Sofia hated to be a tattletale, but she felt she owed it to Luisa to voice her concern.

Luisa shook her head and chuckled. "I know. I told her I would think about it. He seems like a nice young man but he is quite a bit older. He told me that he invited her because she helped him with his English." Luisa shrugged. "But I think Julietta is a little in love with him. I do not want her to get involved in something that will distract her from her studies. But if I forbid her to go, she will still see him at school and it might drive her toward him even more. She is a strong-headed girl. If she feels I do not trust her, she will rebel even more." Luisa sighed. "It is difficult to know how much freedom to give a young girl."

"I know what you mean," Sofia said.

"It was such a relief when Henry was here. He had no problems setting boundaries for Julietta. And she did not resent it the same way she does when I forbid her something."

Sofia nodded. "I can understand that. She probably idealized him."

"Exactly. He could do no wrong. But I am the mean mamma who is around all the time, always making demands." Luisa smiled. "Well, I will talk to Monica's mother and see what she says. We may let them go for a few hours and pick them back up early."

"Sounds like a good compromise," Sofia said.

After Luisa was gone, Sofia remained sitting outside for a while, watching the fields and hills sink into the blue-black night. It was still pleasantly warm and the soft evening breeze brought the scent of the freesia in the corner of the patio and a whiff of sweet ripening grapes.

Sofia thought about her talk with Luisa, which seemed to have brought them closer. Up to this evening, Luisa had struck Sofia as friendly but guarded and somewhat aloof. Now, however, she had seen a more vulnerable side of her, a warmth and passion she hadn't experienced before. She could understand her father's attraction to this somewhat mysterious woman, so unlike the distant and erratic woman her mother, Cleo, had been. Sofia felt sorry for her father who had to hide his love for both Luisa and Julietta for so long. But now Sofia and Julietta had the opportunity to solidify the relationship that her father began.

Chapter 23

With the grape harvest in full swing, Sofia and Julietta were busy most days, working at the different grape fields. Sofia wondered if there was a child labor law in Italy, but if there was, it wasn't enforced on the estate. Julietta, being only fifteen, worked along with the adults. She told Sofia that she did it voluntarily and enjoyed it most of the times. "I do not really have to, but it is our family estate, so I want to help. Besides, I get a lot of extra pocket money," she had said with a wink of her eye.

Today, she told Sofia that her mother was still considering letting her and Monica go to Marco's party. "She almost gave in yesterday, but then Uncle Edoardo said we were too young." Julietta rolled her eyes and glared at her uncle, who worked in the field next to them. "He always puts his nose into my business," she said with a scowl.

"Well, he's your uncle and he feels responsible for you," Sofia suggested.

"He is not my father, so why does he interfere?" Julietta snipped angrily a cluster of grapes and put it into the plastic crate along the rows of vines.

"Perhaps now with Henry gone, he feels he needs to be something like a replacement father for you."

Julietta gave a quick snort. "Papa would have let me go."

"Are you sure, Julietta?" Sofia raised an eyebrow.

"Yes," her sister said angrily. "He knew he could trust me."

"I don't think your mother and your uncle don't trust

you. I think they're just concerned for your welfare," Sofia said.

"Well, then ..." Julietta stopped her work and stared toward the houses. "What is *he* doing here?"

Sofia turned around. A young man came walking toward the field. Sofia had never seen him before. He was of medium height, somewhat overweight, dressed in a light-gray summer suit. "Who is he?" Sofia asked.

"It is Guido, my half-brother," Julietta said.

"Your half-brother? I didn't know you had a half-brother." Sofia was puzzled at the news. Then she remembered Adriano Gori mentioning a son from Luisa's former marriage, who had an interest in her property.

Julietta shrugged. "I do not know him very well. He is from Mamma's former husband. He hardly ever comes here. He lives in Rome with his father."

"Buongiorno," the man gave them a brief nod, then walked over to where Edoardo worked. The two nodded at each other and talked for a while. Then Guido came over to Julietta and asked her how she was.

"*Bene*," she said, then motioned at Sofia. "*Sofia, mia sorella*," she introduced her.

Guido glared at her and gave what looked like a forced smile. "*Buongiorno, signora*." He turned back to Julietta and said something to her, mentioning Luisa's name. Julietta nodded. He left with a brief waving motion to Sofia.

As he was leaving, Julietta looked after him. "I don't like him. He is a crook."

"How come?" Sofia asked.

"He is really greedy and he is into some bad business ... what do you call it 'shady?'"

Sofia nodded.

"He only comes here when he wants money and he makes

Mamma really unhappy." Julietta sighed.

"If he's your half-brother and you're my half-sister, does that mean he is my half-brother, too," Sofia wondered.

Julietta shrugged. "I don't know. Is he?"

Sofia chuckled. "I have no idea, but anyway, he lives in Rome, so I guess he won't bother us too much."

"Yes, I hope not." Julietta began to work again, then stopped. "You know he came here when Papa died and he wanted to have the two grape fields that belonged to Papa. My mother told him that they were going to you. He was all upset and said that they belonged to the family. It is ridiculous because he is not part of the family. My mother and his father are divorced. They divorced a long time ago. Anyway, they screamed at each other, Mamma and Guido."

Another guy who wants my property. Sofia sighed. "What a mess. Anyway, I don't want to worry about it. Let's keep on working. Edoardo is not looking too pleased. We're just standing around." She continued cutting the clusters of plump ripe grapes, pushing the thought about her property away.

At noon, Sofia and Julietta took a break and walked over to the main house. A blue Ferrari was parked in the courtyard and Sofia assumed it was Guido's car. A loud, angry male voice came from inside. Sofia and Julietta looked at each other. The door opened and Guido dashed outside, his face flushed and pinched. Luisa followed and called after him, then threw up her hands, as he ripped the car door open. He revved the engine and drove away.

"What did he want?" Julietta asked.

Luisa answered with a flood of Italian, then exhaled deeply and shook her head. "Sorry," she said to Sofia. "He makes me so angry." She went back inside and Sofia and

Julietta followed her.

"It is always the same," Luisa said. "He is my son from my former marriage," she told Sofia.

"I know," Sofia said. "Julietta told me."

"He came out to the fields and talked to Uncle Edoardo," Julietta explained.

"Yes, he claims that he and his father are starting a new business." Luisa rolled her eyes. "They are always up to something, which ends up being a failure. Then Guido comes here, and all of a sudden we are family again. They want money. He called it a favorable investment for us ... or something like this. What it really means is that they want to borrow money and they never pay it back. I have given him money in the past but no more." Luisa brushed her hand over her face.

Julietta went up to her and hugged her. "Don't be upset, Mamma."

"I am sorry. He just makes me so angry." Luisa hugged Julietta back. She turned to Sofia. "It is such a sad thing. He is my son. I do not know what I did wrong that he turned out this way."

"It is not your fault, Mamma," Julietta said, her arm around her mother.

Sofia felt sorry for Luisa. It was the first time, she saw her so vulnerable. "Family," she said. "They are so difficult sometimes."

"Yes," Luisa said, more quietly now. "But what would we do without them?" She gave a sad smile.

In the evening, just after sunset, Sofia went for a walk. She loved to walk in the late evenings. After the sun had gone down, the heat of the day turned into a pleasant warmth. It was mostly quiet. An occasional laughter from the *cantina*, where the few volunteers had their meals, the barking of a dog in the neighborhood or the whispering of the trees in the evening breeze were the only sounds.

When she came back to the house and went inside, she thought she saw someone behind the house. She'd left the lantern on the patio on. *The old Santucci,* was her first thought. She turned off the light in the living room and stared outside. She recognized the shape of a man next to the shed with the garden tools. It wasn't Silvio Santucci, the man didn't have a cane. Perhaps the gardener, she thought.

She opened the door to the patio and stepped outside. But nobody was there. She shrugged and closed and locked the door, then remembered she had to put the trash outside for the collection in the morning. She grabbed the trash bag and opened the front door. Carrying her trash bag to the main house, she saw Guido, Luisa's son, walking down the path that went by Sofia's house. He faced her for a quick moment, but didn't acknowledge her. He walked toward the car, which was parked in the driveway of the main house. She'd seen him drive away in the afternoon. He must have come back. She was almost certain he'd been the man standing behind her house. *What was he doing there?*

The encounter with Guido felt creepy and reminded her of the night she thought she'd seen the old Santucci during the storm, as well as of the dead animals in her yard. She still wasn't completely convinced that they hadn't been put there on purpose. Perhaps someone in the family tried to make her leave. Was it the old Santucci or perhaps this Guido character? But what would they accomplish? It wouldn't change anything about her inheritance. The fields would still belong to her. Unless they killed her. She thought of the wine barrel that this Umberto person almost dropped on her. That would have done the job. But, no, he looked really contrite.

And he wouldn't gain anything. He didn't belong to the family.

No, she didn't want to feel distrustful all the time. The last few encounters with the family had been pleasant. Luisa was becoming a good friend. Edoardo was still somewhat standoffish but his behavior was a far cry from the sour attitude he'd displayed toward her in the beginning. The old Santucci was still an old grouch but he more or less behaved the same to everyone. He hadn't singled her out anymore.

Going back inside, she locked the door and checked to make sure the patio door was locked as well. Before going to bed, she gathered her bathing suit, a towel, suntan lotion, and a few other things and put them into a bag. Julietta and Sofia were going to Cecina the following day. It was market day there and they wanted to spend some time at the beach as well. She was looking forward to a day off with her sister. They'd become closer, too, and a warm friendship was developing.

Sofia put on her T-shirt she used as a nightie and brushed her teeth. She turned off the lights and looked out the window in the back of the house again but except for the shadows of pine trees lightly swaying in the wind, she didn't see anything.

Chapter 24

Sofia and Julietta were singing *Let It Be* by the Beatles as they drove the two-lane country road toward Cecina. It had been one of Henry's favorite songs and Julietta knew all the lyrics. It was early in the morning. Sofia rolled down the window and inhaled the light smell of resin from the pine forests. Getting up in the morning, she'd noticed a definite cooling. The temperature in September was still warm, even hot, but the mornings and nights were fresher. It would be pleasant to swim in the Mediterranean and take a sunbath at the beach. Later in the morning, they planned to visit the open-air market of the town.

After about forty minutes, they arrived in Cecina and found a parking spot near the sea. They carried their picnic basket and bathing things down to the beach and spread out their towels. The beach was still empty but within half an hour, a group of young men and a few families joined them. When Julietta proceeded to rub suntan lotion on Sofia's back, one of the young guys whistled and strutted over to them.

"Let's pretend we do not speak Italian," Julietta suggested.

That was just fine with Sofia who wasn't interested in the mindless chatters of young guys trying to pick up girls. The pretended language barrier did work after a while and the young man walked back to his friends with a shrug. Julietta giggled quietly. They both stretched out on the towels and sighed. Sofia enjoyed the warm sun on her body and the rhythmic sound of the small waves tumbling softly onto the sand. Unlike the Pacific Ocean she was used to, the water in the Mediterranean was gentler. When she mentioned it to Julietta, her sister said that this would all change in October with the approach of the fall storms.

"Well, we better enjoy it while it lasts. Let's go for a swim." Sofia got up.

"You go first. We should not leave our things unattended," Julietta said. "You never know." She glanced at the young men near them.

"Okay, I'll be back soon." Sofia walked down to the water. It was pleasantly warm, another change from the nippy ocean she was used to at home. She walked in up to her waist, then swam further out. When she looked back, Julietta was waving at her from the beach.

After about an hour, they unpacked their picnic— prosciutto sandwiches with cucumber and tomato slices, hard-boiled eggs, and some candy for dessert. In the meantime, the beach was slowly filling up with people, mainly Italian families with children who enjoyed the last few days of vacation before school started again.

"Are you looking forward to going back to school?" Sofia asked her sister.

Julietta shrugged. "Yes and no."

"What does that mean?"

"Well, usually school is all right, but I hate to be away from you." Julietta's face clouded over. "How long are you going to stay?"

"I guess until after the grape harvest, but I'll be back next year," Sofia said.

"But that is a whole year." Julietta sighed.

"We'll have to find a way for you to come to California. You can stay with me. What about during Christmas or the summer vacation?"

"This would be great. Mamma wants me to go to summer school, though."

"We'll ask her. If you stayed for a few months, you could even take classes in California. That would be really great for your education, wouldn't it?"

"Yeah, that would be fantastic. I would love to visit California. It sounds so exciting. I always wanted to find out where Papa lived."

"I'll talk to your mother," Sofia said.

"Wonderful." Julietta hugged her.

"Let's go to the market now," Sofia suggested. They packed their things and drove back into town. Finding a parking place near the market proved to be a challenge. They had to circle around the area several times, before they found a spot.

The open-air market of Cecina was a colorful display of anything from household goods to clothes and shoes as well as all kinds of groceries. Sofia was surprised to see how reasonable the prices were. Since the introduction of the euro, Italy was no longer the paradise for inexpensive goods, but at this market, the prices were low.

"That is because the market is for the locals," Julietta told her. "The tourist stores are more expensive."

Sofia bought some socks and a couple of long-sleeve sweaters. Having arrived here in the heat of summer, she hadn't brought much for the cooler weather and with the possible October rains and storms, temperatures would drop.

Julietta, who had received some money from her mother for back-to-school outfits, tried on one of the shiny quilted faux-leather jackets that were so fashionable among young people as well as a pair of dress-boots. She was looking at herself in the mirror when they heard a whistle. "*Favoloso*," a voice called. As they turned around, Nicholas was waving at

146

them from the sidewalk. He came over, a shopping bag in hand.

"Nice outfit," he said to Julietta. "Isn't this market fun? Have you seen the food in the next street?" He gave them both a hug.

"Actually, we are on the way there," Sofia said. "We want to buy some vegetables and stuff for dinner."

"Would you like to join us for dinner?" Julietta asked Nicholas. "There is a store nearby that sells really great fresh hand-made pasta. We were going to get some for tonight."

"Sounds wonderful. I'd love to." He looked at Sofia who nodded. "Yes, come on over."

After Nicholas left, Sofia and Julietta took their purchases to the car and locked them in the trunk. Then they went on to the grocery section of the market with its extensive display of vegetables, fruits, meats, and fish. They bought lettuce, broccolini, different types of peppers and other kinds of vegetables Julietta picked out, which Sofia didn't know. They walked along the stands looking for prosciutto. The cheeses and smoked meats looked inviting but when they came to a stand with a whole roasted pig, Sofia flinched.

"Oh, no, look at this. Seeing the whole cooked animal really makes you want to become a vegetarian." She took Julietta by the arm and pulled her to the next stand.

Julietta, obviously used to these kinds of displays, laughed at Sofia's squeamishness. Fortunately, a few stands down the street, there was a more appetizing selection of the famous prosciutto. And as Sofia tried one of the paper-thin slices the merchant cut for her, she changed her mind about becoming a vegetarian. They bought some cheese and smoked ham, then walked back toward the clothing section of the market where the pasta shop was. As they entered, Sofia marveled at the display of different types of fresh pasta.

Plates full of tortellini, different shapes of ravioli, spaghetti, fettuccine, fusilli, and more were arranged artfully along the counter.

They bought enough pasta for the three of them. They added a bottle of mineral water for the road home and hurried back to their car, since it had become quite late.

"I hope you don't mind that I invited Nicholas for dinner," Julietta said as they were driving home.

"No, why should I? He's good company," Sofia said.

"You know after dinner, I will leave you two alone." Julietta winked at Sofia.

Sofia rolled her eyes. "Would you please stop you silly goose."

Chapter 25

In the evening, Sofia and Julietta prepared a mixed salad and made a couple of tomato and pesto sauces for the fresh pasta. Sofia opened a bottle of her estate wine. Nicholas offered to bring dessert and surprised them with a custard made of orange juice, mascarpone and a shot of Grand Marnier. He also brought a bottle of Prosecco.

"How were you able to make this dessert?" Sofia asked. "You don't have a kitchen."

Nicholas lived with the volunteers in a separate house and ate most of his meals in the *cantina*, a communal dining room on the estate.

"Well, okay, actually I didn't make it. This is the dessert for the workers for the night. I bribed the cook to let me have some."

"What was the bribe?" Sofia asked.

"I promised her a lock of my blond hair." Nicholas winked at her.

Sofia chuckled. "That will do it."

It was still warm enough to eat on the patio. They had a glass of Prosecco before dinner and Julietta poured herself some Coca-Cola, one of her favorite drinks. Sofia who didn't care for soft drinks shook her head.

"How can you drink this stuff? You're going to spoil the great food."

"It is Papa's fault. He always let me have it when I ate with him. Mamma won't allow it either. But do not worry, dear sister, I will switch to mineral water with dinner, if you let me have a sip of wine." Sofia and Julietta carried the pasta and the salad outside. Nicholas poured the wine and let Julietta taste a sip. She made a face and switched to mineral water. "I love our vineyards but I have to admit I do not like wine much."

"You'll have to acquire a taste for wine, I think," Nicholas said. "When I was younger I didn't like it at all. Now, I love it." He poured Sofia and himself more wine. "*Salute.* And dinner is wonderful. Compliments to the chefs." He lifted his glass to Sofia and Julietta.

"This was probably the easiest dinner I've ever prepared," Sofia said. "All I needed to do is simmer the pasta and Julietta helped me make the sauce."

"Well, it's a nice change from eating at the *cantina*," Nicholas said. "Although, to be honest, the food there is pretty good and there is plenty of it. I'm glad I'm working hard or I'd put on mounds of fat."

Sofia laughed at the thought of Nicholas putting on weight. He was trim and had a well-developed physique but there was no fat on him. "I think if you haven't gained any weight by now, you should be fine."

After they finished dinner and dessert, they all helped clean the table. Julietta offered to clean up in the kitchen and shoved Sofia away when she wanted to help. "You have to entertain our guest. I will leave you alone. It is past my bedtime." She winked at Sofia who shook her head and grinned.

Sofia and Nicholas sat outside for a while, drinking espresso. It was getting dark, the rust and yellow-colored fields slowly faded into the black-blue of the night with only a sliver of silver along the hills in the distance. After a while, they moved back into the living room. They talked about the work at the estate and Nicholas's plans of having his own vineyard in California.

"You know I really want to import some of the estate wines and sell them together with my grandfather's wine," Nicholas said. "The funny thing is, Santucci senior approached me about it."

"Really?" Sofia was perplexed. "Why would he do this? Luisa told me he hated Americans. He certainly doesn't have any kind feelings toward me."

Nicholas shrugged and took another sip of coffee. "I was surprised myself. Although the old Santucci always behaved rather cool toward me, he was never actually hostile."

"Well, I guess you're not an impostor like me who is stealing his vineyards, the ones he almost ruined with his careless investments," Sofia said in slightly bitter tone.

"Yes, I guess I'm not an immediate threat to him. He probably feels he could make some money going into business with me. Lately he has become almost chatty." Nicholas picked up his cup and downed the rest of his espresso.

"He must be nuts. He doesn't even own the estate anymore. He looks like a jealous lunatic to me," Sofia said.

Nicholas nodded. "He's weird all right, although once in a while he makes a level-headed even intelligent remark about winemaking. At one time, he must have been good at it. He may still have an interest in the estate. Sometimes I see him discuss stuff with his son."

"So what is it he actually wants from you?" Sofia wondered.

"He hasn't said anything specific. He just asked if I would be willing to import some wine and sell it in California. I told him I was going to think about it. It may not be a bad deal, I guess. If I can get a good price for the wine here, I can sell it in

California and make some money from it. Any addition to my savings would be welcome."

"I think the old man can't let go of the business," Sofia said. "It's as if he wants to get involved again. But I don't see how he can do it, since he doesn't own the estate anymore. Unless he does it together with Edoardo." Sofia brushed a strand of hair out of her face. "Anyway, I don't want to spend the evening talking about the old nut case," she said, her voice sounding somewhat irritated.

"Oh, no, neither do I. Sorry I brought it up. Is there any espresso left?"

"Yes, of course, I'll get some more." Sofia was glad they changed the subject. The talk about the old Santucci made her feel uncomfortable. She wondered why he all of a sudden seemed to take an interest in Nicholas.

Sofia brought two cups of espresso and they sat next to each other on the sofa near the floor-length window. Outside the last light of the day faded and it was getting dark fast. A breeze kicked up and brought the scent of dry grass and a whiff of jasmine.

"It's so beautiful here," Sofia said, sipping her coffee.

Nicholas nodded. "It really is. I've been looking forward the whole year to this."

"Are you coming again next year?" Sofia asked.

"I may not be able to, since I'll be busy with the harvest back in California. This year, my brother helped my grandfather but he may not be able to do it next year. What about you?"

Sofia glanced at him and noticed again his dark eyes that formed an interesting contrast to his blond hair. A warm sensation spread through her chest. "I'm pretty sure I'll be back, at least for the harvest. I just realized how much I enjoy the work. It's such a great change from only writing about wine."

"I'd love to read some of your stuff," Nicholas said.

The bougainvillea in the corner of the patio swayed in the breeze. A thin layer of mist hovered over the grass, the first signs of the approaching fall. Sofia got up and turned on one of the lamps, then closed the balcony door to prevent the mosquitoes from flying in. She left the two windows with the screens open. "I have one of the magazines with an article of mine here. You're welcome to read it."

"I know you're very involved in the vineyard here, but ... have you ever thought of getting back into winemaking in California?" Nicholas asked.

Sofia shrugged. "Sometimes, yes. I regret having lost the vineyard after my divorce and also my father's vineyards up at the Russian River. I have fond memories of helping him work." Sofia paused. "But now, having a vineyard here, that's probably going to take up most of my time aside from my job as writer."

"Are you thinking of living here permanently?" Nicholas's voice sounded hesitant.

"I really don't know yet. So many unexpected things have happened this year that I kind of gave up making plans. I'd love to be closer to my sister and be more involved in the day-to-day activities of the vineyard. But I do have ties to California as well, to my aunt, my grandparents, and I have friends there." Sofia stopped, realizing she was thinking out loud. She smiled. "How about that for a non-answer?"

"I fully understand. It's all so new for you and probably confusing. But if you ever think about doing winemaking in California, I'm looking for a partner."

There was an intensity in his eyes that surprised her.

Nicholas averted his gaze and looked down at his slender but strong workman's hands. "I think I mentioned it before.

My plan is to have my own outfit. My grandfather plans to retire one of these years and he wants me to take over his vineyards. Eventually, I would also like to buy some additional property. It will take time and I need a lot more money for it than I have now." He looked at her again, his eyes warm now. "I'd love to work with you. You're perfect for this. You're passionate about winemaking. You love the vines, the grapes, the work. You remind me of your father." He chuckled. "Except you're a lot more beautiful."

Was he blushing? It was hard to tell in the dim light of the lamp. Sofia's heart beat faster. He had hinted at working together before but never so directly and with so much fervor. And there seemed to be more to his offer than just a business proposal. She took a deep breath. "I'll definitely think about it. Once I can figure out what to do with my life. Right now, it's just ..."

"I know," he said. "Just think about it." He took a deep breath. "I better get some sleep. I think tomorrow will be another busy day." He got up and picked up his empty espresso cup.

"Just leave it," Sofia said. "I'll get it later." She followed him to the door.

He turned around. "Thank you very much for an excellent dinner ... and a lovely evening." He hugged her and gave her a light kiss on the cheek.

Alone in her house, she thought about the evening, about Nicholas and his offer. "Winemaking in California, with Nicholas?" It was tempting. He was a nice guy. "Come on, Sofia," she told herself quietly. "He is more than nice." But what would this mean for her work here? As if her life wasn't complicated enough already. She took a deep breath, washed the espresso cups and went upstairs to go to bed.

Chapter 26

After the Merlot grapes had been crushed, they were being pressed. The "must"—skins, pulps, and seeds—which had been fermenting for about a week were being siphoned into the wine press, a large contraption made of shiny stainless steel. Here the last of the juice was extracted from the solids and fed back into the fermentation tanks for the extended fermentation, also called extended maceration, that would last four to six weeks, depending on the type of grape varietal and wine made. Later, the juice was fed into the barrels and aged for several years.

After work, Sofia stopped once again at the cellar. She wanted to check out her barrels without being disturbed. After making sure the forklift was unattended and there was no dangerous machinery around, she entered the barrel room. As she reached the end of one of the rows of barrels, she heard a noise. She stopped, feeling her heart beat pick up speed. *What now?*

"Hello," she called. "*Chi è?* Who is there?"

A figure emerged from behind a row of barrels. It was Nicholas. "Hi there. What's up?"

Sofia exhaled relieved. "Oh, it's you. I just heard a noise. Since my last experience in the cellar, I've become a little, well, let's say, cautious."

Nicholas grinned. "No wonder. It's not every day, someone tosses a wine barrel at you. I was actually checking the status of the wine in some of the barrels." He walked up to her. "Besides I love the cellar. It's the only pleasantly cool place in the afternoon."

"You're right. I just wanted to have a look at the barrels of wine from my father's ... well I guess from my vintage." She sighed. "I'm still not used to the fact that they're mine now."

Nicholas gave a quick nod. "It'll take a while to sink in, I guess." They walked to the rows of Sangiovese and Merlot wines. "Beautiful barrels," Nicholas said. "I bet they're made of French oak."

"Yes, Edoardo told me. They're expensive but then only the best for my father." Sofia smiled and lightly touched one of the light-brown barrels.

"Yes, French oak seems to add just the right amount of spice," Nicholas said.

"It's cold down here." Sofia rubbed her arms.

Nicholas nodded. "Let's get warmed up by the Tuscan sun again. It's actually quite a bit cooler now, at least in the early morning and at night. I even had to pull out my sweatshirt last night," he said as they climbed the stairs.

"You're right and in October and November they expect some storms. I hope we'll be done with the harvest by then ... oh, no." Sofia stopped short as they stepped outside. Silvio Santucci stood in front of the cellar, leaning on his cane.

To her utter shock and surprise, the old man smiled at her. When Nicholas emerged from behind her, Silvio Santucci's face stretched into an even bigger smile. He overwhelmed them with a flood of Italian and from the little Sofia understood it had to do with wine.

Nicholas nodded and turned to Sofia. "He wants me to translate. He wants to know if you would be able to sell his wine in California."

Sofia looked at them perplexed. "I'm not sure how that would work exactly. Is it the wine from my fields or the wine from the estate in general?"

Nicholas said a few words to the old man, who nodded and began to talk in rapid Italian to Sofia in a still friendly tone.

"He means from the estate in general. Remember he asked me the same thing," Nicholas continued. "I think he wants to start some business venture with the two of us, but I'm not sure what it actually is. I think we should ask Edoardo. He would probably know a little more what his father's plans are. I'll tell him, we'll think about it and see if it would be possible."

Sofia agreed and Nicholas said a few words to Silvio who again continued his flood of Italian. It was the first time Sofia heard him talk in whole sentences, let alone carry on a conversation. Up to that moment, he'd mainly mumbled or grunted in her presence. After a while, he nodded and bowed slightly to Sofia. "*Buona sera, signorina.*" He turned around and walked slowly away, supporting himself with his cane.

When he was out of earshot, Sofia shook her head. "I'm totally stunned. This is the first time he talked to me, even smiled at me, instead of shooting daggers at me with his eyes. What happened?"

Nicholas chortled. "I don't know either. He's so strange sometimes. But perhaps he had a change of heart about you."

"Perhaps, but I just don't trust him. He's so erratic with his emotions." Sofia looked after the old man, who made his way in the direction of Edoardo's and Gina's house. "But then again, maybe you're right. Well, it would sure be nice, if he didn't hate me anymore." She glanced back at the cellar and shook her head.

"How strange, every time I come to this cellar, something odd happens. First, some crazy drunk almost kills me with a wine barrel and now the old grouch Santucci made me a business offer. What is it? The magic of the wine?"

157

Christa Polkinhorn

Nicholas chuckled. "Well, in the case of the old drunk, it was more like dark magic."

Sofia accompanied him part of the way to his lodging. "Talk about dark forces. You know I never even thought about this. Our work, I mean turning grapes into wine, can be dangerous for some people."

"True, but alcohol is different things to different people. It is medicine to some, a pleasurable past-time for others and yes, I guess, it can have a damaging effect on people who don't know how to handle it." Nicholas shrugged. "I like to think that my work is geared toward the positive features of wine."

"I guess so," Sofia said. "After all, most things can be used for both good and bad ends." She sighed. "Or is this too pat an answer?"

Nicholas put his arm briefly around her. "Think of what we would have to do to remove everything in this world that could conceivably cause harm to some people. We'd have to root out cocoa beans and sugar cane, because some people eat too much chocolate and sweets and get diabetes, or we couldn't have any fatty food at all because some people are heavily overweight, well you know what I mean." He chuckled.

Sofia laughed. "That's a good way of talking ourselves out of the dilemma, isn't it? Anyway, time for me to get back to my place. I promised to help Julietta with her English homework."

"See you tomorrow then," Nicholas said.

On the way home, Sofia mused about the day's strange event, about the old Santucci who seemed to have made a hundred-and-eighty-degree turn in his attitude toward her. "Italy, you sure are a mysterious country," she muttered and grinned.

Chapter 27

"I do not know, Julietta," Luisa said hesitantly.

Luisa, Sofia, and Julietta sat in the living room after dinner at the main house and discussed Marco's party Julietta was invited to. "I do not really know the family."

"Please, Mamma. I will not be alone. Monica is invited, too. And you have met Marco at my party."

"How are you going to get there?" Luisa asked quietly, as if she were debating the issue with herself. "And how are you going to get home after the party. One of us would have to drive you."

Julietta's face lit up. She seemed to feel her mother relent. "Perhaps Sofia can drive me."

"Yes, I wouldn't mind. No problem at all." Sofia was happy to be able to support Julietta.

"Well, I will talk to Monica's mother about it and we will see."

"Thanks, Mamma." Julietta hugged her mother.

Luisa smiled. "I have not said 'yes' yet."

"I know you will," Julietta said.

Two days later, Sofia helped Julietta get ready for her party. Luisa had talked to Monica's mother who felt it would be okay for the girls to attend. Sofia agreed to drive them to Marco's home and Luisa had insisted on picking them up afterward.

Julietta was wearing a yellow-and-blue patterned skirt and matching top. There had almost been a fight with her mother who felt the skirt was somewhat too short, but Sofia and Julietta convinced her that this was the fashion. Now, Sofia helped Julietta put on some makeup. When she was ready, Sofia looked her over and realized just how beautiful Julietta was with her long wavy chestnut-colored hair and her shiny purple-blue eyes.

"You're going to drive the boys crazy," she said with a chuckle.

Julietta winked at her. "I only hope to drive one boy a little crazy."

Sofia realized that her sister was in love. She put her arm around her. "I hope Marco deserves such a wonderful person like you."

They went over to the main house to say goodbye to Luisa and Donna who both showered Julietta with some last minute advice. Donna kissed her and told her to be careful with those men. Luisa said she would pick Julietta up at eleven, which led to another argument because Julietta wanted to be able to stay until midnight. They finally made a compromise of eleven thirty.

In the car, Julietta gave a sigh of relief. "What do they think?" she mumbled exasperated. "I am not a child anymore. I can take care of myself."

Sofia chuckled. "For your parents and grandparents you will always be a child. Remember that. Even Henry who you know was very open-minded and quite easygoing used to stay up until I came home after a party. He could never go to sleep, not knowing if I was all right or not."

"Yes, last time Papa was here, I went to the movies with a few friends in the evening. When I came back, he was still up and so was Mamma, although they always went to bed quite early. I guess that is natural, no?"

On the way to Marco's place, they picked up Monica. Like

Julietta, she was dressed up for the party. She wore a tight short skirt and Sofia felt her make-up was a little on the heavy side for a girl her age. Monica was a year younger than Julietta. *Am I getting old?* Sofia wondered.

The two girls were soon engaged in an excited conversation interrupted by giggling and from what Sofia could tell, the talk was all about the boys they were going to meet. In another fifteen minutes, they arrived at Marco's house. It was one of those beautiful Tuscan villas, surrounded by a huge garden and one of the ever-present olive groves. The driveway and the road along the property were already filling up with young men and women, all of them dressed in elegant outfits. From what Julietta had told Sofia, Marco's family was quite wealthy. His father was a banker and his mother some kind of high-society celebrity, a former actress. The other partygoers seemed to be quite a bit older than both Monica and Julietta and Sofia began to wonder if the two girls wouldn't feel out of place in this kind of environment.

Sofia parked the car along the road and the three of them got out. "This seems to be quite a fancy event. Who are all these people?" Sofia asked Julietta. "Do you know them?"

"A few of the girls are from Marco's class," Julietta said hesitantly, as she scrutinized the other people. She seemed to have lost some of her enthusiasm and looked a little subdued. Perhaps she'd expected a slightly different crowd as well. But then her face lit up. "There is Marco."

A young man in an elegant suit stepped out of the house and greeted some of the newcomers. Sofia barely recognized him anymore, all dressed up. He had the looks of a high-society offspring and Sofia wondered about his interest in Julietta, who after all was from a different social class. When Marco saw them, he waved and came down the driveway.

"You made it," he said to Julietta with smile. He hugged

161

her and gave her a chaste kiss on the cheek, then turned to Monica, greeting her with a kiss as well. He glanced at Sofia and smiled at her in what she felt was a somewhat seductive way. "Pleased to meet you again." He shook hands with her. "I hope you are going to join us?"

Sofia shook her head and laughed. "I'm just the chauffeur. But thank you for the invitation. I have plans of my own for tonight. Sofia's mother is going to pick the girls up at eleven thirty," she added, thinking that this would signal to Marco that he was dealing with underage schoolgirls. "Julietta and Monica are a little too young to stay out all night."

Julietta rolled her eyes. "Oh, Sofia, you are even worse than Mamma."

Monica tittered and Marco gave another one of his charming smiles. "Do not worry," he said. "I will make sure nothing is going to happen to them. I will protect them like the ... what do you say? 'Apple of my eye?'" He grinned.

"Stop it." Julietta gave Marco a playful punch.

Sofia hugged her sister. "Okay, I'll be gone. You two have fun and either Luisa or I will pick you up. You have your cell with you, don't you?"

"Yes, I do." Julietta sighed, rolling her eyes again.

Marco shook hands with Sofia and with one arm around each of the girls, he led them up the driveway and joined the rest of the people. In the meantime, more guests had arrived, all young, all well dressed, and all wealthy-looking.

When she sat in the car and was about to drive away, she realized she hadn't even checked if Marco's parents were indeed home. She hadn't seen anybody old enough to be his parents and she'd forgotten to ask. It would have been too awkward to go back and ask such a question but Sofia wished she did know. Somehow, the environment, the house, the guests, it all looked less and less like a school celebration and more like a party of wealthy young adults.

I worry too much, Sofia felt. After all, Julietta was intelligent and well brought-up. She knew what to do and what not to do. But she was also in love. Sofia sighed. On the way home, she began to relax. It would be all right, she finally decided. She had to let her younger sister make her own choices. Sofia didn't need to worry like an old fuddy-duddy. Sofia realized with a flash that she had indeed accepted her role as "older sister."

At home, Sofia was getting ready to play a game of chess with Nicholas. Sofia told him that her father taught her how to play. In the beginning, Henry had always won but in time, Sofia had occasionally beaten him. As it turned out, playing chess was one of Nicholas's favorite past times, "aside from reading horror novels," as he had admitted with an embarrassed smile.

Sofia found a chess game in one of the drawers in the study and set it up in the living room. Then she made a large bowl of popcorn and took some lemonade out of the refrigerator.

"Come in," she called when there was a knock on the door.

Nicholas entered, imitated a warrior stance, swinging his arm around, as if he was holding a sword. "Ready to be killed?"

Sofia, with a smirk, "I'm going to pound the heck out of you."

"Oh, yeah? We'll see about that."

They played for about two hours, both winning and losing games. At around ten o'clock, Sofia's phone rang. Julietta's cell phone number was on the display. "Strange," she said and answered the phone.

Julietta sounded distressed. "Sofia, I tried to call Mamma, but she didn't answer."

"She may be upstairs at Donna's or outside. She didn't expect your call that early. What's the matter?"

"Could you please tell Mamma to pick me up?"

"Why? What happened?"

"I will tell you later. I am outside. I am waiting in the driveway"

"Julietta, for heaven's sake. What's wrong?" Sofia got up, getting ready to walk to the main house, her phone still pressed to her ear.

"Problems?" Nicholas asked.

Sofia nodded. "Julietta is upset. She's waiting outside in front of Marco's house."

"Uh-oh. That doesn't sound good." He followed her.

Sofia continued to talk on the phone. "Julietta, are you all right?"

"I'm okay ... but I can't find Monica. She's inside with some boy. They're drinking ... and Marco ..." There was the sound of a sob.

"Julietta, stay where you are. We'll be right there."

Chapter 28

In the main house, Luisa was busy marinating a chicken for the following day. Sofia handed the cell phone to her. Luisa talked to Julietta for a few seconds, then pressed the disconnect button. "She wants to come home," she said. "Something went wrong at the party."

"Come on, let's all go," Nicholas suggested. "You might need some help."

Luisa nodded, grabbed the car key, and the three left. "I had a strange feeling about this party," Luisa said. "I wish I had not let her talk me into letting her go."

"Yes, I felt that all the other guests were quite a bit older and I couldn't figure out why Marco invited the girls. But he seemed like a nice, responsible person. I'm just not very good at figuring out men." Sofia sighed.

"Well we don't know yet what happened, but it sounds like Monica is in trouble somehow," Luisa said.

As they drove the small hill up to the mansion of Marco's parents, the party seemed to be in full swing. Music blared through the open windows and lights flickered on and off. Julietta was sitting on a stone bench at the bottom of the few stairs leading up to the main entrance. When she saw them, she got up. She looked miserable and had obviously been crying, judging from her red-rimmed eyes.

"*Che c'è?* What's the matter?" Luisa asked. She gently touched Julietta's cheek.

"I just want to go home," Julietta said. "But I cannot find Monica anywhere."

"What is happening in there?" Luisa said, scrutinizing the house.

"It was fine at first," Julietta said. "But then they started drinking and I think Monica had something to drink, too. And they started disappearing in different rooms and Marco ..." Julietta burst into tears.

Sofia hugged her. "What is with Marco?"

"He was dancing with me and then, all of a sudden, he was gone and I couldn't find him anywhere. Then I saw him kiss one of the girls from his class and they disappeared in a room ... I think one of the bedrooms."

Luisa, Nicholas, and Sofia looked at each other.

Broken heart, Sofia thought. She put her arm around her sister.

"Well, let's find out where Monica is," Luisa said. She climbed the few short steps to the main door with Sofia, Julietta, and Nicholas in tow. They knocked but realized that nobody would hear them with the music blaring, so Luisa tried the door and it opened. Inside, some people were dancing, others were helping themselves to appetizers and drinks.

Luisa, Nicholas, Sofia, and Julietta walked through an entrance hall that led into what looked like a living room. The inside of the huge home was even more elegant than the garden leading up to it. There were wooden tables and chairs with elegant carvings and other pieces of antique furniture. Paintings, which could have been originals, decorated the walls. A wide marble staircase led to the top floor. When they came in, a few people glanced at them, but then ignored them. Julietta walked up to one the guys and asked if he had seen Monica. He shook his head, then motioned upstairs with a shrug.

"Well, let's find out." Luisa started up the stairs with the others following. When they arrived on the second floor, she called Monica's name. As there was no answer, she began to open one of the doors that lead into a bedroom. Sofia just got a glimpse of a half-dressed couple sitting on a bed and kissing and fondling each other. Luisa slammed the door closed. Sofia could tell she was angry now. She called Monica's name again, loud this time. At the end of the hallway, a door opened and Marco stepped outside. He looked at them stunned, closing the belt on his pants. His black hair was rumpled as if he had just gotten out of bed, which was probably close to the truth.

Sofia glanced at Julietta who stared at him with a painful expression.

"Where is Monica?" Luisa asked him with a stern voice.

He shrugged. "I don't know. I haven't seen her in a while, perhaps—"

"What is going on here? I thought this was a party? It looks more like a *bordello*, a brothel. Where are your parents?" Luisa yelled.

Marco began to look somewhat intimidated. "*Sono andati.* They went out."

"What is this, anyway?" Luisa said in English, probably for the benefit of Sofia. "I thought your parents were home and you would have a class party. Instead people are having sex in your bedrooms and Monica disappeared."

"I'm sorry, really," Marco said. "I didn't know. We are just having a good time, no?" He looked at Julietta imploringly. She, however, glared at him.

"Let me help you find, Monica." Marco walked along the hallway and began to open doors, peaking into each room carefully and closing the door fast. But even that way, Sofia could see that there were couples in some of the rooms in various stages of undress. A few seconds later, another door

Christa Polkinhorn

opened and to Sofia's relief, Monica stepped outside, followed by one of the men. Monica looked frazzled and the top buttons on her blouse were open, but at first sight, she looked unharmed.

"*Cosa c'è?* What's the matter?" she asked. Her face was flushed, either from embarrassment or perhaps from drinking.

"What do you mean '*Cosa c'è?*'" Luisa said in an angry voice. "What are you doing in a bedroom? With a man? What do you think your parents would say to this?"

"We didn't do anything, just kissing." Monica's facial color darkened even more.

Luisa turned to the guy who had been with Monica. "How old are you?"

He gave her a guilty look. "Eighteen," he said, hesitantly.

"Do you realize that Monica is underage? She is not even fourteen yet? Do you know what happens to men like you if the authorities find out? You will end up in jail for having sex with a minor."

"Ho, ho." The young guy opened his eyes wide and raised his hands in a defensive gesture. "We did not have sex, we just talked. I gave her a kiss. That is all. That is not forbidden, no?"

"This is because I interrupted your dillydallying. No telling what would have happened if we had not come along."

Sofia almost had to laugh about Luisa's choice of word. *Dillydallying?* She wondered where Luisa had heard this expression.

Luisa turned to Monica. "Get your things, we are going home." Then to Marco who was standing there with a crestfallen look. "And I will talk to your parents about this."

"Please, we did not mean any harm. I did not realize

168

Monica was in here with a boy."

Luisa glared at him as he finished buttoning his shirt. "Of course, you did not notice. You were busy with a girl yourself, obviously." She took Monica by the arm and they left.

"*Signora* Santucci, believe me, nothing happened. Please do not tell my parents." Monica brushed through her disheveled hair as they were walking down the path to the car.

Luisa stopped and glowered at her. "You go into a bedroom alone with a man. What do you think his intentions are? Just kissing? That is only the beginning. Are you really that naïve? Are you going to ruin your life by getting pregnant as a teenager and forget about your education and everything? And how would your parents feel?"

Sofia put her arm around Julietta who had been very quiet during the whole scenario. "Sorry about Marco," she whispered. Julietta nodded and her eyes misted over.

They all piled into the car. Luisa asked Nicholas to drive and sat next to him. "I am too upset," she said. "I will probably run us off the road."

Sofia sat in the back with Julietta and Monica. The drive home was quiet. Monica had tears in her eyes and she whispered a few words to Julietta.

"Have you girls been drinking alcohol?" Luisa turned around and glanced at them.

"Not me," Julietta said.

"Just a little," Monica admitted.

"That's when you lose control and your good judgment," Luisa said with a stern voice. "You think you are doing the right thing and when you get sober again, you regret what you did."

Sofia wondered if Luisa spoke from experience. Had she

regretted getting involved with Henry? Had it been a similar occasion? Too much alcohol, wrong judgment? Luisa had been a lot older when she met Sofia's father. But there had been a former marriage, an unhappy one.

When they arrived at Monica's house, it was dark. Obviously her parents were either out or asleep. Monica and Luisa got out of the car and they exchanged a few words Sofia couldn't understand. Luisa put her hand on Monica's shoulder. Monica nodded and went inside.

Back in the car, Julietta asked Luisa if she was going to tell Monica's parents what happened. Luisa shook her head. "I do not think so. Perhaps you can talk to Monica. She will listen more to you than to me or her parents. You are her friend. She is a good girl but I think she is too careless."

"Okay," Julietta said. "But please, Mamma, do not tell Marco's parents. That would be so embarrassing and I have to go to school with him. Please."

Luisa sighed. "Well, it is really not my business. Nothing happened to you and I really cannot blame Monica's behavior on him. But Julietta, he is not the right boy for you."

"Mamma, we are not together. He has a girlfriend. I just found out. We are ... just friends," Julietta said hesitantly. "I am not even sure we are still friends." Her voice broke.

"I am sorry, Julietta," Luisa said.

Julietta brushed the tears away. "It's okay. I want to study and I want to visit Sofia in California. It is better not to be ... how do you say? Bound down?" She gave Sofia a quick smile.

"Tied down," Sofia said. "That's good because I want you to come and stay with me. Perhaps, you'll even find an American boyfriend."

"Oh, *per favore*," Luisa said with a groan. "Not you, too." Then she chuckled.

"Well, Papa was a good man," Julietta protested.

"This is true," Luisa said. "But being involved with someone from another country can be a lot of problems." Then she smiled. "You did the right thing, Julietta, to go outside and call us. I am glad you did. And Marco, perhaps it is better you find out now. Better being sad now than miserable later. He has other interests. He is just a little too old for you."

Julietta nodded. "I know, Mamma, but it still hurts. I really thought he loved me." Her voice trembled.

"*Cara*, he does not know what love is yet. Right now, he is more interested in sex than in love." Luisa glanced at Sofia with a smile. "Your Papa used a funny expression for that. I cannot remember it exactly. Something about planting oats? Do you know what I mean?"

Nicholas laughed out loud. "You mean he is sowing his wild oats." Sofia chuckled and even Julietta cracked a smile.

At home, Nicholas went back to his place and Julietta spent the night in Sofia's house at the encouragement of her mother. Luisa felt that the company of her sister who was closer to her in age would be able to help her deal with her first heartbreak. Julietta and Sofia sat at the table in the kitchen, drinking a cup of herbal tea Sofia had prepared. Now, at home, where it was quiet and peaceful after the evening's upheaval, Julietta was able to give in to her disappointment and hurt. Angry at first, she screamed a few juicy expletives at her cheater of a boyfriend, then put down her head on her arms.

"I cannot believe he would be so mean, all of a sudden," she said, looking up again. "We had such a good time together. He told me how much he admired me. He said I was beautiful. He invites me to a party and then goes off with

171

another girl and ..." Julietta sobbed. "How could he do this to me?"

Sofia let her express all the anger and sadness without saying much. She just patted her back. Having had her share of heartbreaks, she could readily identify with her sister's feelings. She suspected that Julietta had probably read more into Marco's compliments and his flirting than he meant to convey. She was in love with him and any positive remarks on his part had probably been overblown in her mind. But that didn't make Julietta's pain any easier to bear.

"Did he give you the feeling you were his girlfriend. Did he say he loved you or something like this? Did he come on to you?"

Julietta hesitated. "No, not directly, but we were hanging out together after class. And he said nice things to me. And he kissed me."

Sofia hugged her. "You know, I think he was flirting with you but perhaps he didn't mean it as seriously as you took it."

"Maybe. But he didn't need to invite me to a party and then ... make out with another woman. That stupid Mona. I hate her." The tears were back.

"I agree. It wasn't right to lead you on if he wasn't serious. But you know, Julietta, you are a beautiful girl and smart and a wonderful person. You deserve someone who respects and loves you and not someone who has other girls on the side."

Julietta nodded and gave a weak smile, but Sofia knew it would take a while for her sister to get over her first broken heart. After turning in for the night, Sofia read for a while, then checked on Julietta, who to her great relief was asleep.

Chapter 29

It was a pleasantly cool and quiet September Sunday morning. After seeing that Julietta was still asleep, Sofia went downstairs, put water in the espresso pot, and waited for it to bubble. She poured herself a cup, stepped outside barefoot and was surprised at how cold the stone floor was. Fall was approaching and with it the harvest of the red grapes. Sofia was looking forward to the activity in the fields.

Standing at the door to the patio, she gazed at the fields of grapevines, full of plump, ripe fruit. She inhaled the pungent sweetness of the early fall, the scent of sage and the Tuscan roses in the garden.

Getting hungry, Sofia took a loaf of bread out of the breadbox, cut off a piece and ate it slowly. She gulped the last sip of coffee down when she heard footsteps upstairs. Julietta was up, slowly making her way down the staircase in her pajamas. Her eyes were half-shut and her long hair hung in tassels over her shoulder and into her face. Sofia could tell from the scowl on her face that her sister wasn't in the best of moods.

"Good morning. Want some coffee?"

Julietta shook her head and yawned.

"What about hot chocolate? I was going to make breakfast."

"Not hungry," Julietta grumbled.

Sofia suppressed a smile. Her sister's bad mood reminded her of her own post-party blues. "Oh, well, perhaps later. I'm going to have something though."

Julietta plopped down on the sofa and brushed strands of hair out of her face. Sofia got bread, butter, and jam from the kitchen and made more coffee. She sat down at the table in the dining room.

"You're sure you don't want anything?"

Julietta shook her head. "I am going to take a shower and get dressed."

"Okay, that'll make you feel better." Sofia watched as her sister made her way back up the stairs with the slow demeanor of an old woman. "Perhaps we can do something fun afterward," she called after her. "Go to Cecina, for instance?"

The only answer was another grumbling noise. Sofia shrugged and poured herself another cup of coffee, ate a second roll with a piece of provolone cheese and a slice of melon. She was trying to think of something that would cheer up her lovesick sister.

A while later, there was a knock at the door. Nicholas, all perky and cheerful, stood outside. "How are you ladies on this lovely morning?" He gave Sofia a quick hug, and motioned with his eyes toward the second floor. "How is our party-girl?"

"Not in the best of moods, I think," Sofia said. "Want some breakfast?"

"Thanks, I ate at the *cantina*. But I won't say no to a good cup of coffee." He followed Sofia into the kitchen where she poured him a cup. A few minutes later, Luisa stood at the door. She came inside, smiled at Nicholas, and looked around the living room.

"Is Julietta not up yet?" she asked.

"Yes, I am." Julietta came walking down the stairs. Having showered, dressed, and combed her hair, she looked refreshed and a little happier.

174

"You have a visitor," Luisa said and went to the open door.

"Who?" Julietta squinted her eyes and followed her mother.

Luisa motioned with her head over to the main house. Marco stood in the driveway. He was looking down, kicking at some pebbles on the ground.

Julietta's face tensed. "I do not want to see him."

"Come on. He wants to talk to you, apologize. I think it would help." Luisa gently took Julietta by the arm. They walked over to Marco who looked up and gave a guilty smile.

"Well, I sure didn't see that coming," Nicholas said in between sips of coffee. "He must be more decent than I took him for. At least he has the guts to come by and apologize."

Sofia nodded. "Yes, I guess so. I hope he's not going to confuse Julietta even more."

"Yeah, I hope not either. Anyway, I thought perhaps we could go to town, to a movie. I saw they're playing *Midnight in Paris* by Woody Allen. It should be lighthearted and fun, something to take her mind off her man." Nicholas chuckled.

"Great. I've seen it before and I loved it. I wouldn't mind seeing it again," Sofia said.

"How about if I pick you girls up at six, then we'll have time for pizza before the show?"

Sofia nodded. "Sounds good. I hope I can convince Julietta to come." She glanced at the main house where Julietta and Marco stood next to each other. Julietta, her arms crossed in front of her chest, looked down and Marco seemed to be talking. After a few seconds, they both walked away and turned the corner toward the front of the house and disappeared. "I guess it depends how she feels after her talk with Marco."

"Okay, I'll check on you guys later. Thanks for the coffee."

175

Nicholas handed her the empty cup.

Sofia went inside and washed the coffee cups, then sat down in the living room waiting. Julietta came back after half an hour and sat next to Sofia on the sofa. "Men," she grumbled, then smiled a little.

"So how did it go?" Sofia wanted to know.

"All right. We talked. He said he was sorry the party got out of hand. He should have been more careful about Monica and all that." Julietta shrugged. "He also said he did not mean to deceive me. He liked me a lot but he had a girlfriend and he wanted to be my friend."

Sofia put her arm on Julietta's shoulder. "How do you feel about it?"

Julietta shrugged again. "Okay. I mean, I still like him a lot, but perhaps I did read more into his behavior than he meant. You know? Just what you said."

"I'm sorry, Julietta." Sofia hugged her sister.

"It's okay," Julietta said. "I am glad we talked. At least now it will not be that strange meeting him again."

"Good," Sofia said. "Nicholas asked if we wanted to go to town, have pizza and then go see a movie, *Midnight in Paris*, have you seen it?"

Julietta shook her head. "No, but … well, okay, let's go."

"Oh, good. It'll take your mind off your problems."

Julietta snickered and rolled her eyes. Then she faced Sofia. "You know, you never told me about your love problems, your divorce and all that."

Now it was Sofia's turn to sigh. "Oh, no, do you really want to know? It's not very pleasant."

"Only if you are okay about telling me," Julietta said.

"Okay, but for that we need some comfort food or drinks." Sofia got up.

Juliette followed her into the kitchen. "What is comfort

176

food?"

"Something that makes you feel good like chocolate or apple pie or macaroni and cheese. In Italy, it would probably be ice cream or biscotti or pasta or something like this."

"Okay, what about hot chocolate?" Julietta said.

"Perfect." Sofia grabbed a can of chocolate powder while Julietta took a carton of milk out of the refrigerator. After heating the milk and filling two large mugs with hot chocolate, they sat in the living room next to the window.

"Okay, tell me. Why did it go wrong with your husband?" Julietta brushed a milk mustache from her upper lip.

"Well, for one thing I got married much too young. I was smitten with James and he could do no wrong. Henry warned me not to rush into it, but of course I thought I knew better. You know you always think you know better than your elders."

Julietta chuckled. "Yes, for sure."

Sofia told her how happy she had been at first, how she enjoyed working at his parents' vineyard, but that she soon begun to notice that James was a real control freak.

"Control freak? I love that word," Julietta said.

"Yes, but having to live with one is not too pleasant. Anyway, we started fighting and then one day, I caught him in bed with one of my friends. I know it sounds like a cheap movie."

"Oh, my God, that is terrible."

"Well, that was the straw that broke the camel's back, so to speak. After that, I didn't trust him anymore. We did try some counseling, but James didn't want to or couldn't change. So we separated and I moved back to Santa Monica to live with Henry. And finally, we got divorced."

"He sounds like a real *verme*, how do you say? Creep?"

Sofia shrugged. "Yes, but it wasn't only his fault. I was just too young and idealistic. I didn't know that you have to work to keep a relationship going. I just took it for granted that everything would work out perfectly. Stupid of me. Anyway, I learned something from the whole story and perhaps James did, too. One thing he seemed to realize was that he needed to change his work. He wasn't into winemaking; he only did it because his family expected it."

Julietta took a sip of hot chocolate and was quiet for a while. Then with a sigh. "I am happy you told me all this. Now, I am glad it did not work out with Marco. I am too young, too."

Sofia hugged her. "I agree. You have your whole life ahead of you. Focus on your studies and find out what you want to do."

Julietta nodded. "You know, Sofia, I am not sure I want to become a vintner or winemaker either. I hope my family understands if I chose a different profession."

"I'm sure they will, Julietta. You have to choose something that suits you. Because if you don't, you won't be good at it and you'll be unhappy."

Julietta nodded, then hugged Sofia eagerly. "I am so happy you are my sister."

"Thank you. I'm happy too to have you as a sister." Sofia's eyes misted over. She cleared her throat. "What would you like to be?"

"I am not sure yet. But I really love science. Biology or chemistry, or perhaps even architecture," Julietta said.

"Ah, science, just like Henry. You know he studied and taught microbiology and chemistry, don't you?"

"Yes, he told me." Julietta smiled.

"I think that's a great idea. You'll have lots of possibilities." Sofia had seen Julietta's report card. Her sister

178

had aced all her science classes.

Later, Nicholas picked them up and they drove to Cecina, where they had pizza at one of the trattorias and then went to the movies. The movie theater was modern and like American theaters sold an assortment of candy and soft drinks, but unlike in the United States, the concession stand served alcohol as well. They also sold popcorn but it was bagged popcorn not the fresh kind they had at home. They bought soft drinks and a bag of popcorn and found seats in the middle of the theater. To Sofia's surprise, people here didn't spread out over the whole theater as they did in California, where they would sit as far apart from each other as possible. Although the cinema was half-empty, other moviegoers sat right next to them. *Just goes to show, Italians are a lot more sociable than Americans are.* Sofia snickered. Nicholas raised an eyebrow and grinned, probably thinking the same thing.

Another pleasant surprise was that instead of reams of commercials and previews, the movie itself began right away. Sofia was a little disappointed when she realized that the movie was shown in the English original with Italian subtitles. She'd hoped it was in Italian so she could practice the language. Since she'd seen the film before, she was able to focus a little on the subtitles.

After the movie, they went for a drink in a nearby coffee bar and then drove home. Julietta proudly proclaimed that she didn't read the subtitles at all and understood everything.

"Great," Sofia said. "At least *you* were able to practice the language."

"I really liked the guy who played the writer. So cute," Julietta said. "His fiancée, however, was so stupid. Are all Californian men as cute as that guy and you, Nicholas?"

Julietta asked, smiling.

"No, we're the exceptions." Nicholas wiggled his eyebrows.

Sofia was happy to see that Julietta was her old self again. It seemed that heartbreak Marco was slowly being replaced by "cute Californian guys."

Chapter 30

A few days later, Sofia needed to drive to town to buy stationery. All through her time in Vignaverde, she had written articles for the magazine she worked for in California, describing the work and the progress at the vineyard. She'd taken along her laptop and had sent her articles including photos over the Internet to her boss.

Sofia felt more enthusiastic about her writing since she was able to combine the physical work with its description on paper. Even her boss noticed her renewed enthusiasm and encouraged her to keep sending him her articles.

It was an unusually muggy day. Sofia glanced at the few dark clouds in the sky, hoping it wouldn't rain. They were in the middle of harvesting and rain could damage the ripe grapes, causing them to burst.

It didn't look as if heavy rain was expected though. The clouds didn't look ominous enough and the weather forecast indicated a few possible light showers for the day and then it was supposed to clear up again.

As she walked to the driveway at the main house to pick up her car, she saw Julietta pushing her bicycle. She was getting ready to go to school. Sometimes, her uncle or her mother drove her to school, particularly when the weather was bad. But most of the time, she rode the relatively short distance on her bike.

"Want me to give you a ride?" Sofia asked her. "I can pick you up after school."

"No, thank you. I am going to Monica's for lunch today

and we will go on a bike ride after school."

"Okay, see you later." Sofia waved. She was glad her sister and her friend liked to exercise outside once in a while rather than sit in front of the computer and spend all their free time with electronic gadgets as was the case with kids in United States. Not that Italian children were any less interested in electronics. Sofia was always amazed to see them walk around with their cell phone constantly attached to their ears.

Julietta had a cell phone but her usage was limited because she had to pay for the calls with her pocket money. And perhaps growing up on a vineyard and being used to working and playing outside gave her a more balanced outlook on how she wanted to spend her leisure time.

Sofia got in the car and drove the gravel path to the paved road, which dropped down a steep hill and then merged with the highway leading to Vignaverde.

As Sofia approached the highway, one of the agricultural vehicles working in the adjacent field was driving slowly into the road. Sofia tapped the brakes and got ready to slow down to let the tractor pass. To her shock, her car kept going instead of slowing down. Her heart leapt and she pressed the brake again, but there was no resistance. Her foot went all the way to the floor, but the car accelerated even more down the hill.

"My God," Sofia screamed and kept on pumping the brake pad. Panic seized her, and she began to strip off her seatbelt, thinking she might have to jump out of the car. She punched the horn several times, hoping the tractor would stop or speed up or something. "No, I can't lose my head." *The hand brake.* She looked down and pulled the hand brake, which made the car swerve. In her panic, she yanked the steering wheel around to prevent hitting the vehicle. But it was too late. The left side of her car bumped against the

The Italian Sister

vehicle and Sofia hit her head hard on the side window of the car, which fortunately didn't break. The car turned around and hit the vehicle again, then came to a halt.

Sofia felt an intense pain in her left arm and the blow to her head almost made her lose consciousness. Then everything became hazy. She heard a voice and saw a frightened male face look at her through the window. Someone called her name and she saw Julietta's face, her terrified eyes. Sofia blacked out.

Some time later, she found herself stretched out on a gurney. Around her lights flashed from police cars and a weeping Julietta stood next to Sofia and kept stroking her face. There were people who looked like emergency crews in yellow and blue outfits. She was lifted into a van. Julietta was sitting beside her, talking on her cell phone. Sofia closed her eyes again and moaned from the pain in her head and left arm. She felt a cool hand on her forehead. A few seconds later, she was overwhelmed by a feeling of nausea.

"I'm getting sick," she moaned. Someone lifted her head gently and turned her a little. She vomited into some kind of a bowl someone put in front of her. As she lay back down, tears were streaming down her face.

She tried to remember what happened—the brakes, the vehicle, the crash ... but why was Julietta here? She felt confused and closed her eyes again. Fading in and out of consciousness, she noticed that they had arrived somewhere and she was wheeled into a building. Her head and her left arm hurt and whenever they moved or lifted her, she moaned in pain. People in white and green coats stood around her. They began to ask her a bunch of questions in Italian, which she barely understood.

"The brakes didn't work," she said to a friendly but serious man whom she took for the doctor.

He looked perplexed, then talked briefly to a woman who seemed to be a nurse. A little later, she saw Julietta beside her who proceeded to translate. She seemed to have gained some of her composure again. "What happened?" she asked. "I was just starting to drive my bike down the hill when I saw it, the tractor, and then I heard the bang and your car all messed up. I was so afraid," Julietta's voice trembled.

Sofia told her about her brakes failing and that she hit the agricultural vehicle. She couldn't remember anything after that. "It's all fuzzy. I just know that my head and my arm hurt and I feel nauseated."

Julietta put her hand gently on Sofia's forehead and explained to the doctor what she'd said.

"The doctor said it might be a concussion. That is why your head hurts and you feel confused and sick to your stomach. They are going to take x-rays and check out your arm. I will stay here with you and I called Mamma. She was out in the fields but she will be here soon."

Sofia nodded. The next hour or so, she was wheeled in and out of rooms and into what she assumed were x-ray machines or perhaps MRIs. Someone gently touched and checked her arm. After all the prodding and testing, she found herself in bed in a room with Julietta and Luisa by her side. Luisa was pale but composed, unlike Julietta, whose eyes were still red from crying.

"You have a concussion and a sprained left arm," Luisa said. "But fortunately, the arm is not broken and you do not seem to have any internal injuries. They want to keep you here for one or two days for observation. Just to make sure that everything else is okay. After that you just need to take it easy for a while." She took a deep breath and touched Sofia's hand. "Julietta told me that the brakes in your car did not work?"

184

Sofia nodded, then touched her head. She felt a large bump next on her left temple. The headache had diminished a little and turned into a periodic throbbing. "Yes. I stamped on the brake like crazy. Then I tried the hand brake, but it was too late. I'm still confused about what really happened after that."

"Well, you did hit the tractor with the left side of your car, the driver's side. You really were very lucky. You hit your head and they said you were not using your seatbelt," Luisa said.

"I always have my seatbelt on," Sofia said. "I don't know. Perhaps I opened it because I wanted to jump out ... I don't know, but I did have it on in the beginning. I think at least. I'm not sure, not sure of anything." She sighed. "I still feel a little nauseated."

"That is because of the concussion," Luisa said. "Try to lie still and relax. The police were here and they will question you, but I told them to wait until tomorrow. They want to know what happened."

"Where is the car now?" Sofia asked.

"They towed it somewhere. But I will let the police know about the brakes. They need to check the car. If the brakes did not work, then the rental agency may be responsible."

"It's so strange," Sofia said. "They have always worked ... I'm so tired."

"Rest now. Do not worry about anything. We will look into the matter with your car. We will come back later. Right now, try to sleep." Luisa gently stroked Sofia's arm.

Sofia nodded and tried to smile.

After Luisa and Julietta left, a nurse came into the room and asked Sofia how she felt. She spoke heavily accented English but at least Sofia could understand her.

"My head and my arm hurt and I still feel a little queasy

but not as much as before."

The nurse brought her a glass of water and some pills. After taking the medicine, Sofia became drowsy and fell asleep.

PART FIVE: BETRAYED

Chapter 31

"I am afraid, I have to tell you that your brakes have been tampered with." Sofia and Luisa stared at the fat police officer. He looked at Sofia with a stern face. "The brake pipe was cut."

Sofia thought she had heard wrong. "What did he say?" She stared at Luisa in shock.

Luisa shook her head, then talked in rapid Italian with the officer. Finally, Luisa turned to her.

"This is terrible. I do not know what to say. They believe that someone had done this on purpose. The brakes themselves are fine, but the brake pipe was cut with a tool."

"What? But who...? *Dottore* Santucci?" It was out before she realized it.

Luisa stared at her. "What do you mean?"

Sofia bit her lip. She didn't want to accuse someone without having any proof. "It's just ... sometimes I think he hates me. But I'm not sure. He changes all the time. Once he even talked to me in a friendly way and asked if I would sell the estate wine in California. But a few days later, he treated me as hostile as in the beginning. I can't figure him out."

Luisa shook her head. "He can be unpleasant. And you are right, his emotions are not ... how do you say ... stable, but I do not think he would do something like this." Luisa scrunched her forehead, as if she was thinking long and hard about the possibility. Then she shook her head again. "He could not have done it. He and my mother are away. They have been gone since a few days ago. Before the accident

189

happened. It could not have been him."

"You're right." Sofia felt embarrassed. "I'm sorry."

"He is not always in his right mind. But I do not think he is dangerous," Luisa said. "But I want to have this investigated thoroughly. Someone wanted to harm you. We must find out who it was. I will go and talk to the police some more." She touched Sofia's arm. "Do not worry now. We will find out what happened. Julietta will come to visit you after school."

When Sofia was alone again, she tried to come to terms with the shocking news. Who could have done this? What a terrible situation. She could've been killed or someone else could've been hurt. She remembered offering Julietta a ride, which her sister had turned down. What if she'd been in the car as well? What a terrible and senseless thing to do. Who?

Her headache was getting worse again. She wanted to lie down and rest, but she couldn't relax. She thought of all the people she'd met. Who could have been the culprit—Luisa? Not likely, unless she was a real fake. Sofia didn't even consider Julietta. Who else? Edoardo? He had warmed up to her while they worked together in the fields. They weren't really close yet, but she couldn't imagine him doing something so mean and stupid. And Gina, his wife? She'd been somewhat aloof but never hostile. Then again, John told her once that in cases where families contested a will, for instance, it was often not the children themselves but the spouses who were the driving forces behind the fights. Nicholas? Impossible. But who? Umberto? He wouldn't gain anything by harming her. No, he was simply an alcoholic and a little crazy. Of course, there was Guido and his interest in her vineyards. But he wasn't even around. Or was he?

Sofia felt tears streaming down her face. She had felt more

accepted and part of the estate and she thoroughly enjoyed working at the vineyards, but now the growing friendship and trust between her and the family had been shattered again. It was just too awful. What should she do? She couldn't really talk to the police. Most of the policemen didn't speak English. She had to depend on someone to translate. But could she trust anyone completely until she knew who had done it?

Sofia thought of Adriano Gori. He had told her to call him if she needed help. He would be the one to confide in. He seemed to be the only one she could fully trust now. Sofia wiped the last tears away, called the nurse, and asked her for her cell phone. Fortunately, it still had enough of a charge. She must remind Julietta to bring her the battery charger. All her important phone numbers were on her smart phone.

When a woman answered her call, Sofia asked her in broken Italian for *signor* Gori. The receptionist answered her in fluent English that Mr. Gori was out and asked her if she could leave a message. More relieved that she could converse in English than embarrassed about her lack of Italian, Sofia asked for Mr. Gori to call her back and that it was urgent.

Ten minutes later, her phone rang and she heard the friendly voice of the lawyer. "Sofia, good to hear from you. How are you?"

"Not very good." She suppressed a sob and told him about the accident and the fact of the tampered brake.

There was a moment of silence. Then Adriano's voice again, serious now. "Have you talked to the police?"

"Yes. The policeman told me about the cut brake ... brake cable or something. I can't remember the exact term."

"Okay, Sofia. Do not talk to anybody else about it. I shall visit you tomorrow."

"Luisa already knows. She was the one who translated for

191

---

the policeman," Sofia said. "And I'm sure by now the family knows about it."

"This is okay. Do not worry. Rest and relax. We will find out who did this. I shall see you tomorrow."

Relieved to hear his warm and concerned voice, Sofia lay back and closed her eyes.

Chapter 32

The following day, Adriano Gori came to see Sofia. He brought along a charming, well-dressed woman, probably in her fifties, with short blond hair and blue eyes. He introduced her as his wife Gerda.

"I thought that perhaps female companionship will help you a little. Gerda can make sure you get the best possible treatment here in the hospital. She is a former nurse and she knows a few people from the staff here," Adriano said.

Gerda greeted Sofia with a hug. The light lavender perfume had a calming effect on Sofia. Gerda spoke fluent English with an accent that was different from Adriano's.

"My wife is originally from Germany and has lived in the United States for a few years," Adriano explained.

"In California," Gerda said. "And I loved it." Gerda's enthusiasm was contagious and Sofia immediately liked her. They talked a little about California.

"I would like to go back again for a visit. If my busy husband will ever take any vacation, that is." She glanced at Adriano with raised eyebrows.

"I will, I promise," he said and gave a quick smile, then became serious and faced Sofia. "We need to talk about that unfortunate accident, or whatever it was."

"I'm going to visit a friend of mine here," Gerda said. "Should I tell the nurse to bring you some coffee or tea?"

"Are you up for it? How are you feeling?" Adriano asked Sofia.

Sofia felt a little better than the day before. "Coffee would be great."

Gerda left the room and Adriano pulled up a chair and sat next to Sofia's bed. He briefly touched her hand. "I talked to the police here in Vignaverde. They assured me they would investigate. Let's see what they come up with. I also have a friend who is a detective, a private investigator. If the police drag ... their feet—is that what you call it?"

Sofia nodded. "Yes, drag their feet or drag their heels."

"Okay, if they do not produce results soon, I shall ask him to help." He raised his hand, as if to ward off possible concerns Sofia might have. "Do not worry about payment. He owes me a favor. I helped him out a few times." Adriano chuckled.

Sofia wondered what kind of fixes a private investigator got himself into. "Thank you very much for your help."

"Now, tell me exactly what happened before and during the accident." Adriano took a small notepad and a pen out of his briefcase.

Unlike the day before, Sofia remembered the situation in more detail. Adriano listened and wrote down a few brief notes. Sofia also told him of her initial suspicion that the old Santucci might have done it. "But that's not possible. He and his wife have been gone for a few days. He wasn't at the estate before or during the accident."

Adriano looked at her pensively and nodded. At that moment, the door opened and the nurse came in, bringing a tray with two cups of coffee. After tasting the somewhat weak brew, Sofia made a face.

Adriano laughed. "Not exactly the best espresso, no?"

"It's okay," Sofia said, then sighed. "Anyway, I've been racking my brains about who would do something like this. In the beginning of my stay, I would have suspected everyone in the family, for instance Edoardo or perhaps even Luisa, but we've become much closer and I couldn't imagine any of them doing something so ugly. Luisa certainly not and I don't think Edoardo would stoop that low." Sofia rubbed her forehead. "But then again, I don't know. Then there was this weird thing with Umberto, a friend of the old Santucci." Sofia told him of the incident with him in the cellar.

"Well," Adriano cleared his throat. "As you know, if something happened to you, the property would go to Julietta and indirectly back to the family. Julietta is the next of kin. So everybody in the family would have a motive. But I don't think either that Edoardo or Luisa would do something like this. And Santucci senior would not gain anything by it financially ... Umberto? I have met him a few times. He is a strange old man but I think he is harmless. Although dropping a heavy wine barrel is extremely dangerous. They better not let him work any equipment anymore.

"Actually, I am more worried about this Guido Berlusconi," he continued, "the son of *signora* Santucci from a former marriage. I think I mentioned him. He is a real crook, that man. He lives in Rome, but I shall tell the police about him. They can find out if he was anywhere near the property the past few days."

"Oh, yes, he was here. But that was a couple of weeks ago. I actually met him briefly. He's a very unpleasant man." Sofia's eyes filled with tears. "Oh, Adriano, I've become very happy here. And now I suddenly feel that everybody hates me or there is someone out there that wants to harm or even kill me. It's so scary."

"I know. I can imagine how you feel. I am not the police but I shall use whatever influence I have to make sure the culprit is found and brought to justice." He patted her arm. "Right now, you need to focus on getting well. You are safe here in the hospital, and if you need anything, please let me know. You can also call my wife when I am not available." Adriano handed her a card with his private phone number.

"Thank you so much. I'm so grateful for your help."

"You are very welcome. Try to relax and do not worry."

At this moment, Gerda entered the room again. Adriano got up. "Call us if you need anything."

"Yes," Gerda said. "You can call me anytime at home. And once this matter is over with, perhaps we can get together and talk about California. I want to show you some pictures."

"Oh, oh." Adriano grinned. "Make sure you have enough time for this. My wife's picture sessions last a long time."

"Stop it," Gerda said and playfully slapped his arm.

After the two left, Sofia leaned back in her pillow. In spite of the unsettling situation, Sofia felt better. The Goris had been able to disperse the worst of her fears. She knew that Adriano would do anything to find out who hurt her.

Later in the afternoon, Julietta came by. Sofia asked her about her day at school, but the conversation shifted to the accident right away.

"Someone wants to harm me," Sofia said, her voice shaking.

Julietta nodded. "But who?" She narrowed her eyes. "Could it have been Guido? I don't trust him. But he was not here. At least I do not think so."

"Yes, Mr. Gori mentioned him too," Sofia said. "But if he was in the neighborhood, wouldn't we have seen him?"

Julietta shrugged and looked at Sofia pensively. "I don't know." Then she hugged Sofia. "I am so glad you are going to be okay. I was so afraid." Her voice broke.

"Ouch, my arm." Sofia gently pushed Julietta away.

"Sorry. Does it still hurt a lot?"

"Only when I move it. I hope it won't last long. I still want to help with the harvest. At least, it's my left arm. Perhaps I can still help pick."

"Do not worry about picking," Julietta said. "We have enough volunteers. There is still a lot of work to do later. Mamma and Uncle Edoardo said they want you to help them with the blending."

Sofia smiled. "Yes, that would be fun. I can try." If Edoardo and Luisa wanted her to help, they certainly wouldn't have tried to kill her. She probably could safely scratch them off the list of suspects, or could she? They could also use it as a ruse to deflect her suspicion. But she couldn't get all paranoid about it.

"Uncle Edoardo says hello. He will pick you up when you get out of the hospital," Julietta said.

The door opened and the nurse came in, carrying a large bouquet of flowers. She put the vase with the flowers on the table and gave Sofia a card. Sofia opened the envelope and saw Nicholas's signature underneath a brief message: *Sorry to hear about your accident. Julietta told me you would be okay. I was worried. I'll come and visit you tomorrow. Kind regards, Nicholas.*

"Look at those beautiful flowers," Julietta exclaimed. She read the card and winked at Sofia. "He likes you a lot. I bet he is in love with you."

"Oh, nonsense, Julietta. He's just a concerned friend." Sofia's face, however, stretched into a smile.

Chapter 33

Sofia stood at the conveyor belt where the picked grapes were manually checked once more before they were dumped into the crusher. It had been a week since she was released from the hospital. Her headaches were mostly gone and her left arm felt better. She was still wearing a brace over her wrist and couldn't lift anything heavy. Physically, she felt almost normal again but her emotions were in turmoil. The police hadn't found the culprit yet, although they'd come by several times and questioned everyone at the estate. Sofia suspected Adriano's influence had something to do with their increased attention to the case.

A stern but polite inspector, who fortunately spoke English, had arrived to talk to Sofia. She told him about the strange occurrences, the incident with Umberto and the wine barrel, her suspicions about Guido and her misgivings about the old Santucci as well as the dead animals. The inspector told her basically the same thing as Adriano had mentioned, namely that everyone in the family would have a motive. He dismissed with a smile the dead animals, but assured her that every single person on the estate would be thoroughly investigated. He warned her to be circumspect and not to go out at night by herself, and he gave her his phone numbers and told her to call him anytime.

Sofia glanced at the workers around her. All of them were intently focused on the task of spotting damaged grapes. At first glance, nothing seemed to have changed since her accident. After her return from the hospital, many of the workers welcomed her enthusiastically and expressed their dismay at what happened to her. When it became clear, however, that someone among them might have been guilty of tampering with the brakes on her car and that they might be suspects, their attitude began to change. A cloud of distrust and resentment hovered over the whole estate. During the day, people were friendly and helpful but when she tried to join them as they relaxed after work, she noticed the difference in their attitude. The workers and volunteers who had been laughing and talking became unusually quiet and tense when she showed up. As soon as she left, she heard them laugh and talk again. She felt a jab in her chest. The convivial friendship she enjoyed with them was gone.

More and more she began to withdraw as well. After work, she stayed at her house and waited for Julietta to come home from school. Her sister and Nicholas as well as Adriano, who called her regularly, were her closest allies now. Nicholas often joined them in the evening for a while. Luisa came by regularly, asked her how she felt and reassured her that they wouldn't give up until the guilty person was found. Edoardo was attentive to her during work and insisted she take it easy. As much as Sofia wanted to feel close to the family again, she couldn't entirely dismiss the suspicion that they might be involved in the crime. She didn't want to believe their friendliness and care were fake, but she couldn't completely trust them either.

After school and homework, Julietta often walked around the estate, joined the workers and listened to their conversations. She seemed to feel like a detective and clearly enjoyed her self-appointed role. When she came back, she reported anything suspicious, which was usually not very helpful. Sofia was amused at her sister's eagerness to play Sherlock Holmes, but warned her not to get herself into trouble.

"Do you really think whoever did this would confide in you, knowing you're my sister?"

Julietta raised an eyebrow and smiled. "You never know. In all the detective stories I read, the criminal always gave himself away eventually."

"Honey, those are stories, not reality."

"Just leave it up to me," the young sleuth said in a mysterious tone.

Sofia sighed. "Don't do anything dangerous, please. It's enough that one of us got hurt."

One person's behavior toward Sofia didn't seem to have changed as a result of the accident. The old Santucci still displayed his erratic emotions toward her. He glared at her viciously one day, treated her with cold indifference the next and then all of a sudden he gave a quick smile and waved at her. His behavior totally confused her and she didn't trust him. However, since he had a foolproof alibi, Sofia attributed his strange behavior to his general mental instability. One day, however, new suspicions flared up again.

Chapter 34

Sofia and Edoardo were at one of the vineyards, testing the grapes. Edoardo measured the sugar content and the ripeness of the grapes with a refractometer. He checked the small instrument and nodded. "It looks like we can pick really soon," he said to Sofia. "We will collect some grapes from the whole field, crush them, taste the juice, and check the sugar content with the hydrometer. That's much more accurate than with this little thing." He pointed at the refractometer.

Sofia nodded. "I remember. We call it 'batch sampling' in California."

Edoardo nodded and gave a quick smile, then became serious again. "You do not need to help picking. I would prefer if you did the final checking as before. We have a whole crew of experienced pickers."

Sofia, however, wanted to help, since it was her Sangiovese field they were getting ready to harvest. "I would like to try. If it hurts too much, I'll stop."

Edoardo shrugged. "Suit yourself. But remember. The last test before the crushing is very important. It is the place where we catch the remaining bad grapes and guarantee a good wine."

"I guess you're right. It's just, it's my own field but perhaps I'm being sentimental."

"It will not be the last time you are helping with your fields. You have time," Edoardo said.

So, he was expecting her back for the next harvest? Sofia was surprised. It was the second time he made a reference to her continuing to be involved. He'd encouraged her to help with the blending as well. He seemed to have accepted her as part of the estate. She glanced at him. He was gazing over the field toward the pine forest. As she looked in the same direction, she saw Edoardo's father standing next to Nicholas. They seemed to be having an animate but friendly talk. The old man pointed with his cane in a few directions. At one point, Nicholas seemed to laugh out loud. A little later, the old Santucci walked away, supporting himself with his cane. Nicholas continued to work.

Sofia scrunched her eyes. She remembered their talk when the old Santucci had asked her about importing wine to California. However, she was surprised how friendly Nicholas and he seemed together. They looked like old pals. Perhaps they planned to go into business together after all. Nicholas, who had been so passionate about inviting her to become his partner during that dinner before the accident, hadn't mentioned it anymore. Then again, so much had happened. They didn't really have the opportunity to talk about it. Sofia shook her head. *I can't get all paranoid.* She followed Edoardo who went on picking a few more grapes and tasting them.

On the way back to her house, she saw Nicholas and Silvio again. They were standing next to Nicholas's car, talking. The old man pulled out an envelope from his pocket and gave it to Nicholas who held it, nodded, and got into his car. Sofia stopped and looked at them stunned. Did they make a business deal? Was it money? Did Silvio pay Nicholas for something? A terrible thought rose in Sofia's mind. Was Nicholas…? No, no way.

By then, she had reached his car. Nicholas was getting ready to drive away. When he saw her, he gave a quick smile, waved, and left. Was it her imagination or did she detect a

The Italian Sister

guilty look on his face? Sofia's heartbeat had doubled, her head hurt her again, and she felt nauseated.

She went back to her house, poured herself a glass of water, and sat down in the living-room, trying to come to terms with what she'd witnessed. It couldn't be. She must be imagining things. Nicholas couldn't be the culprit. What would he gain by killing her? Then again, she knew he needed money to invest in his vineyard back in California. Perhaps Silvio Santucci or someone else from the family had promised him a lot of money if he hurt Sofia, perhaps the offer had been too tempting. But no, Nicholas had been so kind to her. He'd been really concerned when she was injured. No, it was just ridiculous. One thing, however, was sure. Sofia no longer knew who or what to believe. More and more, she felt persecuted from all directions. But she couldn't let herself go insane.

203

Chapter 35

"Do you think Nicholas could have something to do with the brakes?" Sofia sat next to Julietta who was busy finishing her homework. Sofia had helped her with her English assignment. In her advanced English class, the students now studied American and English literature.

"What? No, of course not. He is such a nice man. Why would he ...?" Julietta looked at her stunned.

"I don't know, Julietta, I'm just confused." Sofia hesitated to tell her sister about the exchange between Nicholas and the old Santucci she'd witnessed in the afternoon. She didn't want to give her the impression she still suspected her grandfather or anybody else of her immediate family of having a hand in the crime. But how else could she explain her suspicion that Nicholas was somehow involved.

"I'm sorry. I'm probably paranoid." Sofia decided to keep her suspicions to herself for the moment.

Julietta closed her books, came over, and sat down next to Sofia. "Do not worry, they will find the bad guy. The police, I mean."

Sofia sighed. "I'm not sure they will. I haven't heard anything. And how could they if nobody saw the person do it?"

"Fingerprints," Julietta suggested.

Sofia shook her head. "You can be sure that whoever cut the break pipe was wearing gloves."

"Hmm, you may be right." Julietta studied her finger-nails. She had painted them a glossy green. "But not

Nicholas," her sister said.

Sofia sighed. "No, I don't think so either. I know I'm not very good at judging people's characters, especially not men." She gave a quick snort. "But I couldn't be that wrong. He seems to be a genuinely good person."

"Yes, and he likes you. Why would he want to hurt you?"

He needs money. Sofia shook her head to chase the thought away. "I don't know," she said. "I'm just worried sick that whoever did it is going to try again. I'm even afraid to drive anymore. Sometimes I feel like packing up and leaving."

"No, do not leave, please." Julietta held Sofia's arm. Her eyes pleaded with Sofia.

Sofia put her arm around her sister. "Don't worry. I won't. I can't, really."

There was a knock at the door. Julietta got up and opened. It was Nicholas.

Speaking of the devil. Sofia shook her head. *Stop the stupid thoughts.*

He came in and smiled at her. "How are you ladies?"

"Sofia is afraid," Julietta said.

"Why? Because of what happened?" Nicholas looked at Sofia.

She tried to analyze his expression but there was no guile in his eyes. She nodded. "I see ghosts everywhere."

"Well, I don't blame you. Do the police have any new information?" Nicholas sat down on a chair across from Sofia. He put a paper bag on the coffee table. "I got you some white peaches in town. I bought too many. They're really sweet."

"Thank you, that's nice," Sofia said.

"So any news at all?" Nicholas asked.

"No, not really." Sofia glanced at him, wondering if he was truly concerned or just curious. "So, is Santucci senior still interested in doing business with you?" She tried not to sound distrustful.

Nicholas gave her a questioning look. "Actually, no. He was asking me a bunch of questions about other things."

Sofia was surprised at Nicholas's answer. If he was no longer interested in going into business with the old Santucci, then why the animate discussion she had witnessed from far and what was in the envelope? "I saw him give you an envelope in the afternoon," she said.

"That's true. He asked me to mail something for him, since I was going to town anyway. I mailed it at the post office. Why?"

Sofia shook her head. "Just wondering."

"You mentioned once that a man from Rome had caused a commotion ... what's his name?" Nicholas said.

"You mean Guido, Julietta's half-brother?" Sofia said.

"Yes. Do you think he could have something to do with it?" he asked.

"He is a crook," Julietta said. "But we don't know if he was near the estate when the accident happened."

Sofia got up and walked over to the window, then turned around. "The fact is I don't know who could have done it. I'm clueless. And it scares the heck out of me."

Nicholas walked up to her and hugged her. "I'm sorry. I wish I could help. But I'm sure the problem will be solved." He took a step back. "In the meantime, be careful. Don't walk around by yourself after dark or go to places alone. Have one of us accompany you, either Julietta or me. If you need to go to town, I can drive you. Okay?"

Sofia nodded.

"Anyway, I need to leave. Edoardo wants me to help him with something. I'll be back later. Stay safe." He gently squeezed Sofia's arm.

"Thanks, Nicholas." She looked after him as he left. *If I*

could only trust you completely. If I could only trust someone.

Chapter 36

A few days later, Sofia and Edoardo walked along one of the fields where Edoardo was checking the grapes again. Sofia was in low spirits. She couldn't relax and she had trouble sleeping at night. Julietta was back in school and stayed at the main house. Luisa had invited Sofia to stay with them so she wouldn't be alone at night. Sofia, however, said she would be all right. Julietta spent the weekends at Sofia's place and during the week, Sofia noticed that Edoardo would walk around her house late at night, probably making sure she was all right, or, as she sometimes thought to herself, wait for another opportunity to harm her. She didn't really believe the latter, but she made sure all the doors were locked at night.

And to make matters worse, Guido had been around again. Sofia had seen him talk to Nicholas a few days ago. It raised Sofia's distrust of Nicholas again. The short exchange she'd witnessed from far could've been entirely innocent. However, if Guido still had an interest in her fields, he may have tried to bribe Nicholas. *Stop it, Sofia, this is ridiculous. You've become a victim of a crazy conspiracy theory.*

But even without her perhaps unfounded suspicions, the situation was getting unbearable. Sofia asked herself once again, if she should just leave and hand over the vineyards to the family. But that was probably exactly what the criminal, whoever it was, had in mind. And she didn't feel like giving up that easily. She would stick it out.

Edoardo tapped her on the shoulder and woke her from her musing. "You seem preoccupied." He gave her a probing

208

look. "You are worried about what happened." It was a statement not a question.

Sofia's eyes filled with tears. "It's just so scary" Her voice broke.

"I understand. But we will not give up until we find who did it," Edoardo said in a reassuring tone. "The police checked out Guido Berlusconi, the son of Luisa from her former marriage. He was here a few weeks ago. Remember?"

Sofia nodded. "I know who he is. Julietta and Luisa told me about him."

"Yes, well he is not very trustworthy. He has been in jail for some criminal activity. It is tragic the way he turned out. I think it is his father's fault, but Luisa really suffers because of it." Edoardo sighed. "And he expressed an interest in your vineyards."

"Yes, I heard about it," Sofia said.

"So far it looks as if he was in Rome at the time. But he is still one of the suspects. And then there is one of the workers. He disappeared over night without giving notice. We don't know why. However, the police are looking for him. They follow every lead." Edoardo gently touched her shoulder.

Sofia was moved by this friendly gesture. She sighed. "But why would a worker I don't know and who doesn't know me do something like this? It doesn't make sense."

Edoardo shrugged. "Perhaps he ..." He shook his head. "Perhaps he is insane. We don't know him very well. He is new. But we will know more when we find him."

Sofia nodded but didn't feel convinced.

"We will get to the ground of this," Edoardo said. "Do not worry."

Sofia had to smile at his slightly mistaken use of an idiom.

"We are ready to pick another field," he said matter-of-factly.

"I'll be there," Sofia said, then walked toward the main house. She felt strong enough to help pick again. The work would take her mind off her fears and sadness. She saw Nicholas drive up and park, then get out of the car and wave at Edoardo. The two began to talk. Sofia glanced wistfully at them, then walked to her house.

Chapter 37

During the first week in October, all the workers and volunteers were out picking grapes. A cool and dry northern wind made the temperature drop to a pleasant twenty degree centigrade during the day but at night it went as far down as twelve degrees. This kept the now fully ripe grapes dry and created the perfect condition for the harvest.

Sofia, together with Edoardo and Luisa, worked at another one of the estate's Sangiovese fields. Fully recovered from her accident, she inhaled the sweet and pungent scent of the ripe grapes. Concentrating on her work, she was able to forget her fears for a while. She focused on cutting the clusters and listened to the sound of the truck, which carried the picked grapes to the winery, as well as the occasional laughter and talk of the workers. The peaceful atmosphere and her intense concentration and hard work were the perfect antidote to her troubles.

"Hi Sofia, how are you feeling?" She was surprised to hear Nicholas's voice. He began to work at the row next to hers. His smile seemed genuine and she hated herself for not being able to fully trust him.

"Great, thanks," she answered. "Working helps my strained nerves."

"I understand," he said, then went on with his work.

Sofia took a deep breath and continued to snip off clusters of grapes, putting them into the plastic containers along the rows of vines.

After a few hours, Nicholas and Sofia walked over to the

winery and helped to do the quick final check of the grapes before they were crushed. Nicholas stayed with the others after work, chatting and laughing. Sofia, however, didn't feel comfortable anymore just hanging out with the workers, so she went home.

Back at the house, Julietta came toward her with a basket in each hand. "Want to come and help pick *porcini*? I saw some in the forest there." She pointed at the woods next to the property.

"Do you know the poisonous from the edible ones?" Sofia asked.

"*Certamente.* What do you think?" Julietta rolled her eyes. "Besides, we are going to show them to Edoardo before cooking. He is an expert."

Death by poisonous mushrooms. That's all I need. Sofia shook her head and grinned.

"What?" Julietta stared at her.

"Nothing. Yes, let's go." Sofia grabbed one of the baskets and they walked the short path to the small forest. Julietta obviously knew her way around the dense brush.

They didn't have to walk very far to see the first of the large brown and white mushrooms that were so delicious when prepared with risotto, pasta, or as a ragout. It was quiet and peaceful in the forest. Circles of dappled light from the sunrays shining through the trees covered the ground. Sofia inhaled the scent of pines and the earthy smell of the ground cover.

After about an hour, they'd picked enough mushrooms for a dinner. It was late afternoon and the light began to dim in the forest.

"Hear that?" Julietta grabbed Sofia's arm. They stood still and listened. A thrashing noise nearby became louder. It sounded like a mixture of thunder and snapping tree branches. "*Cinghiale*," Julietta whispered and pulled Sofia behind a cluster of trees. "Wild boar." They saw the huge animal with its powerful tusks bolt through the trees. As soon as it had appeared, it was gone. Sofia and Julietta breathed a sigh of relief.

"They are usually not dangerous, but if they feel threatened, they can attack," Julietta explained. They walked on and came out of the forest without further interruptions.

After having the mushrooms checked by Edoardo and Luisa, they cleaned them. Luisa invited Sofia to have dinner with them. "It will be just the three of us, Julietta, you, and me. My parents are eating at Edoardo's tonight."

Sofia gratefully accepted the invitation. Julietta set the table and Sofia helped Luisa prepare dinner. Luisa cleaned the mushrooms and cut them into thin slices while Sofia heated the olive oil and sautéed the garlic for a couple of minutes. "Make sure it is not getting brown," Luisa warned. Sofia then added the mushrooms and Luisa turned up the heat, because the mushrooms needed to be cooked on a high flame, as Luisa told her. Sofia cooked them for about ten minutes, added salt and pepper halfway through the cooking time, then added parsley in the end. "If it gets too dry, you can add a little broth," Luisa told her. "Good, now set it aside."

Luisa got ready to prepare the risotto with Sofia watching her. Luisa heated butter, then added some olive oil. "So the butter doesn't get brown," she explained. She sautéed onions, poured in the dry rice and stirred it until it was translucent. She added the white wine and continued to stir until the wine evaporated. "It has to fully evaporate, otherwise the rice may taste bitter." Then, she began ladling the hot bouillon, one spoonful after the other, making sure the rice was always covered with liquid, so it didn't dry out. She sprinkled the saffron over it, let everything simmer for about fifteen minutes and continued adding the broth.

Soon the kitchen smelled delicious and Sofia's stomach grumbled. Shortly before the rice finished cooking, Luisa poured in the mushrooms, mixed everything, added some butter and the grated Parmesan cheese. She stirred the dish and asked Sofia to taste it. "Is it seasoned well enough?"

"Ah, this looks and smells so good," Sofia said. She picked up a little with a fork and tried it. "It tastes delicious, absolutely wonderful," she moaned.

"Good," Luisa chuckled at Sofia's display of pleasure. She poured the rice and mushroom mixture onto a heated platter.

They ate it together with a salad and with a glass of white wine and some lemonade for Julietta. It was a simple but truly delicious dish, made even better by the fact that they had picked the fresh mushrooms themselves. Sofia liked being alone with Julietta and Luisa, the two people she felt most comfortable with by now. The company, the food, and the wine calmed her enough that she was able to enjoy herself once again. They talked and sat around, Luisa and Sofia drinking espresso and Julietta eating a bowl of ice cream. Since it was a Friday and Julietta didn't have school the next day, she spent the night at Sofia's. The two walked to Sofia's house together.

After Julietta had turned in for the night, Sofia sat in the living room, drinking a cup of soothing herbal tea. Now, by herself, the old fears began to rise again. There was still someone out there, someone who hated her and wanted to harm her.

A while later, she went upstairs and stood by the open window in her bedroom, staring into the approaching night. As most evenings since the accident, she saw Edoardo in the back of the house walking around the property. This evening, however, he wasn't alone. A second person walked with him. He was on the far side of Edoardo and Edoardo's body hid him from view. Then they both stopped and looked around and now Sofia saw that the second person was Nicholas. Sofia was just about to call to them, then changed her mind and tried to listen to their conversation. She was surprised they spoke English. Usually, Nicholas conversed in Italian with the Italian members of the estate. He knew the language fluently. But she also noticed that Edoardo liked to practice his English.

"What can we do? What's the best way?" Nicholas asked.

Sofia couldn't hear Edoardo's answer well, since he stood with his back to her. She thought she heard him say. "Kill ..." the rest she didn't understand.

Then Nicholas. "Shoot ...?"

Sofia's heart stuttered. *What were they talking about? Or who?* Sofia wasn't sure if he said "it" or "her."

Edoardo talked a little louder now. "I am not allowed to do it. I would end up in jail."

Nicholas seemed to shrug. "We'll think of something. We need to do something to protect the fields and ... could ruin everything." The two men walked away and Sofia couldn't hear the conversation any longer.

She stood by the window and tried to make sense of the snippets of talk she'd overhead. Shooting or killing something or someone? But Edoardo couldn't do it. He would end up in jail. Did they talk about her? Shooting her to save the fields? Her two fields? Sofia closed the window and sat on the bed.

"That's absurd," she told herself. No, they must have been talking about something else. Perhaps she misunderstood. She really was beginning to lose her mind.

Chapter 38

The day after picking the Sangiovese grapes, which were now hissing and gurgling in the fermentation tanks, Sofia grabbed the bike to drive to Vignaverde to pick up Julietta after school. Although she'd been driving Edoardo's car a few times, which fortunately was an automatic as well, she still felt uncomfortable. Riding a bike was not only good exercise, but there was less that could be tampered with, she told herself.

Just as she pushed the bike toward the path to town, she saw Nicholas walk across the courtyard and wave at her. He asked her if she needed a ride.

"Are you going to town?" Sofia asked.

"I wasn't planning to but I can give you a ride. No problem."

"Thanks, but it's not necessary. I'm taking the bike. I'm meeting Julietta and we're going on a short bike ride. Besides, it's good exercise."

Nicholas smiled and waved at her, then kept on walking toward the building where he lived with his co-workers. Sofia thought about the odd conversation between him and Edoardo she'd overheard the night before. She wished so much they would find the criminal, so she could trust people again.

Out of habit by now, Sofia tested the brakes before driving down the steep hill. Reassured that they worked, she let the bike roll down, enjoying the breeze on her face. She carefully checked for traffic as she eased her way onto the two-lane highway to town. There was very little traffic but since the road was fairly narrow and there was no sidewalk, Sofia preferred to ride on the shoulder wherever possible. Inhaling the scent of pines and the occasional whiff of dew-soaked grass, she enjoyed the peaceful atmosphere.

After a while, she heard the engine of a car approaching. She glanced back and was surprised when she recognized Nicholas's red Fiat. She knew it was his because of the yellow rack on top of the car. He must have changed his mind and decided to come to town after all. Sofia stopped her bike by the side of the road and looked back. The car coming toward her slowed down a little, but then instead of stopping it picked up speed and swerved toward the side of the road.

Sofia's breath caught. She stared at the now speeding car, which drove straight toward her. Paralyzed with fear, she kept staring at the car, then her survival instinct kicked in. She dropped the bike and ran into the meadow just before the car hit the bicycle and threw it up in the air. It fell down on the concrete with a loud bang, skidded along the road, the basket flying off and hitting the grass next to the road. The car sped off and drove around a bend in the road, tires screeching.

Sofia, her knees weak and her heart thudding, sat down in the grass and covered her face with her hands. She was trembling all over. It was Nicholas after all. The thought flashed through her mind and the pain of the realization squeezed her throat shut. *Why? Why?*

She heard the sound of a car engine again. Getting up with wobbly knees and tears streaming down her face, she glanced in its direction. The car stopped and Edoardo jumped out. He stared at her with a terrified look in his eyes. "Are you all right?"

Sofia nodded, then shook her head and sobbed. "Someone

was trying to run me over with his car."

Edoardo walked toward her and put his arm around her. "Are you hurt?"

Sofia shook her head. "It was Nicholas," she cried.

Edoardo hugged her. "No."

She was surprised at his gentle gesture. "But ..."

"It was his car. But he was not the one driving." She looked at him. His face was pale and haggard. A deep crease had formed between his eyebrows.

"Then who?"

He shook his head and his voice trembled as he spoke. "Come." He took her by the arm and led her to his car. He rushed to pick up the damaged bicycle and carried it to the side of the road. "We will pick it up later." They got in the car. Edoardo's cell phone rang. He answered it, listened, then nodded. "*Capisco.*" He slid the phone into the halter on the dashboard and started driving in the direction where the other car had disappeared. His face was hard and cold, giving nothing away.

"What's going on?" Sofia asked.

He sighed and glanced at her, the frozen features in his face softening a little, and his eyes registered pain. "I am so sorry. You may have been right from the beginning."

As they drove around a bend, a terrible picture presented itself to them. The red Fiat had hit a tree and was badly crushed. Sofia's heart lurched. She still hadn't quite digested the fact that it wasn't Nicholas in the car. A police car was there, sirens screeched and more police cars and an ambulance were racing to the scene.

Edoardo stopped his car a few yards away. They got out and started walking toward the scene of the accident. Emergency crew workers were prying the car open and were in the process of lifting someone out. As if in trance, Sofia

218

walked toward the damaged vehicle. She felt Edoardo's hand on her shoulder, holding her back. "You do not want to see this. Wait here."

Not sure what to do, Sofia waited. Edoardo walked toward the stretcher where the injured or possibly dead person lay. Sofia couldn't imagine anybody surviving such an accident. She watched as Edoardo bent over and seemed to say something to the person lying on the stretcher. Perhaps he or she had survived. Then everything went fast. The stretcher was hauled into an emergency vehicle, which sped off with blaring sirens. People were standing around the crushed car, talking. A police officer was talking on his cell phone.

By then Sofia had arrived at the scene of the accident. She touched Edoardo's arm. "Who is it?" she whispered.

Chapter 39

Edoardo put his hand on Sofia's shoulder. "Umberto."

"What?" Sofia was flabbergasted. "But ... why?"

"We will find out." Edoardo brushed his hand over his face. He motioned at the car. "Let's go home."

"Is he going to live?" Sofia asked as they sat in the car.

Edoardo shrugged. "I don't know. I will go to the hospital later to find out."

"What about Julietta?" Sofia remembered that her sister was probably still waiting for her in town.

"I will call her." Edoardo pulled out his cell phone. He called and said a few words in Italian, then pushed the button.

"Did you tell her about the accident?" Sofia asked.

"No. I did not want to scare her. She will find out soon enough," Edoardo said with a grim face.

They drove on in silence. Edoardo stopped to load the broken bicycle into the trunk and then continued.

At home, there were two police cars in front of the house. Several of the people working at the vineyard were standing outside talking animatedly. Nicholas and Luisa were standing next to each other. Only now did Sofia fully realize that Nicholas wasn't responsible. She felt ashamed having suspected him, but how was she supposed to know he wasn't the driver?

When she got out of the car, he came rushing toward her and embraced her. "My God, I'm so glad you're okay. He took my car and ..."

"I know," Sofia said. She began to tremble as the tension gave way to relief and sadness. She put her face on Nicholas's shoulder and began to cry. He patted her back and held her.

"I still don't know what happened. Umberto was in the car." She wiped the tears from her face.

"I am going to the hospital," Edoardo told them, then hesitated. "He was conscious for a while at the accident scene. He told me that my father asked him to do it." Edoardo gave Sofia a quick glance, then walked to the car. She thought she had seen tears in his eyes.

A loud argument broke out inside the house. Two officers were leading the old Santucci in handcuffs out the door. He yelled at the police and when he saw Sofia, he stopped and stared at her, an insane gleam in his eyes. "*Impostore, nemico,*" he yelled at the top of his voice. Sofia's heart clenched in the face of so much hatred.

Luisa hugged Sofia. "They think he blackmailed or bribed Umberto to hurt you," Luisa said. "This is terrible. I am so very sorry. We should have known. He has been acting weird lately, stranger than usually. I just never thought he would do something like this." Her voice gave out.

"It's not your fault," Sofia said. "So I was right with my initial suspicion?"

"Yes." Luisa nodded. "Let's go inside."

Nicholas, Luisa, and Sofia went to sit in the living room. They were quiet for a while, trying to digest what just happened. Sofia was still trembling a little. Nicholas sat down next to her and put his hand on her shoulder.

After a while, Luisa took a deep breath. "Umberto and my stepfather have been friends since childhood," she began. "Edoardo knows more about their relationship. But from what I know, Umberto has been working for my stepfather for a long time and my stepfather has helped him out financially several times. You see, Umberto is a gambler and has problems with alcohol. My stepfather has given him money and jobs at the vineyard. When we took over, we kept him, although he was getting old and could not work much, but we figured he belonged to the family. Lately, however, his drinking was getting worse and I know he got into arguments with my stepfather, who always tried to bale him out."

At that moment, the door opened and Julietta came inside. She was close to tears. "Is it true? About Nonno?"

Luisa nodded. Julietta sat down next to her and started to cry silently. Luisa hugged her. After a while, Luisa got up. "I am going to make some tea. Once Edoardo gets back from the hospital, we will find out more." Julietta followed her into the kitchen.

Sofia and Nicholas looked at each other. Nicholas's face was somber. He shook his head. "I'm still trembling. I was so afraid something was going to happen to you. Umberto opened the door to my car. First I thought he was looking for something. I called him but he didn't react. He just got in and started the car and drove off. I was totally flabbergasted. But then, I remembered that you were on your bike. I thought of the incident with the wine barrel and I got this really bad feeling. I called Edoardo and told him about it. He jumped into his car and drove after him."

Sofia nodded. "I heard a car and looked back and saw it was your car. I thought you were on your way to town and then the car drove right toward me." Sofia covered her face with her hands. She didn't want to admit that she thought it was Nicholas behind the wheel. "First I was like paralyzed and then at the last minute I jumped into the meadow."

"Jesus Christ, you probably thought it was me." Nicholas got up. "What a bastard that man is."

The Italian Sister

Julietta and Luisa came back with a pot of tea and cups. Luisa poured the tea and put a plate of cookies on the table. They sat around in silence, sipping tea.

Sofia tried to come to terms with the jumble of thoughts and emotions that flooded her. She had been right all along, it had been the old Santucci. She didn't dare to think about what it all meant in the end. She looked around at the other people. They all looked somber and sad.

Half an hour later, Edoardo came back. He stood awkwardly in the room for a moment, then sat down next to Luisa.

"How is Umberto?" Luisa asked, exhaling deeply.

Edoardo shook his head. "The doctors do not think he is going to make it. It is probably better he does not survive. He would end up in jail for the rest of his life for attempted murder," he said with a grim voice.

Sofia's heart ached. *I destroyed the family.* The realization hit her full force. If she hadn't come here to claim her property, none of this would have happened. "I feel so bad. I should never have come here. It's my fault."

"This is not true." Edoardo faced her. He spoke sharply. "This is not your fault. This is my fault. I should have known my father better. His mind had been deteriorating for some time and he became more hateful. He even beat my mother. I should have seen the signs. I did not want to believe that he could be so mean, so insane."

"What I don't understand," Nicholas said. "How did they think they could get away with this? I mean their behavior, their plan, they are so stupid. Okay, so the thing with the brakes might have worked. But stealing my car and running Sofia down on the open road. It was obvious that Umberto would be caught. How? I don't understand."

Edoardo sighed. "This is because you look at it with a

223

sane mind. Obviously, my father was not in his right mind. This is the plan of an insane person. He never got over his experience during the Second World War. His family was hurt badly by some American soldiers. And because of this he hated Americans. It made him blind. He thought that by using your car, you would become a suspect. That way he could hurt you, too. In his troubled mind, you are the enemy as well. My father is mentally ill and I think Umberto's mind is gone too. Too much alcohol." His voice broke. He brushed his hand over his face and got up. "The police will be here soon. I need to go and talk to my mother."

After he left the room, it was quiet again. Then Nicholas got up and walked toward the window. He turned around and shook his head. "I feel I'm a character in some absurd movie."

"Well, we do not know what will happen to these two men, but they will not hurt you anymore." Luisa's voice was sad but composed. "We owe you a big apology. This should never have happened. And I want you to know that we love and appreciate you for being here. You have helped us a lot during this harvest. And, Sofia, it was very important for Julietta to have you here ... for all of us."

Sofia nodded. "Thank you. It will take me a while to digest all this."

Julietta who had stopped crying got up and sat down next to Sofia. "Please, do not leave." The two hugged.

Chapter 40

Later that afternoon, a police officer came by and told them that Umberto had died in the hospital. He'd made a full confession and told them that Silvio Santucci blackmailed him and threatened to expose a crime Umberto committed a few years before that the old Santucci had helped him cover up. The officer did not give any details about the alleged crime and he couldn't tell them what would happen to Silvio Santucci. For the time being, he was in the local jail. They would probably indict him for attempted murder and blackmail.

The mood had been somber and sad. Sofia felt depressed and even guilty. She knew it wasn't her fault but she couldn't help thinking that she had inadvertently caused a major tragedy in the family.

Luisa had invited her and Nicholas to have a light dinner with them. Sofia turned the invitation down. She was exhausted from the physical and emotional strain and wanted to be alone. She wondered how Donna Santucci felt. They hadn't seen her since the upheaval. Julietta said she was upstairs and that she would stay with her this evening and sleep at the main house.

At her house, Sofia made herself a cup of herbal tea, hoping it would calm her down. She sat in front of the floor-length glass door to the patio and stared into the approaching evening. Normally, she loved watching the sun set and the colors spreading over the fields and woods. Tonight, the beauty of the landscape was lost to her.

She was relieved that the criminals had been found. But she certainly wasn't happy at the outcome. It made her reassess her whole involvement in this estate. Now she felt as removed from everyone as she had in the beginning. It was even worse now. When she first came here, she knew it would take time to connect with the family. But there was hope and for weeks that hope had been nourished by an ever increasing feeling of closeness.

Now, the closeness was gone. Even her relationship with Julietta had changed. How could it not have? Because of Sofia's presence, her grandfather had been arrested and indicted and would most likely end up in jail. His close friend, Umberto, was dead. Julietta hadn't given Sofia the feeling that she had a very close connection to the old Santucci, but he was, after all, her grandfather, her *nonno*. And Donna, Santucci's wife, must feel terrible now. Sofia knew that Luisa didn't much care for her stepfather. But Edoardo must feel crushed. His father was a criminal, and it all came out because of her, Sofia. She'd seen the despair in his eyes.

All these thoughts made Sofia feel more and more unhappy. She was too distraught to cry; she felt cold inside. And she missed her father. Perhaps Henry could have prevented this disaster. Then again, it was her father who was indirectly the source of all the misery. Had he been more honest early on, perhaps a less stormy and problematic relationship between her and the Italian family would have had a chance. But for this, it was too late. It was now up to Sofia to deal with this whole mess. But how? Should she give up the two vineyards, give her part of the estate to the family, to Julietta? She could just leave and go back to her old life in California. She remembered Nicholas's offer to become his partner. But she didn't know if he still wanted to work with her. She seemed to bring bad luck to everybody.

Too upset to think clearly and with a headache coming on, Sofia got up to go to bed. As she was climbing the stairs, there was a knock at the door. It was Nicholas.

"Sorry for dropping in like this. I can come back another time, if you're too tired." As he looked at her with his kind, warm eyes, something in her broke and tears flooded her eyes.

"It's okay. Come in," she said with a sob.

"Are you sure?"

"Yes, don't mind me. I'll be okay."

He entered hesitantly. She pointed at the living room and suppressed the tears. "Would you like a glass of wine? I could go for one ... after all the turmoil." She wiped her eyes and smiled.

"Sounds good to me, if you're up for it."

Sofia got two glasses and a bottle of wine. She sat on a chair next to Nicholas and poured. When she handed him his glass, he lifted it, and smiled at her "cheers." He put the glass down and shook his head.

"'Cheers' may not be the appropriate term at this point. I know you must feel bad, but at least the terror and the guessing are over with. I don't think, we'll see much of Silvio Santucci anymore," Nicholas said.

Sofia nodded. "It's going to take a while to deal with this. I can't help thinking that I'm in part responsible for the tragedy. If I hadn't been here, this would never have happened."

"True, the old guy wouldn't have attacked you, but he eventually would have hurt someone else. He's insane, Sofia. He needs to be put away for good. He could've killed someone. What about Julietta? You guys were driving around in your car."

227

Nicholas put his hand on her shoulder. "In fact, you did them a favor. You coming here did bring his hostility and hatred out in the open for everyone to see. You got hurt in the process and because of it, he's being put away to prevent him from committing another crime. You don't need to feel bad."

"I know, but I can't help it." Sofia shrugged. She sipped her wine. "I know I'm not responsible for what he did, but it does make me reevaluate what I'm doing here, what I want to do with my property ... with my future."

"Well, that's of course something you need to decide for yourself. Just remember, you do have other options. My offer of becoming my partner back in California still stands." He gave her a warm smile.

"Thanks, Nicholas. I'm so relieved this is over with. I began to suspect everybody. It was horrible not knowing whom to trust. For a brief moment I even suspected you might have something to do with it. When I saw you having a cheerful talk with Silvio Santucci, I got suspicious. And then, the other night, I overheard a snippet of conversation when you and Edoardo walked around my house."

Nicholas wrinkled his forehead, as if trying to remember. "What did we talk about?"

Sofia waved her hand. "It's not important. I shouldn't even have paid attention to it."

"I'm trying to remember ..." Nicholas gave her a questioning look.

Sofia sighed and felt embarrassed. "You said something about ... shooting and killing something or someone to protect the fields. And for a moment, I thought that maybe you meant me. You know, protect them from me. And then Edoardo said he couldn't do it. He would go to jail. Oh, it's so stupid when I think about it now. I was getting so scared. I misinterpreted everything. I'm sorry."

"Huh? Shooting you to protect the fields?" Nicholas looked at her dumbfounded, then he grinned. "Oh, I see, oh, my God. Now, I get it. Helping the family to get rid of you to protect the grape fields from you."

Nicholas burst out laughing. "Oh, my dear," he guffawed. "I'm sorry, I don't mean to laugh at you. I know a lot of bad things have happened today, but this is hilarious." He slapped his thigh.

"I remember now. Edoardo complained about one of the vineyards that had some major damage and it was clearly from an animal. He suspected the wild boar that's been roaming the neighborhood lately. They can be a real pest and create a lot of destruction. So I asked him if he couldn't shoot it. But he has no hunting license and they are quite strict here. If you get caught shooting an animal without a license you could really end up in jail. We talked about different other methods like building fences and all that. See, this is the first year, wild boars came that close to the property, so they aren't really prepared for it."

Sofia sat down and covered her face with her hands. "Oh, God, I should've thought of this. Julietta and I actually saw the boar when we picked *porcini* a few days ago. This is so embarrassing. I should've never suspected you. You never gave me any reason to distrust you."

"Don't feel bad," Nicholas said. "Had I gone through what you went through, I would've been distrustful of everyone as well. Besides, it was exactly the goal of the old Santucci to make me look suspicious. You know, Edoardo told me that before Umberto died, he told him that the plan was to run you down, then drive back, put the car back to where it was before. They wanted to make it look like I was the culprit."

"It's all so insane." Sofia took a deep breath. "I may just

229

take you up on your offer about California. I could hand over the property here to the family."

"Why hand it over?" Nicholas shook his head. "Perhaps, you could come to an agreement, where they work the vineyards and get part of the proceeds from the wine, and you could sell some of the wine in California. That way everybody would profit."

Sofia nodded. "I'm sure there's a way. I would have to talk to Adriano Gori, the lawyer, about it. He may have some suggestions."

"See, you already feel better. You're making plans." Nicholas put his arm around her and pulled her close. Sofia faced him and was intrigued again by his dark-brown, shiny, warm eyes, which reminded her of dark honey. His face was close enough that she smelled his discrete but pleasant aftershave. He gave her a questioning look, then smiled and kissed her lightly on the cheek. His lips brushed over hers and she closed her eyes. He embraced her. His body was firm, warm, and comforting, an invitation to let go and plunge into the waves of passion that washed over and through her, a passion that had been lingering for some time but was kept at bay by the disturbing events of the past weeks. And now, she wanted him but felt that somehow it wasn't the right time with all the family disasters around them. They kissed for a long time, then he pulled back at little and gently touched her cheek.

"I love you, Sofia, and I want to make love to you," he whispered. "But I want it to be on a quieter, relaxed day. I …." He hesitated.

Sofia hugged him. She was surprised at his sudden confession, yet she knew deep down it was right. She'd had feelings for him for a while but hadn't been able to give in to them because of her distrust. She kissed him again lightly, then pulled back. "I love you, too. But I agree we should wait. It wouldn't be right today."

He got up and pulled her up. "Are you sure you're going to be all right by yourself tonight."

"Yes, I'm fine. I need some time to think things over, you know about the vineyard here and everything. But no matter what I decide, I would love to work with you in California."

Nicholas's face lit up and his eyes gleamed. "Great, that would really be wonderful." They hugged. As Nicholas stepped outside, they saw Luisa walk toward them. Now, Sofia was relieved they hadn't given in to their passion. It would have been extremely awkward if Luisa had come to the door and somehow realized they were having sex on the day her family had fallen apart.

Chapter 41

Are you all right?" Luisa asked as she stepped inside. She walked up to Sofia and hugged her.

Sofia, surprised at the warm gesture, felt a knot in her throat. "I don't know what to feel." She waved Luisa to the sofa and sat down in the chair across from her.

"Sofia, it is over. You can relax. I am so sorry we put you through this. It is just not right."

"It's not your fault," Sofia said. She got up and brought another glass from the kitchen and pointed at the bottle of wine on the coffee table. "Want some?"

Luisa nodded and gave a weak smile. "Yes, thank you." She watched as Sofia poured the wine. "It *is* our fault. We tried to ignore the fact that my stepfather has serious mental problems." She took a sip of wine. "You know when the thing with the manipulated brakes happened, I thought immediately of him and also of Guido. It is sad to say that I even suspected my own son. But Silvio was gone and Guido was in Rome, so I figured it could not have been them. I just did not think my stepfather was devious enough to ask someone else to do it for him. And his oldest friend of all people. It is very sad." Luisa's voice faltered.

"What's going to happen to him?" Sofia asked.

Luisa sighed. "We do not know yet. Edoardo hired a good lawyer. We will also ask Mr. Gori what we should do. What we would like is that instead of jail, although he certainly deserves it, he would be put into a mental facility. There he could get the treatment he needs. You know, I never warmed up to my stepfather, but he was not always a bad man. At first, when he married my mother, we were quite happy together. But as he got older, he became more and more unpredictable and erratic. I know some of it has to do with what happened to him during the war. But you cannot blame everything on the war." Luisa took another sip and shook her head. "He needs to be supervised but jail would just kill him." She gave Sofia a questioning look.

Sofia got up and stepped to the floor-length window. "He obviously needs help and I agree, jail would probably not be the right place." Sofia had heard horror stories of treatments and conditions in Italian jails, but of course, she didn't know if they were true. "I just hope this whole thing isn't going to destroy your family. How is Donna?"

Luisa got up and stood next to her. They were gazing at the peaceful landscape outside, so unlike the inner turmoil Sofia was feeling.

Luisa exhaled deeply. "She will be all right. She has had a difficult time with her husband. Believe it or not, she is relieved. I mean, she is relieved that he is away from her. Of course, she feels sad about the whole thing. It is her husband after all. But she will be okay."

It was quiet for a while. They were both watching the fields and woods fade into the descending darkness. A strip of purple grazed the horizon, before it slipped into the night.

Sofia took a deep breath. "It's so beautiful here."

"Yes." Luisa put her hand on Sofia's shoulder. "It will be okay."

"What about Edoardo? It must be hard on him."

"Oh, yes, it is. He is torn apart inwardly. He, too, has had his problems with his father. But it is his father and he loves him, in spite of everything." Luisa shrugged. "You know how it is. You watch your parents or children make mistakes, even commit crimes, but they are still your family. You stick up for them. Family is very important in Italy."

Sofia nodded. "Yes, I know. It's also important where I come from. Perhaps different, but ... when I found out about my father's secret life, I was really angry and upset. But I can't stop loving him. After a while, I was happy to find out I had a family far away. My father and Aunt Emma were the only close family I had left. When he died, it was hard."

"I understand." Luisa put her arm around Sofia. "We are your family, too. I know it is not the same as your family in California, but we love you and we are very happy you are here. Do not forget this."

Sofia looked at her. Luisa's large, black eyes shone with kindness. "Thank you. I can't believe you still care for me after all this upheaval, but I'm happy to have you for a family."

They hugged and Luisa gently brushed a tear from Sofia's face. "You should rest now. We will not be working tomorrow. Take a day off." As she was at the door, she looked back and smiled. "I like Nicholas. He is a great man. You two make a beautiful couple."

Sofia opened her mouth, but she was too surprised to say anything. "How did you know?" she finally whispered.

Luisa gave a quick pearly laugh that was so unlike her normal serious demeanor. "Ah, Sofia, I was young once, too." She opened the door. "Anyway, Julietta and I decided she would stay at the main house for a while to give you some privacy." She laughed again.

"I cannot believe you," Sofia said, grinning. "I thought you Italians were strict Catholics."

"Little did you know." Luisa waved at her and left.

Sofia let herself fall on the sofa and shook her head. Then a feeling of joy flooded her. Things would be all right after all.

She wanted to talk to Edoardo though, to let him know that she didn't bear a grudge. Of all the members of the family, she felt most sorry for him. He'd changed from the time she first met him. He'd been cold, even disapproving of her. But in time they had warmed up to each other. He'd been supportive and had encouraged her, even praised her work at the vineyard. She hoped they could remain friends and he wouldn't withdraw from her again.

PART SIX: THE GRAPE HARVEST

Chapter 42

The herbal and earthy smell of dew-soaked grass marked the full arrival of fall in Tuscany. The October mornings were cool, even nippy, but during the day, the sun warmed and dried the fields. Now, the workers at the vineyard got ready to pick the last two fields of Cabernet Sauvignon grapes. They began to work as soon as the sun dissipated the dew.

When Sofia left the house to go to the vineyard, she saw Edoardo and Julietta sit on the flatbed truck, getting ready to drive to the first field. Julietta, who had a day off from school, waved at her. Sofia climbed onto the truck and Edoardo greeted her with the flicker of a smile.

"How are you?" he asked.

"A little better." Searching for words to express her inner dichotomy, she sighed. "I'm relieved and also sad," she said. "Sad about what happened to your family. I'm sorry about your father."

"Sorry?" His voice was gruff, then he shook his head and said more kindly: "You should not feel bad about him. He almost killed you."

"I feel bad because no matter what he has done, he is your father and this tears apart your family."

Edoardo stopped the truck at the side of the road next to the vineyard with the Cabernet Sauvignon grape varietal. He faced her. "We will get through this. We are a strong family. Do not worry. Yes, it hurts me that my father did this. But it hurts me even more that I refused to see the signs. You were hurt badly during the accident. You could have been killed.

Umberto was killed. I guess I should be grateful you are well again and nothing worse happened to you. I was an imbecile."

It was the longest speech Edoardo had ever made and the most emphatic. His facial color had darkened and Sofia thought she saw his eyes tear up. He turned his head and looked toward the grape field.

"You're not an imbecile," Sofia said. "It's natural that you didn't want to believe your father was capable of doing something like this. It's your father after all. Nobody wants to believe that one's parents are capable of evil. That's hard. I don't blame you. Really."

Edoardo turned to face her again. "Thank you. You are very kind."

"It is true, *Zio* Edoardo," Julietta said. "I didn't believe it either."

"Well, maybe not." Edoardo sighed. "What is done is done."

"How is Donna?" Sofia asked.

"She is all right. She said she was relieved it was over," Julietta said and hugged her. "She hopes you are not going to leave because of this. She likes you. We all love you."

"Yes." Edoardo gave her one of his rare smiles. "In spite of everything, I am glad you are here with us. I hope you will stay and help with the blending." He put his hand on Sofia's shoulder. "Thanks to your family, your father, we are here today on this estate."

"Thank you." Sofia was touched by his kindness and warmth. "I hope your father will get the psychological treatment he needs."

"We hope so too. Time will tell. But I think it is time we did some work."

They jumped down from the flatbed truck and walked to

the field where a lot of workers were busy picking grapes. While Edoardo went up to speak to the foreman, Sofia and Julietta grabbed their shears and began cutting off the clusters of grapes.

A smiled teased Sofia's lips. For the first time in weeks, she felt at home again in this environment. She waved at Nicholas who was helping to load the full plastic crates with the picked grapes onto the truck. He threw her a kiss.

In the evening, Sofia joined the other helpers and Nicholas, who sat around one of the outside fireplaces, drinking lemonade and wine, sharing some appetizers—nuts, olives, and cheese. With the crimes solved and the suspicions gone, everybody relaxed. The mood was friendly and warm again. People talked openly about the situation and expressed their sadness and outrage about Umberto's and Silvio Santucci's attempt to hurt or even kill Sofia.

Most of them thought of the men as a little odd and unpredictable but would have never suspected them of being outright criminals. A few of the workers spoke broken English, but Sofia tried to answer in Italian as much as possible. She and Julietta had been practicing together. Sofia was able to understand the general gist of a conversation, as long as the speakers didn't talk too fast or, what was worse, in a local dialect. She noticed, however, that they made a real effort to include her in their conversations. Nicholas, who knew Italian fluently, translated for her.

One of the men, a teacher from a nearby town, played his guitar and soon everyone was singing. Sofia who didn't know the words to the songs hummed the melodies. She shared a blanket with Nicholas who had wrapped his arm around her. She leaned against his shoulder, feeling the warmth of his body. They watched as the sun disappeared, leaving a strip of crimson on the horizon, and Sofia felt more joyful than she had in a long time.

The October evening air got cool quickly. Sofia pulled her jacket closer and Nicholas hugged her tighter. "Getting cold?"

"A little." She tried to find a good opportunity to invite him home without being too obvious. He didn't seem to have the same qualms.

"I would love to watch the sunset from your home," he said, kissing the corner of her mouth.

"Then let's go," she said with a smile.

The last purplish hues on the fields faded. The light breeze brought a scent of lavender. Nicholas and Sofia stood outside on the patio, their arms around each other. Nicholas gently traced his fingers over Sofia's jawline, which sent ripples of desire through her. Her heart was thumping. She bent her head back to look at the sky. "Have you noticed how much brighter the stars are in Tuscany than in California?"

She didn't really mean to say that but she was nervous. It'd been several years since she'd made love to a man. She'd been twenty-two when she and James divorced after their failed marriage of barely three years.

Nicholas raised an eyebrow and chuckled. "I guess it's because there aren't any big cities nearby. City lights dim the glow from the stars," he responded to her remark. He let his hand softly glide down her back, then kissed her earlobe. A moan of pleasure escaped her.

"Come," he said and lead her inside.

They didn't make love in the bed upstairs. Instead they were lying down on a thick throw-rug next to the floor-length patio door. They had left one of the windows ajar and the honey-sweet fragrance of a patch of gardenias drifted from the corner of the patio. Nicholas was gentle but intense, lapping her skin with his tongue and filling her with heat, and Sofia knew she'd been given another chance at love.

Later, Nicholas lit the wood in the fire place. The dried-out branches almost exploded and the flames shot up, then nestled more gently around the logs. They drank a glass of Sofia's estate wine and made love again. Toward morning, they went upstairs to rest for a few hours.

As Sofia was succumbing to sleep, her father's face flashed up before her eyes. She was sure he'd been smiling. He must approve of Nicholas.

Chapter 43

When Sofia woke up, the bed next to her was empty. For a second, she was afraid Nicholas left. A moment later, she smiled as she inhaled the smell of coffee. Nicholas brought two cups, which he put on the nightstand.

"Coffee in bed, what a treat," Sofia said, sitting up.

"That way you don't have to get up." Nicholas handed her a cup and took a sip from his. After letting her drink a little, he put both cups on the nightstand. He slipped into bed again and kissed her breasts, tracing a line from her chest to her abdomen with his fingers.

They had breakfast on the patio. It was a warm October Sunday and the estate was quiet with everyone taking the day off.

"I just realized something," Sofia said as she bit into a piece of white bread slathered with butter and jam.

"What is it?" Nicholas asked.

Sofia swallowed. "I don't even know your last name. I can't believe I never asked. Just goes to show how involved I was with my own stuff."

Nicholas smiled mischievously. "You mean to say you slept with a man whose name you don't even know?"

Sofia grinned. "Terrible, isn't it. So what is your last name?"

Nicholas hesitated and sipped his coffee. "Well, my full name is Nicholas Roberto Segantino."

Sofia stared at him. "You mean ... from the Segantino

winery?"

"Yes," Nicholas said. He blushed a little. "One of the early Italian immigrant families."

"Wow, they are big from what I heard," Sofia said. "Why did you never tell me?" Sofia tried to wrap her mind around the fact that she had been working and associating with a member of one of California's famous early winemakers and vintners.

"Well, you never asked. And, besides, I don't like to mention it. First of all, I'm a student of winemaking in Tuscany and I don't like to brag about my family's name. Besides, I'm not exactly one of the 'chosen few' of the family."

"Meaning what?" Sofia asked.

Nicholas shrugged. "My father assumed all his children, meaning my brother, my sister, and I, would in one way or the other go into the business of winemaking. Since I am the oldest, he expected me to take over the family estate. But I had other plans and this was a big disappointment for him."

"Oh? Why?"

"Well, for one thing I wanted to learn as much as I could about winemaking and not just from my family. I wanted to study in other places. My father was okay with this but he expected me to come back once my schooling was done and run the family business together with him until he was ready to retire. I didn't do this."

"Why not?"

"My family's estate is too large for me. It has grown so much that my father seems to do everything but grow vines and produce wine. He constantly travels, takes part in prestigious contests, spends an enormous amount of money on advertising and all kinds of entertainment for the visitors. A few years ago, he installed a huge real underground cellar. It's beautiful but in my opinion it doesn't make the winemaking process any easier or better. It's more of a show piece for tourists." Nicholas took a deep breath.

"I don't want to do this. I'm more like my grandfather. He tried to keep his winery small enough so he could work it without a lot of outside help. His outfit consists of two buildings, the winery and a storage shed. In the winery, everything is under one roof: the fermentation tanks, the barrels, and the bottled wine. He keeps the machinery he doesn't use all the time in the shed. That's it. He doesn't have a separate fancy tasting room. He has a tasting area in the winery itself. Very convenient, compact, and simple."

"It sounds a little what my father and his friends had up at the Russian river. Very functional, nothing fancy, but from what I heard, they made pretty good wine," Sofia said.

"Yes, exactly," Nicholas continued. "But my grandfather realized that my father had big plans and that by being so old-school, he was holding him back. So he split the estate. My grandfather kept the old winery and three of the vineyards with the Italian varietals for himself and handed the rest over to my father."

"That's generous of your grandfather," Sofia said.

"Well, he knew that there would be tension between him and my dad with their different approaches. I think he was smart. He still works his three fields and produces some excellent wine. I like his approach. In fact, I get along better with my grandfather than with my father, at least when it comes to winemaking."

Nicholas brushed his hand through his hair. "I work with him taking care of his vineyards. He also told me he would hand the fields over to me as soon as I was ready to be on my own."

"That sounds great," Sofia said.

"Eventually, I would like to buy the land next to it for a

fourth varietal, not sure yet what. Most likely Zinfandel."

"How is your relationship with your father now?" Sofia asked.

Nicholas shrugged. "Fine, in general. My father is still a little resentful, but I hope he'll get used to me being my own person. He finally accepted the fact that he had to find another heir for the estate and now my younger brother and sister are running it together with my father and will take over once he is ready to retire. I'm happy about this. That way, the estate remains in the family.

"I admire my father. He has a lot of courage and he taught me a lot and he will always be one of my important mentors."

Sofia felt Nicholas's enthusiasm and it spurred her own passion. "I look forward to working with you, Nicholas."

He bent over to kiss her. "I look forward to it, too. And I'm very happy it won't be merely a working relationship."

Sofia chuckled. "I think we eliminated that possibility last night."

Chapter 44

Sofia was getting ready to drive to Florence to pick up her aunt at the airport. Emma had two weeks off from teaching, a sabbatical of sorts, which she decided to spend visiting Sofia in Tuscany. Edoardo, going out of his way to make up for the damage his father caused, gave Sofia free use of his car, a dark-red sporty-looking Fiat that didn't seem to fit Edoardo's serious character and conservative attitude. Perhaps it reflected his wilder inner-self he would never show openly. Sofia smiled at the thought. Edoardo and wild didn't seem to go together but who knew? He'd also paid for the damage to hers and Nicholas's rental cars. Fortunately, they both had insurance, which covered part of it.

Sofia started the car and drove the gravel path to the road. As always since the accident, she tapped the brakes to make sure they were working. She assumed this habit would stay with her for the rest of her life.

The air was crisp this October morning but the sky was clear and the sun would warm and dry the now dew-soaked grass. Sofia inhaled the whiff of eucalyptus in the air. As she drove by the neighbors' olive groves, she waved at a few of the workers, who checked the olives and were getting ready to pick them. The Santucci family and their neighbors, the Brunellis, helped each other out during the grape and olive harvest. The farmers supported each other during this crucial harvest time when everything depended on the weather and the right timing of the work flow. It was one of the things Sofia enjoyed most about farming. No matter how many modern machines and instruments the farmers had, in the end it was up to nature and the help of loyal friends that made all the difference.

As she slipped a CD with songs by Andrea Bocelli into the CD player, she thought of Nicholas and smiled. Who would have thought a couple of weeks ago that things would turn out so well and that she would be happy here and even find love in this place? She hummed the song and let her eyes wander over the fields and vineyards and the occasional small village and farm houses.

When she got closer to the edge of Florence, she took a deep breath and focused intensely on the now increasing traffic, hoping she wouldn't get lost. She was somewhat worried about driving alone to Florence. She would have preferred having company but Julietta was at school and she didn't want to ask Nicholas because they were still very busy at the vineyards. Besides, she wanted to prove to herself that she was independent enough to fight her way through that crazy traffic. Fortunately, Edoardo's car had a GPS and she'd activated the English language function at home. Now, the mechanical-sounding male voice guided her safely to the airport. She parked the car and breathed a sigh of relief.

From what she remembered when she arrived here three months before, the airport was modern and quite easy to get around. She found the arrival gate where Emma would appear. She had to wait for about half an hour until the passengers disembarked. Scanning the arriving people, she saw her aunt right away. Emma looked lively and didn't seem to show any signs of the long, tiresome flight.

"Look at you and that great tan. Have you been lying on the beach all the time?" Emma said, greeting Sofia with a kiss.

"No, not lying on the beach. That's from hard work and picking grapes, Emma." Sofia chuckled.

Christa Polkinhorn

"I'm so happy to see you. Is everything okay now? You really gave me a shock when you told me what happened to you. Why didn't you call me? I would've taken the next plane to come and get you."

"That's why I didn't do it, Emma. I didn't want you to worry. And yes, everything is okay now. The old lunatic is in jail and I feel so much better again."

"Great, and how about that nice young man of yours?" Emma winked at Sofia.

"I'll tell you all about him," Sofia said. "Let's go home though. You must be tired from your trip."

"Na, I'm fine. Jet lag will hit me later."

At home at the main house, Luisa stepped outside when Sofia parked the car. At the same time, Edoardo came walking over from his home. Emma got out of the car and waved at Luisa and Edoardo. Unlike Sofia, who'd approached the people at Vignaverde with caution, Emma seemed to have no such concerns. She went up to Luisa and stretched out her arms in a welcoming gesture.

"I'm so happy to finally meet my Italian sister-in-law," she said. "It's a crime and a shame that it took us so long to get acquainted." She hugged Luisa who looked startled at Emma's enthusiasm. Then she embraced her and smiled at Sofia amused.

"This is my brother, Edoardo," Luisa introduced him.

"*Benvenuta, signora*," Edoardo said in his serious manner.

"Oh, for heaven's sake, forget the '*signora*'," Emma said and hugged him. "I'm Emma, your sister-in-law ... I guess that's what we are, isn't it? Henry was my brother and you're the brother of his significant other, so yes, indirectly I guess we are related."

Edoardo seemed to have trouble understanding Emma's

250

explanation of their shared family history. He smiled indulgently at the American woman's exuberance. "I am very happy to meet you, Emma," he said and hugged her back.

"And where is Julietta?" Emma asked looking around.

"She is over at Sofia's house getting her things, so you can have her bedroom while you are here," Luisa explained. "She has been staying with Sofia once in a while but now, she will stay in her room in the main house."

"Oh, no, I don't want to chase her away. I can sleep on the couch for those few days," Emma said. "Is there a sofa?"

"There is an extra bed in Henry's former study," Sofia said. "So it wouldn't be a problem. There is enough room really."

"Well, we want you and Sofia to have some privacy," Luisa said.

"Oh, stuff and nonsense." Emma waved her hand. "We can have all the privacy when we're back in California, can't we, honey?" She patted Sofia's arm. "I'd really love to get to know my Italian niece. If this is all right with you?" She smiled at Luisa and Edoardo.

Luisa and Edoardo glanced at each other. They seemed to be surprised and somewhat flabbergasted at Emma's enthusiastic acceptance of them as family.

"I guess if you insist." Luisa gave Sofia a questioning look.

"Yes, let her stay, please," Sofia said. "You know, Aunt Emma raised me. She's great with kids and young people."

"All right." Luisa smiled. "Would you like something to drink? Lunch will be ready in about half an hour."

"May I offer you some wine as an aperitif?" Edoardo asked with a warm smile in Emma's direction. He seemed to be charmed by Emma's outspoken nature.

"Actually, I wouldn't mind freshening up a little beforehand," Emma said. "It's been quite a long trip. But I would love some wine a little later on," she added. "I heard only good things about your wines."

Edoardo nodded. "It will be waiting for you."

Chapter 45

Sofia suppressed the giggles. "You charmed the man, Emma," she said on her way over to her house. "I've never seen him so lively. But be careful, he is married."

Emma chuckled. "I have no intention of complicating my easygoing life with a married man, thank you very much. I leave such entertainment to your father. Sorry that was bad taste." She patted Sofia on the back.

Sofia laughed. "Bad taste or not, it's true."

Over at Sofia's house, they found Julietta, stuffing her nightgown and a few toiletries into her bag. She looked up as they entered, tears running down her face. "*Mi dispiace*," she muttered and grabbed a Kleenex from the box.

"What's the matter, Julietta?" Sofia asked stunned, getting ready to hug her.

"Sorry," she said again, looking at Emma. She turned around, blew her nose and faced them again. "It is nothing."

"What do you mean, it is nothing?" Sofia said. "You're crying your eyes out and claim it's nothing?"

Julietta shook her head. "I am just having a bad moment," she said, then smiled at Emma through her tears. "Hello, I am sorry."

"Well, hello, Julietta. How wonderful to meet you. I've been looking forward to this for a long time." Emma went up to her and hugged her, then took a step back and gazed at Julietta. "You look so much like your father," Emma said with a dreamy voice. "But you have your mother's gorgeous hair." She brushed a strand of Julietta's mahogany hair out of her face. "But tell me, why are you crying?" She embraced the girl again.

Emma's motherly warmth triggered more tears. Julietta hid her face on Emma's shoulder and sobbed. "There, there." Emma tapped her back. "Let's sit down somewhere and you can tell me all about it."

Sofia couldn't help smiling. Emma's behavior reminded her of her childhood and the times she'd cried on Emma's shoulder. She pointed at Julietta's bag. "You can stay with us. Emma will sleep in the study. There's enough room and Luisa said it was okay ... if you want to that is."

"Thank you," Julietta said and took a deep breath.

"Okay, that's settled," Emma said. "Now, sweetie, let's talk." She pulled Julietta down on the sofa in the living-room. Sofia sat across from them. Emma looked around the living room. "What a lovely house." Then she turned to Julietta again. "Is it a boy?"

Julietta looked at Emma surprised, then managed a weak smile. "No."

"Then what?" Emma gently touched Julietta's face.

"It's just ... Sofia is going back to America and I shall not see her for a long time. And we will never really be together and I miss Papa so much."

"Oh, sweetie." Emma hugged her. "We miss him, too. Don't we, Sofia?"

Sofia nodded. She felt a knot in her throat and her eyes teared up.

"It is just all so complicated. I want to come to California to live with Sofia, but then I will miss Mamma and my friends and ... I will always miss someone." A sob escaped her.

Emma continued to hug her. "I know what you mean. You have family in two places, you had a father in California and you only saw him once a year. And now he's gone. You met your sister, but the two of you don't live together. You're being torn between two places and two sets of loved ones. It's difficult. I'm not denying this."

Julietta nodded. "I do look forward to visiting Sofia," she said with a quick smile.

"Yes and we look forward to having you. You can always stay with us. And your mother and your uncle can come too. They have vacation once in a while, don't they?"

"Perhaps Mamma can come. She always wanted to know where Papa was from," Julietta said.

"That would be wonderful. See, you're already making plans and thinking of the good things. You have family and friends in two places. And sometimes this is painful, but at other times it's fun. You get to live an exciting life."

"*Si*, yes," Julietta said. "Thank you."

"Luisa agreed to let Julietta visit for Christmas," Sofia said.

"This will be a lot of fun. I'm sure our Christmas celebration is a little different than the Christmas here. But I think you'll like it," Emma said.

Julietta took a deep breath and wished the last tears away.

"So, why don't we both freshen up a little and then go over and try some of this excellent food Sofia told me about?" Emma said to Julietta. "I'll unpack a few things and then I'm ready."

Over at the main house, it smelled of herbs and saffron. When Sofia, Julietta, and Emma entered the living and dining room, Nicholas who had been invited for lunch, got up and Sofia introduced him.

Emma took a step back, smiled, and looked Nicholas up and down. "So you are the smashing young man my niece raves about. I have to say she has excellent taste."

Sofia was amused to see that Nicholas blushed. Sofia and Julietta went into the kitchen to check if they could help. Donna gave them a jug of lemonade and a tray with glasses, which they brought into the living room.

In the meantime, Edoardo and Gina had arrived. While Emma was talking to them, Nicholas came up to Sofia with a wide grin on his face.

"Your aunt is a crack-up," he said.

"I know," Sofia said. "She made even Edoardo loosen up."

Soon lunch was ready and everybody was sitting around the dining-room table. Donna, who was eating with Luisa and Julietta all the time now since her husband had been arrested, sat next to Emma. The two were soon engaged in a lively discussion in Italian and English. Sofia noticed once again how much the atmosphere at the Santuccis had lightened since the old lunatic had left.

Donna was happier, Edoardo smiled more often and even joked sometimes. Luisa, too, was livelier and Gina, who'd always been polite and cool, went up to Sofia and to her surprise began a conversation with her. And fortunately Julietta, who a few moments ago had been in tears, seemed happy again.

Lunch was delicious, veal cutlets with parmesan, zucchini squash, porcini mushrooms, and Luisa's excellent risotto. Edoardo opened a bottle of the Sangiovese and Merlot blend.

"From Sofia's vineyard," he said, poured everybody a glass and toasted Sofia.

In the evening, Emma, Julietta, and Sofia had a light dinner of soup and salad at Sofia's place. Since Emma was fading fast and Julietta had to go to school the following morning, they both went to bed early. Sofia stayed up for a while, finishing one of her articles for her publisher. Since Emma was sleeping in the study, Sofia brought her laptop to the living room. Just when she closed it, she heard someone walk down the stairs.

"Jet lag, after all," her aunt said. "I thought I was tired, but the minute my head hit the pillow, I was wide awake again."

"Want some red wine or herbal tea?" Sofia asked.

"Herbal tea, if you have some. I had enough wine with lunch." Emma sat on the sofa. She pointed at Sofia's laptop. "I chased you out of your study. I'm sorry."

"No problem, Emma. I often write down here and I'm done with my article." Sofia boiled some water and made two cups of ginger tea.

They both sat on the sofa facing the balcony door, where the sun had set and the darkness enveloped the fields and forests. There was a patch of dark violet clouds on the horizon and the weather forecast was for showers, but so far the October storms had been kept at bay. Since the grapes were all picked and safely stored in the fermentation tanks, the people on the estate were ready for the fall and winter rains. In fact, the dropping temperatures would give the plants time to rest and the soil needed the water from the rain.

"I have some news for you," Sofia said, sipping her tea.

"Yes, I figured that much," Emma said with a smile. "And it must have something to do with Nicholas. A very nice man, by the way. Your father would approve."

"Yes, I love him," Sofia said. "I didn't intend to get involved with another vintner or winemaker from California after my disastrous experience with the last one. But Nicholas is very different. He is kind and considerate and his heart is really into winemaking. And, he wants me as a partner." Sofia told Emma about her plans to move up to the Central

Coast and work together with Nicholas. She asked her if Emma would consider moving into Sofia's house in Santa Monica.

"That way, I wouldn't have to rent it out to a stranger. I wouldn't charge you rent. I know you would take good care of it."

"I'll definitely think about it," Emma said. "In fact, this sounds like a great solution. I love the house and that way you and Nicholas would always have a place to stay." She nodded enthusiastically. "But, I insist on paying rent." She raised her hand. "Dear, Sofia, you need to become a better business woman. You'll need the money to help Nicholas pay rent as well. And you'll need money to support yourself."

"I'll keep my job as editor and writer, at least for a while, until we rake in the big bucks," Sofia joked. "Also, Nicholas mentioned that his grandfather and his father will help us. They'll lend us their volunteers for planting and harvesting. I'm really happy about this, since his father was at first somewhat disappointed that Nicholas went into business on his own."

"This all sounds very promising. I'm so happy for you, Sofia." Emma hugged her.

Chapter 46

Sofia woke up early and opened the window to a clear, brisk, and sunny late October day. It was Sunday and quiet at Podere Ginori. The vines were resting and the vintners who cared for them did the same, enjoying the relaxing time after a busy and strenuous harvest. Of course, their work would continue, but on a slower and more relaxing pace. The wine in the barrels needed to be racked regularly. Fields were going to be fertilized and vines must be pruned to prepare them for the following cycle of growth. But now it was time for the winemakers to show their art and science. It was also the time for blending wines which had been aging for a while.

Sofia sat together with Nicholas, Luisa, Edoardo, and Emma in the tasting room on the property. Last time, Edoardo and Henry had done the blending of the estate wine together. This year Edoardo insisted that Sofia take Henry's place. Sofia was looking forward to the process although she was nervous. She felt she didn't have enough experience to do a good job. She'd done blending together with her father but it had been merely for fun. They'd invited a few of Henry's friends and it had been more of a party than a serious undertaking.

To Sofia's relief, however, the process of tasting and blending turned out to be pleasant and easygoing. Each person had a measuring glass, a sheet of paper, the tasting notes, where they wrote down the percentage of the blends, some remarks and an evaluation. In addition, each taster had a spitting bowl.

"It's almost a pity to spit the wine out, but I guess you don't want to get drunk," Emma said.

Edoardo laughed. "That's one of the reasons. But the primary reason is the fact that tasting wine without drinking it gives a more accurate representation of what a wine tastes like. When you spit it out, you are left with a cleaner palate before tasting the next wine. Drinking a wine leaves an aftertaste and the aroma from the first wine lingers in your nose when you taste the next one."

In the middle of the table, there were four different types of red estate wine that they used for blending: Sangiovese, the most popular grape in the region, Merlot, Cabernet Sauvignon, and Cabernet Franc.

Sofia knew that her father's blend from the past years had been a mixture of ninety percent Sangiovese and ten percent Merlot and she was initially planning to keep the blend the same. Edoardo, however, told her not to stick slavishly to what her father had done but to taste the wines. "Make your own decision. As you know the character of the grapes changes each year."

He poured Sofia some of the Sangiovese into her wineglass. She swirled the wine and smelled it. "Whoa," she said. "Strong, earthy?"

Edoardo: "Try it."

Sofia took a sip and left it in the mouth for a while. "A little harsh? Lots of tannin."

"Yes," Edoardo said. "Remember I told you we had quite a cool early summer last year. Sangiovese grapes can develop an astringent tannin in cooler weather. That is where the Merlot comes in. It adds fruit, body, and softness to the blend."

Sofia tried the Merlot and smiled. "Yes." She suggested to add more Merlot and less Sangiovese. After trying several blends with different percentages, she decided that eighty percent Sangiovese and twenty percent Merlot was the one she liked best.

Edoardo and Nicholas tried the blend.

"Brava," Edoardo said.

"Excellent," Nicholas added.

Emma tried the mix as well and nodded approvingly.

Sofia took a deep breath. She felt she'd past the test. They continued tasting and testing the blends from the estate. Feeling more relaxed, Sofia thoroughly enjoyed the rest of the tasting session. There was a lot of humor and laughing.

However, despite the fun and the relaxed atmosphere, the final outcome of the tasting and blending session was serious business. It would decide what kind of evaluations the wines would receive from the experts and critics as well as from wine lovers all over.

.

Chapter 47

On the day of the grape harvest festival at Podere Francesco Ginori, the late October sun bathed the vineyards, now stripped of their fruit, in a golden haze. Every year after all the grapes had been picked and crushed and pressed and were doing their magic in the fermentation tanks, the family invited the workers, volunteers, and everybody who contributed to the estate for a big celebration.

"We celebrate the coming together of nature and man and give thanks to the sun and the rain and the soil and all the many people who have contributed," Edoardo said. He helped some of the men carry large tables outside. It was just warm enough to eat in the courtyard in front of the main house. On the lawn next to the house, a small playground had been set up for the children. Sofia, Julietta, Emma, and Nicholas were setting the tables.

Luisa and Donna together with a few volunteers had helped prepare some of the food the day before. There was all kinds of antipasti, smoked meats—salami and the famous prosciutto—vegetables such as artichoke hearts, beans, corn, tomatoes marinated in olive oil and balsamic vinegar. In the kitchen, Donna and Luisa and a few of their friends were preparing huge pots of risotto with mushrooms and plates with pieces of chicken and seafood. Jugs with lemonade and water and, of course, bottles of wine from the former *vendemmia* were spread out over the different tables.

It was boisterous affair. People talked, laughed, and sang. Some of the workers brought an instrument, a guitar, and a few harmonicas. Children played in the field, picking the last fall flowers, or tried out the swings and the slide in the playground. Cars with invited guests from outside the area began to arrive. Sofia saw Adriano's silver Lancia drive up. He'd brought his wife and son and daughter. She went to welcome them. Adriano and his wife hugged her.

"I am very happy you are better again," Adriano said. He introduced his children, a young man who seemed to be a younger version of his father, and a girl with Gerda's blond hair and blue eyes.

"Yes, things have improved a lot," Sofia said. She sat at the table together with Emma, Edoardo, Gina, and their children as well as Nicholas and Julietta. Adriano shook hands with Edoardo.

He put his hand on Edoardo's shoulder and whispered something in Italian Sofia couldn't understand. Edoardo's face clouded over for a brief moment, then it lit up again. He nodded and said in English with a quick glance at Sofia. "We just found out that my father was moved to a mental clinic."

Sofia smiled. "I'm glad to hear this." She wondered if Adriano had something to do with the decision. As she had realized in the meantime, knowing the right lawyers seemed to be as important in Italy as in the United States, perhaps even more so.

Then, the eating and drinking began. Plates of antipasto were passed around. Edoardo and Nicholas poured the wine and after a few moments, Luisa and Donna joined them while a few of the volunteers brought the plates with the risotto. The scent of meat, herbs, and spices made Sofia's stomach growl. For a while, it was quiet with people eating and savoring the estate wines.

Sofia noticed that Julietta next to her had been unusually quiet and suspected her sister felt the pain of the upcoming separation. She put her arm around her and looked at Luisa. "Are you going to tell her?"

Luisa nodded and turned to Julietta. "*Cara,* I made the reservations for you for Christmas. You will be able to spend three weeks with Sofia in California."

Julietta's mouth fell open. Then she screamed and laughed. "Thank you, thank you." She rushed over to her mother and hugged her. "This is going to be so cool."

Sofia took a sip of wine, put down the glass, and looked around. So many happy people all celebrating together. Only a couple of weeks before, it had seemed impossible that she could be happy here again. Now, however, a feeling of joy and gratitude filled her. She glanced at the landscape around her, the vineyards, woods, and the olive groves on the neighbor's property. She would miss it all but she would be back.

A few days before, Sofia had a talk with Adriano, Edoardo, and Luisa. She wanted to include Luisa and Edoardo as co-owners of her two vineyards. Edoardo steadfastly refused to accept the offer, since he felt he had no right to the property after what his father had done. The only way he would agree to a deal would be if he could pay for his and Luisa's half. The estate had done well and they could certainly afford the money. And it would be the least he could do to compensate her for the pain they had inflicted on her, he felt.

Sofia had talked the proposal over with Adriano who told her she would be more than stupid not to accept Edoardo's money. "First of all," he said. "You give Edoardo Santucci the possibility to make amends for his father's actions. It would make him feel better. And besides," he continued, "you told me you wanted to go into partnership with Nicholas. Wouldn't a little extra money help you two?" He'd been right. She could contribute some of her own money and then they would be equal partners. She hadn't mentioned anything to Nicholas yet. She figured she would surprise him with the offer once they were back in California.

Sofia, Nicholas, and Emma were going to fly back to Los Angeles a week later. They'd been able to change their return flight so they could all travel home together. Sofia had invited Nicholas to spend a couple of days in Santa Monica with her. Later, she would join him at his place in the Paso Robles area.

"A penny for your thoughts." Sofia felt Nicholas's breath on her cheek. She smiled at him and he gave her a long leisurely kiss. She heard a chuckle and when she turned her head, she saw Adriano and Gerda look at them with a big smile on their faces.

"Ah, how romantic. Love in Tuscany," Gerda said and Adriano lifted his wine glass and toasted them.

"Remember, Sofia, when you were concerned about being part of the family?" he said.

Sofia nodded. "Yes, it has happened. I found my Italian family."

"And, not only that," Adriano said. "You also found a *ragazzo*, a boyfriend. Congratulations."

"Yes, I'm grateful for everything. It's wonderful to have both my Italian and Californian family here with me." She hugged Emma and Julietta. "And to be able to celebrate with all my friends." She lifted her wine glass. "And to Henry, who in his admittedly unusual way made it all possible." A few people chuckled.

"To Papa," Julietta said.

Gina and Edoardo toasted them. "Let this be the beginning of a new relationship between California and Toscana and our wines," Edoardo said.

"*Congratulazioni.*" Donna held up her glass of wine and

gave them a warm smile.

Sofia took a deep breath and felt her eyes tear up, this time from happiness.

The End

Acknowledgements

This book has been a collaboration between myself and many kind and helpful friends. To mention them all by name is a challenge but I'll do my best. Through my research into the world of winemaking, which is an important topic in this book, I met a lot of interesting and very helpful people and made some lasting friends. I would like to thank first and foremost Mark and Dave Caparone from the Caparone Winery in Paso Robles, California. Mark showed me around their winery, let me taste their excellent wines, and spent hours answering my many questions. A thank you also goes to the Ginori Lisci estate in Querceto, Tuscany, Italy, which gave me the first glimpse of Tuscan winemaking, to the Obrecht Family in Jenins, Switzerland, who took time out of their busy day during the grape harvest to explain the process from picking grapes to bottling wine. A big thank-you to my patient family and friends whom I dragged around vineyards and wineries in Tuscany and Switzerland: my nephew Rico, my niece Claudia and her husband Alberto, to Claudia and Weltsch Bamert and their son Severin and Severin's friend Megan, to my great-niece Risayra and her boyfriend Oliver, to Vreni Nieth who accompanied me to Jenins, to Silvia Delorenzi-Schenkel who shared her knowledge of growing grapes and making wine and who introduced the Obrecht family to me. I also want to thank travel guide, Annie Adair in Volterra, Italy whose videos on Volterra helped me a lot in my research. This hill-town served as model for my imaginary town of Vignaverde. Thank you dear Beta Readers/Editors for your valuable feedback: Helen Ginger, Linda Cassidy Lewis, Susan Dormady Eisenberg, Lindsay Edmunds, Silvia Delorenzi-Schenkel. Thanks to Linda Cassidy Lewis and Diane Busch for the final proofreading and thank you, Diane, for the lovely cover. And last but not least: A big thank-you to my editor, Sharon Stogner, for her keen eye for detail and the many helpful suggestions.

Christa Polkinhorn, originally from Switzerland, lives and works as writer and translator in Santa Monica, California. She divides her time between the United States and Switzerland and has strong ties to both countries. She is the author of five novels and a collection of poems. Her travels and her interest in foreign cultures informs her work and her novels take place in several countries. Aside from writing and traveling, she is an avid reader and a lover of the arts, dark chocolate, and red wine. She can be reached by email at cpolkinhorn@msn.com or you can visit her at her website www.christa-polkinhorn.com or her blog http://christa-polkinhorn.blogspot.com.

Made in the USA
Las Vegas, NV
12 August 2023

76002579R00163